protagonist's interior world into a whole lush landscape and filled it with desire, loss, tenderness, humor, and tragedy. The result is a novel full of wild, irresistible life."
—CLARE BEAMS, author of *The Illness Lesson*

"*In the Lobby of the Dream Hotel* is a truly brilliant novel. This is a story about madness and music, forbidden love, entrapment and escape—all written in Plunkett's electric and propulsive prose. It's the most compelling novel I've read all year; I couldn't put it down. Stunning."
—ANNA HOGELAND, author of *The Long Answer*

"*In the Lobby of the Dream Hotel* is a beating heart of flowing paths and urgent questions: How do we tell the difference between our dreams, our fantasies, and our possible futures? How do we step from one life into another, not knowing if the earth under our feet will hold? In this sensitive, suspenseful novel, Genevieve Plunkett fearlessly dances between past and present, between wanting and having, between loves laced with cruelty and loves aching with tenderness and possibility."
—CAITLIN HORROCKS, author of *Life Among the Terranauts*

PRAISE FOR *Prepare Her: Stories*

"Dreamlike, atmospheric stories that revel in haunting, protracted tension . . . If art is control and precision, the unbridled life that inspires it is too sweeping and wild to be accurately captured. Yet Plunkett is a writer of such extraordinary power that she's able to summon the unknowable chaos into a spellbinding story."

—Rachel Yoder, *The New York Times Book Review*

"Plunkett's striking debut puts a series of women's interior lives in stark relief . . . Plunkett's keen observations will pique readers, and the stories pay off with dividends."

—*Publishers Weekly*

"[A] nuanced debut story collection . . . With bracing honesty, Plunkett's richly drawn narratives bring emotional depth to the characters' struggles and internal conflicts." —*Booklist*

"[A] vivid and emotionally raw look at the less-picturesque side of small-town Vermont life . . . Plunkett's writing is mesmerizing . . . The neatness and precision of [her] writing is well-suited for the quiet but emotionally deep nature of her characters, who straddle the line between a too-lucid understanding of the world and a longing to escape into the imaginative realm of the ever-evasive could-be."

—*Shelf Awareness* (starred review)

In the Lobby of the Dream Hotel

ALSO BY GENEVIEVE PLUNKETT

Prepare Her

In the

Lobby

of the

Dream Hotel

✦ *a novel* ✦

Genevieve Plunkett

Catapult
New York

Copyright © 2023 by Genevieve Plunkett

ISBN: 978-1-64622-048-9

Library of Congress Control Number: 2023931312

Jacket design by Nicole Caputo
Jacket art: crouching nude © Oana Stoian / Trevillion Images;
glitter © Istock / Dimitris66
Book design by tracy danes

The title page is set in the typeface Le Murmure, designed by Jérémy Landes

Catapult
New York, NY
books.catapult.co

Printed in the United States of America

1 3 5 7 9 10 8 6 4 2

For Jamie

In the Lobby of the Dream Hotel

Waitress Mark

◯─◯THE BOY WANTED TO KNOW ABOUT THE mark on Portia's neck. Over the course of four days, it had turned from a reddish color into something more clearly defined and purple and, finally, to a softer, although no less alarming, green-blue smudge. It seemed that the boy could no longer bear the grotesque mystery of it.

"What happened to your neck, Mommy?" he asked, running his thumb over it. They were sitting on the futon together, just to sit. The boy, Julian, was seven years old and still very affectionate. He liked to slide his hand up the back of Portia's shirt, to rub or gently scratch the spot between her shoulder blades. Sometimes he would hum to himself or recite under his breath the prime moments of his fictional inner world, as if broadcasting the score of an imaginary game.

This habit had been adapted from old habits, the first from when he was nearly two, when he would lie with Portia in her bed, squeezing her breast, sometimes rolling the nipple with his finger. The sensation that this yielded, a sickening, unforgiving feeling of frustration, was only tolerated because it was the quickest way to get the boy to sleep. Eventually, and with patience, Portia was able to coax the boy's hand from her breast to her stomach, where he would mash the flesh of her belly, indulgently, like a cat kneading a cushion. It was not much better, but it felt like progress. Over the years, his hand had migrated to her side, then to her back, where it would return throughout the day, reclaiming this one small need.

Motherhood had proven to be stranger and more intimately compromising than Portia had expected. Her biggest difficulties were not external—the grocery store tantrums, the lack of sleep, the many domestic injustices of the day. Instead they seemed to rise from her gut, like fermentations—wordless burdens, unanticipated sorrows, and all the worrying. She worried about the improbable, mostly, the heavy tree branches that might fall on the child, diseases that he might pick up in the sandbox. When he was a newborn, she had entertained a very brief but horrifying notion that she would go mad and drop him in the fish tank. She had stacked books on the lid, to deter her crazed, hypothetical self. It would take long enough to remove them, she reasoned, that the impulse would pass, the child would be spared. She would come to, like a sleepwalker. There were so many of these morbid, imaginary bargains to be made, now that her son was in the world and she could not stop the world from taking him if it wanted to.

The morning after Julian was born, the doctor who had delivered him came to Portia's bedside. He was a man with a rounded gray beard and immensely hairy hands. How could those hands catch a baby? Portia thought. Or dip into the tender cavity of a cesarean section? In the end, her own baby's birth had been a cesarean, and Portia was left bedridden, her battered, swollen stomach stapled together, a catheter bag slung over the side of the hospital bed, filling slowly with urine. The doctor looked at the bag. He said, "Women have it hard."

Portia thought that he might be talking about the way that she had cried before the surgery, when the feeling in her legs began to fade, as if she were being erased from the bottom up. She would flinch for years afterward when anyone brushed against the small of her back, where the cold epidural needle had touched her spine.

"Since they are little girls," the doctor continued, "women are taught to hold their bladders. At school, on long car trips—they are too afraid to say, 'pull over,' and instead, they watch the exit signs roll by until someone else speaks up." Portia looked into the man's brown, close-set eyes, trying to figure out what he meant. His eyes were wet with compassion, warm, fatherly compassion, like a preacher, touched by his own words. She waited for him to arrive at his point, but he only rested those deep eyes on her until they seemed to reach their own private satisfaction.

"Take care," he said, and he touched the cheek of the sleeping baby on her chest.

Portia pressed the bruise on her neck and thought of her lover, Theo, the tender force of him, the shockwaves that traveled up through her and lodged, like tears, or ecstasy, in her throat. A soft, involuntary sigh escaped her.

"It's just a waitress mark," she told her son. "Waitresses get them from carrying large trays on their shoulders. The edges of the trays push into their necks and leave a bruise. We all get them." The boy studied her face, and Portia saw a sweet, accepting smile appear on his lips, as if it made no difference and all the difference in the world. As if he understood her plight, the complicated burden of what she had to endure. As if to say, "Poor Mommy!"

Three Men

PORTIA WAS ANGRY WITH THE PSYCHIATRIST for calling her "ripe." It was all that she could think about, even as they lay her on the stretcher and tightened the strap around her hips, so she would not roll around when the ambulance took a corner. They kept it dark in the back of the ambulance; the faces above her, the EMTs who had to accompany her, were mostly in shadow, although they were occasionally swept over by passing streetlights or blinking reds.

"Boring night," one of them said.

Portia's psychiatrist, Dr. Shay, had probably wanted to make light of the situation. He might have thought that he and Portia were close enough, after so many years, that he could make a joke at her expense. They often laughed together during appointments. Sometimes Dr. Shay told Portia that she was "fascinating" and that he wished that they could meet out of session just so he could "pick her brain." He talked about Kurt Cobain and Virginia Woolf. He lent her books, which she always managed to lose or damage carelessly—a copy of *The Magus* dropped below the passenger seat, the cover pulverized by winter boots. Portia could sit on his porch, he said. He would make lemonade in a big glass pitcher, with basil picked from the garden. He had a greyhound named Baby, rescued from the racetrack. And he had just redone the siding of his house with cedar shingles, which seemed to Portia to be somehow stylish and resourceful, although Dr. Shay had never explained to her why he had done this. The richness of his life was all implied, the best-practice quirkiness of it all, the ease. *I'm more like you than you know,* he seemed to say to her.

Portia had been curled up on her parents' couch for about two weeks, too tired and depressed to do anything else, when they dragged her in to see Dr. Shay.

"She hasn't showered either," Portia's father added, after they had been over the list of his concerns. That was when Dr. Shay had leaned forward, flared his nostrils, his gray, handsome face commanding and official.

"Boy," he said. "You *are* ripe." And Portia, betrayed, had fallen mute.

She was offered a shower when she got to the hospital. They allowed her to lock the door to the bathroom, which insulted her further, as if she were not at all dangerous enough to need supervision. No one was taking her seriously. She was twenty years old. A college dropout. Old enough to make terrible decisions.

Some minutes into the shower, there was a soft knock on the door.

"Still here," Portia called out. "Still alive." And she waited for the knock to come again, letting the warm water trickle over her body in the unnervingly large shower stall—large enough for a horse, she thought. Large enough for a whole crew to come in with brooms to scrub her raw. Then she would not be ripe anymore.

She was shown to her room, where there was a bed, bloated down the middle, the rubber mattress split, revealing a layer of grayish insulation. Whenever she turned over in the night, the springs creaked, making her sleep patterns known, it seemed, to the whole world.

Portia had been living with her parents and sleeping on their couch since leaving college. Her parents were stubborn about technology and kept a black rotary telephone with a tightly coiled cord on the corner table in the living room, as well as one beside their bed upstairs. A phonograph, shaped like a tall cabinet, stood in the main hallway. There were two doors on the lower half, with delicately sized knobs, that opened outward, to let out the sound.

A man had been calling her, usually every night, but sometimes he would not call and Portia would fall asleep with her hand on the receiver, ready to choke the ring as soon as it sounded, so that her parents would not hear. But one night, her father did hear, and he lingered on the upstairs line, listening briefly but long enough. He heard what she said to the man on the telephone, how she whispered to him in a voice that he must not have recognized—a voice that he would have never wanted to hear from his daughter. It did not matter that none of the acts, as they were highly exaggerated for effect, were ever performed.

"You can rip me in half," Portia said.

The man on the phone had liked that one.

Portia's father had not. "All right," he said, his voice coming through the line, like a voice over her shoulder. "That's enough of that." Portia had slammed the heavy receiver onto its hook so suddenly that it caused the bells inside to echo out into the room.

As Portia lay awake in her bed, she thought about the man on the phone, never a boyfriend, barely a lover. It was difficult to remember how it had all started. She knew that he had often come to the bar of the restaurant where she worked. Since then, the two of them had always been in the periphery of each other's life, weaving in and out throughout the years as familiar faces, a sly, unspoken mutual attraction. He was still getting over an ex-girlfriend, who they sometimes included in their fantasies, who they sometimes abused hypothetically, locking her in the bathroom, pouring cold water over her, shaving off her eyebrows. What her father could not understand was that it was not real. They were only words. What he did not understand was that Portia could tell the difference—even the man on the phone could tell the difference. The man on the phone, whose name was Tracy Eugene Browning, had been to jail. Portia had only ever known him as Skip. According to the police reports, Skip had thrown a blender at his ex-girlfriend in a drunken fight, and, although he had missed her, she had called the cops. He would not have gone to jail if he had not swung at one of the officers and called him a swine. It sounded just like Skip, to consider himself above saying the word *pig*.

Portia did not miss Skip, but she missed his voice, the authority and sadness of it.

"Get it out of me," he used to say over the phone, as if he were asking her to suck venom from a wound.

There was a commotion in the hall then: clipped, incoherent voices and grunting, the scuffing of shoes. Portia pulled on a sweatshirt and walked out, following the sounds, which were not as close as they seemed but were coming from the common area, near the entrance to the wing. There she found three men in nursing scrubs, embracing a fourth man, holding him as he resisted them. There was something slow and religious about it, how his feet hovered off the ground and his eyes rolled upward, as if in exaltation. The men were too occupied to tell Portia to leave. She should have left, but she was fascinated by the sight of them, the signs of their struggle surrounding them: overturned metal chairs and a mess on the floor, like someone's dinner plate had been smeared facedown. The struggling man seemed to come back from his trance, his eyes slipping down from inside his head and fixing on Portia. They were blue and intelligent. The man was sweating from his forehead and in splotches on his shirt and under his arms. Portia realized that the sweet, faintly bitter smell in the air was the smell of the man's sweat. It was the sweat of fear and adrenaline. He was speaking to her now, but the nurses spoke over him.

"Please," one of them said to Portia. "Return to your room."

"What?" Portia asked the sweating man. "What did you say to me?"

"Please," a nurse said again. His biceps bulged. The tendons in his neck were tensed. It seemed to Portia that the nurses were no longer keeping the man from simply breaking free but instead holding him back from getting to her. She watched the muscles in their arms lock as the man tested their grip.

"I know you," the man said.

✦

Portia and her boyfriend, Nathan, liked to tell people the truth when they asked how the two of them had met.

"Well, she had just gotten out of the mental hospital," he would begin, straight-faced, until someone chuckled, expecting this to be the setup to a joke.

"No, really," Portia would chime in. "I still had the plastic bracelets on when we had coffee for the first time." There was usually a moment of embarrassment, of recalibration, as the tone was reset with these new elements in mind. It was not so much that mental illness was considered taboo among their acquaintances but that people often became involuntarily prudent toward her. They seemed to soften when speaking to her, to avoid a certain level of conversational commitment. It took years for Portia to pick up on this. Her and Nathan's fun was probably not worth the small thrill of the social deviation. It would always make people uncomfortable. It would always be just a little too sad.

That Portia had spent time in a mental hospital did not bother Nathan. It may have even raised in him a sense of daring or intrigue. Portia was also much younger, by more than a decade. She was young and troubled, and there was some allure to that. What Nathan could not accept was what she had done to the inside of her thighs. He could not fathom it, and he wanted it erased from history.

He had not had a chance to notice her thighs at first, having turned down her advances on their first and second dates, but he did not have the willpower to do so on the third. In his bed, Portia had slipped him inside her without pause, or warning, without even opening her eyes. About this, she would always feel sorry—that, even though he had been perfectly willing, she had not asked him if he had a condom or if he was ready.

Afterward, he had flipped on the light and offered her his undershirt to clean up with. She brought it involuntarily to her face, breathing him in, before wiping herself down. Sometimes she felt closer to Nathan through his smell, closer than when he was right in front of her.

"What's this?" He was pointing to her legs. She looked

down at what the marks had become: scabbed slightly, the skin around them no longer angry and sore. They spanned the length between the inside of her knee and the crevice of her thigh, neatly, like the rungs on a ladder.

"Who did this to you?" he asked. His face was narrowed in concern and the anticipation of outrage. Portia saw that he was already dressed, his shirt tucked halfway into his pants, the open buckle of his belt clinking loosely. And for a moment, she wished that she had a better excuse—a random attack in an alleyway. Something freakish and faultless.

✦

Portia eased herself back onto the stiff, bloated hospital bed and pulled the covers around her, even though she was flushed with heat. She was thinking about what the sweating man had said to her, how the thick arms of the nurses had locked and how they had finally raised their voices at her. She did not have to obey them, she knew that, just as the sweating man, who was growling and spitting, would not face any lasting repercussions for what he was doing.

"I know you," he had said, and his eyes were wide and suddenly full of humanity. He had the look of someone who had just been snapped out of a spell of hypnosis.

"How?" Portia wanted to know. "How do you know me?"

"Miss, please," the men were warning her. There seemed to be no one else there to attend to her and they could not let go of the man, so there was a moment where it seemed that they were stuck, holding on to him for the sake of this strange conversation.

"I know who you are."

"Who am I?" Portia was wide awake, rapt. The men could see that this was not going anywhere productive, so they began hauling the sweating man away, and, as they did this, he strained against them to look at her. For a moment, she believed him to be completely sane, caught in the wrong body.

"You're the Whore of Babylon," he said, and then twisted his neck unnaturally to spit a bean-sized drop of mucus onto the cheek of his captor.

The next morning, Portia met the sweating man at breakfast. He looked like any other young man who had had a bad night, scruffy and dark beneath the eyes. He sat across from her with his breakfast tray and glanced at her, as if he had no recollection of what had happened just hours before.

"What's your name?" Portia asked him, although she knew better. She should not start a conversation with a person who required the strength of three large men to keep him from doing whatever it was that he was inclined to do. And what would that have been? Portia wondered. She remembered the sober way that he had looked at her—"Whore." The word had not been delivered with disgust but, instead, something like wonder.

"I'm Portia," she said. "We met last night." The man was trying to stab a straw into the aluminum-covered hole at the top of an apple-juice carton, but he could not seem to align the point of the straw with its target. He told her that his name was Jerry. Like Tom and Jerry. He said this last bit without annoyance, but rather as if it were an obligation. As if he had been saying it since childhood.

"I suppose it would be better to be Jerry than Tom," Portia said. Jerry took another stab at his juice box, missing and bending the straw.

"To be honest, I've never known which one was which," he said.

"Oh," Portia said. She felt that he was not asking her to tell him now. She had no business telling him. It would have seemed like a terrible encroachment. She should have, of course, left it at that, but she got up to help him with his straw. This move was not entirely innocent. In fact, it was very much the opposite. The other version of Jerry, the one from the night before, when he had been focused on her, seething, like an animal, was far more interesting than the distracted but courteous man before her now. She wondered what it would take to bring back that version of him. It was easy to believe that she was not responsible for her actions. It was easy to believe that she was safe, so she touched him.

She had seen a woman throw a tantrum over the color of a Jell-O cup, get right up on the table with her bare feet and threaten the nurses' station.

"Do you know who my husband is?" she shouted. Her toenails were jagged and yellow. The nurses were not insulted, and they did not belittle the woman. They understood that this was not something that she was in control of; otherwise she would not be there. This sense of recklessness had rubbed off on Portia, even though she, herself, had the wherewithal and self-control to stay off the tabletops. She stood behind Jerry and wrapped her arms around him, hoping to help guide the straw into its hole. He smelled strongly of body odor, but it was not unpleasant, as if through his sweat, his body had expelled a sweet-smelling alcohol. She thought of how the stalk of a weed bleeds a milky and bitter substance when it is broken, that smell of injury or distress. Jerry's body stiffened beneath hers. He stood. He was not a large man, but he was fit, in a stocky way. From where she was, still standing behind him, Portia could see the nurses at their station and how their faces changed. She saw one nurse take off her reading glasses and set them on the counter. Her expression seemed to say: *And now this*. Portia, worried that she might be in trouble, turned from them and walked quickly to her room without looking back. What she heard when she got there sounded like a brief scuffle. Someone hooted in approval, and then the sounds faded and there was some calming, authoritative speech. Keys jingling. Relief. Portia was suddenly exhausted, and she felt herself dragged into sleep. It was a dark, aggressive sleep that lasted the rest of the morning.

✦

When Portia was a child, her friend, Meredith Leek, often appeared on Portia's swing set in the backyard, twisting herself idly around on the swing, her mother crying, her father drunk again. Meredith had seemed tired more than anything, filled with weary acceptance—a taxing comprehension—of her dysfunctional home. She moved across the country as soon as she graduated from high school, and she and Portia lost touch, but Portia still ran into Mr. Leek, Meredith's father. He seemed to show up everywhere, walking his dog, making small talk about his life as a retired man.

Portia had been dating Nathan for about nine months by then, and they had recently moved into an apartment downtown, newly renovated, above a lawyer's office. The landlord had called them the perfect "young professional" tenants, although this had only applied to Nathan, Portia a college dropout, still babysitting for her old professors. She liked how the balcony of the apartment looked out across a parking lot behind the downtown businesses, providing a view of the weedy, gated alleyways, the dumpsters, and the loading docks. The opposite, front-facing apartment had a balcony over Main Street, and this small disparity bothered Nathan. He did not seem to appreciate the charm of what Portia considered to be the more intimate view: sometimes people sat on the hoods of their cars and smoked or threw litter from their pockets, thinking that no one was watching. Cats cut through with bodies aligned and focused, unlike the occasional loose dog, who stopped to sniff at car tires or to perk up at the sound of a distant voice. In the evenings, the puddles would shine metallic and magenta in the sunset.

Mr. Leek frequented this place also. He liked to take the shortcut through the alley and walk his dog around the edge of the parking lot. Portia had noticed that he had a habit of stalling behind the video rental to give his dog time to defecate by the back entrance, as if he had a score to settle with the place. Portia ran into him occasionally when she was carrying groceries from her car to the apartment. Mr. Leek would drop the dog's leash and take some of the bags for her, his dog, a gray-muzzled Doberman, following obediently, if not dejectedly, knowing very well that it was free to go but was past its prime. The Doberman reminded Portia of Mr. Leek: perhaps once a symbol of something irrefutable, righteously masculine and aggressive, now reduced by time. Meredith had estranged herself from her father and was engaged to a woman. Her mother had divorced him and was mildly successful selling knitted homemade goods at local businesses—something that could be considered unabashedly female and uncomplicated. Portia imagined that all of this might have hit a nerve in Mr. Leek.

There was one day that Mr. Leek asked Portia about her personal life. Did she live in this nice apartment all by herself? He had never seen a man come to help her with her bags.

"My boyfriend works during the day as a prosecutor," she said. "I try to get the shopping done before he gets home, so I don't have to be out when he is around."

Mr. Leek nodded.

"You know how to manage your time," he said with approval. The Doberman meandered off to sniff a discarded coffee cup, then slunk back to the heels of its master, as if humiliated by the transgression.

"You young folks are right about one thing," Mr. Leek continued.

"What's that?" They had come to the door, and Portia had to set everything down to search for her key at the bottom of her purse. An apple rolled out of one of her grocery bags into a greasy puddle on the blacktop. A receipt came fluttering out of a pocket, like a moth. Mr. Leek leaned closer to her.

"Sleeping together before you get married," he whispered. "Wish I'd thought of that forty-five years ago."

Later, Portia would tell Nathan about what Mr. Leek had said next about his ex-wife, Meredith's mother. It had been the first time that Portia had heard anyone use the term *bipolar* as if everyone were familiar with it, as if it had the same toxic connotations for everyone. Until then, *bipolar* had been a private suggestion, a diagnosis paper-clipped to the top of Portia's chart. A theoretical twist in Dr. Shay's brow.

"He said that sometimes the stress of her illness was unbearable," Portia told Nathan. "He said that he sometimes thought about getting his handgun, and putting them both out of their misery." Nathan shook his head. He heard stories like this all day at the prosecutor's office—domestic disputes, drunken fights, insane people getting themselves into absurd and dangerous situations. Meanwhile, everyone was cheating the system, while the law slogged ahead, bilious and bloodshot. Eventually, it seemed to Portia, Nathan must have been forced to start filing all this information into the categories of *good people* and *bad people*, or else he would lose his mind trying to understand it all. She watched as he blinked away her story about Mr. Leek, back into his filing cabinet head.

"Stay away from him from now on," he told her.

✦

The night that Jerry appeared in her doorway, Portia did not stop him. She had been sleeping restlessly. The new medication that they were giving her had an unfortunate side effect that made her want to crawl out of her skin. She wanted to climb walls, scratch her scalp, grind her teeth. She had bit all her fingernails down to the red, painful quick. She was not even sure why the medication had been given to her, what it was that they wanted her to feel or to avoid feeling.

"It doesn't have to be permanent," the doctors assured her of the medication. "Think of it as a kind of chemical vacation."

"Okay," Portia said, and she chewed the inside of her mouth until it felt like raw meat.

Portia had seen Jerry only a few times since the incident at the breakfast table. The staff, for the most part, kept him secluded, but she had seen him once or twice being led down the hallway by the hand, his eyes swollen and slow. So Portia was at once surprised and not surprised to see him standing there, in the light of the doorway, awake and staring at her. It seemed that somewhere, in the depths of her mind, there was a story being pieced together. A story about desire and desperation and mutual recognition.

"Hi, Jerry," she said. He was tugging gently at the drawstring of his hospital pajamas, muttering something that Portia could not hear. She sat up in bed. It was a rule that patients could not enter the rooms of other patients, but they would often linger in doorways, sharing headphones across the threshold or talking quietly, playing cards. All of this could have been done in the common area, where there were fewer restrictions, but Portia wondered if it did not seem more intimate, more quietly subversive, this way.

"I can't hear you," Portia said. "Come closer." She watched Jerry shuffle into the room, still holding his drawstrings, eyes downward. The urge was undeniable: to touch him, to press her restless, affection-starved body against his. Nothing of consequence would have to happen, she reasoned. She would not be giving up her integrity but just neglecting it for a moment. She could shed herself and then crawl back inside, and no one would have to know. Jerry came closer, and Portia saw what he was doing. He had not just been playing idly with the drawstrings of his pants but working to undo a large knot. She watched him pull it loose and then slip his thumbs under the waistband. It had been a long time since Portia had seen a naked man. Skip had liked to describe himself to her over the phone in ways that were often cartoonish or cliché. She liked it better when he left it up to her to imagine: "If only you could see what you are doing to me."

Now, with Jerry's pants around his ankles, she could see it fully—what she had done to this man in her room, what she wanted to believe was her doing, for in every other aspect of her life, she was powerless.

"Oh," Skip used to say. "Get it out of me." Like he was full of disease. Like he was begging her to save his life.

✦

"At the hospital," Portia told Nathan, as she was sitting on his bed, "they took away my shoelaces and my underwire bra." He nodded, full of knowledge and sympathy, and sat beside her so that he could place his arm around her. She had tucked his undershirt between her legs to cover herself.

"But they let me hang on to my wallet. There wasn't any money in it—just my ID and a phone card that I had used on an exchange trip to France." Portia paused. She remembered the slow clarity of that day, the way the sun had been shining through the blinds, the heat of it on her bare skin, as she sat half-naked on the busted mattress. The plastic phone card snapped easily, the bend in it turning pale just before breaking. What proved to be more difficult was getting through the skin. She had to hold the flesh of her thigh taut, to swipe the jagged edge of the card quickly over the surface, sometimes more than once, for it to work.

"I knew that if I cut myself, then I'd be too embarrassed to sleep with him when I got out," she said. "It made sense at the time." She felt Nathan's hand fall away from her shoulder. From the corner of her eye, she saw him roll his head on his neck, eyes closed.

"Who? Who did you want to avoid sleeping with?" he asked, finally.

For their first anniversary as boyfriend and girlfriend, Nathan and Portia spent a weekend in New York City. Nathan had a college friend, a woman who worked nights, who let them stay in her apartment, even sleep in her bed, while she was at work. They would not have had anywhere else to sleep, the apartment was so small. There was one other room, besides the bedroom, the kitchen, and the bathroom, that seemed to want to be a living room, or study, but it was no bigger than a closet and served mostly as an entryway, overtaken by a stack of the college friend's black shoes. Although the friend had never said so directly, it was implied that Nathan and Portia should be there as little as possible during the day, while she was asleep, so they had planned to stay busy. Nathan had lived in the city during his late twenties. Portia expected that he would be comfortable finding his way around, navigating the subway maps, which reminded Portia of the path of a virus, or something equally terrifying and unhelpful. She was surprised when, after a morning at the Museum of Natural History, Nathan stopped in the middle of the sidewalk and turned to her.

"It's your turn," he said. Portia did not understand. It had started to rain lightly, and umbrellas were going up all around them.

"I mean, it's your turn to lead the way." Nathan lifted his eyebrows. "Oh?" he asked her. "Did you expect me to do all the work?" Portia was wearing a tank top and jeans. She was wearing cheap sandals, which she had realized were wrong the minute that she stepped off the train that morning. She saw the exhaustion in Nathan's eyes, the way he removed his glasses and pinched the bridge of his nose.

"You have no idea," he tried to explain to her, "how hard it is for me to take on all of the responsibility. Doing everything for you." He wanted to know, Who had bought the train tickets? Who had driven them to the station?

"I don't have a map," Portia managed to say. She had not thought to bring a map. Her throat felt enlarged. The rain was cold now on her cheeks, as her face became hotter. Nathan had seemed happy to plan the trip, so she had not questioned him, but maybe she had missed some crucial sign, or an opening, somewhere during the previous week, where she should have offered to do something more.

"Go on," he said, smiling. He extended a hand. "Lead the way."

There was nothing to do but to go back to the apartment—much too early—and the college friend had woken up, confused. She walked by them, in her underwear, and spent a long time in the bathroom, running the water. Portia had not been able to find her way back to the apartment by herself; she had not been paying attention to the route that they had taken to the museum—she had been so distracted by the flimsiness of her sandals, by the unnerving scale of their surroundings. There were sometimes people lying motionless on the ground. She could not tell if they were breathing.

"It's fine," Nathan had told her, and walked quickly ahead, with his collar pulled up by his ears, and she had had no choice but to hurry after him, the remorse building inside her until it was nearly unbearable.

"I understand it now," Nathan said as they arrived in the cramped front room. His dark hair was wetted into little points across his forehead. His eyes were fierce with the awe of his own epiphany.

"I understand what Mr. Leek was talking about," he said. "About his wife. The misery."

Through the bathroom door, they heard the friend cough, followed by the hiss and sputter of the shower being turned on. Portia allowed herself to hear what Nathan was saying, to hear his words without denying or rejecting them, as if she could somehow open her body to them and let them be hurled inside her. Nathan shut his eyes and lowered himself to the floor, offering Portia the one chair, but she could not take it. From now on, she would have to be careful about what she was accepting from him. She would have to make sure to keep it fair, to be always on her guard.

She walked into the kitchen, a sliver of a room, barely wide enough to open the oven door, and went to the window. From there she saw the pavement, the glass and the metal, the strange, jerking movements of the city. There was no horizon, nothing slow and distant—no trail of geese or the ripple of a line of trees. No soft mountains fading into clouds. Instead she saw the tight, awkward progression of traffic below and the well-dressed people, who were surely thriving, or else why would they be living there?

Hearts

PORTIA SPENT MUCH OF HER CHILDHOOD alone. She loved the quiet of her room, the warmth that overtook her mind when she was concentrating on something that was just her own. There was something exhausting about being caught in the gaze of another person, to be obligated to keep her face from exposing her feelings and intentions. For Portia, the peak of humiliation was to be predictable, to have someone guess her next move—to say, "That's *just* like Portia."

She remembered being immersed in her games of make-believe, unable to anticipate interruption or distraction. Her ability to focus was so pure that her forehead would begin to throb and her back would become warm. It was the warmth of total security, like being wrapped in a blanket, facing the doorway, knowing that no one could see you or come up from behind you. The pleasure of moving her dolls around the bedroom and knowing exactly what they would do, mouthing the syllables of their carefully chosen names, would keep her from feeling hunger or fatigue. She often had to be reminded to use the toilet.

To Portia, at that young age, there was nothing more intimate and scandalous than the human heart. If a character were sick in one of her games, it could only be a malady of the heart: heartbreak, an arrow shot right through. If she imagined a witch, then it was a heart-craving witch. She might cast a spell on your heart or rip it cleanly out. Hearts were to be protected. They were also to be listened to in secret. Perhaps the finest act of adult love was to lay a head on the chest of a lover to see if he was still alive. Daggers were pulled from them. Vows were made on them. At night, Portia would sometimes hear the heart in her pillow, drumming into her ear, as interesting and unbearable as seeing an adult cry, as wonderful and nauseating as two people kissing on the television. And when the Tin Man came onto the screen with his womanly lips and his wet eyes and sang his song, Portia would hold her hands over her ears and crumble inside, in sympathetic agony.

There were other things that fascinated her, of course: the enormity of whales, how her grandmother licked envelopes so seriously, and how Portia felt ticklish and disgusted whenever she watched her cat retract its claws. Life was full of surprises and private betrayals, and all the while, the grown-ups were there, acting incorrigibly.

There was a museum in Philadelphia, where Portia's grandmother lived, that had, as part of a children's exhibit, a giant heart that could be climbed through and explored, the arteries like curving blue and red hallways. Although her family may have visited the museum only two or three times, Portia found herself dreading the giant heart, quite regularly, for its exorbitance and for the fuss that her parents made over it, because they must have sensed that it disturbed her.

"Uh-oh," they would say. "It's the *Big Heart!*" And for some reason, she always felt obligated to crawl inside with the other bewildered children, where she would meet their eyes and exchange a look that said, *Here we are, in this giant world.*

Acorns

NATHAN DID NOT APPROVE OF THE WAY that Portia failed to pursue critical information.

"For months I've assumed that our neighbor's name was Gladys," she had confessed to him.

"Oh?" he asked. "What made you think that?"

"Because she looks like a Gladys. She has big glasses and *glasses* sounds like Gladys. They're beige."

"But why not just ask the woman her name?" Nathan was exasperated. There were so many ways to solve these types of problems. So many easy ways.

Portia shrugged. "I like Gladys."

Nathan could not accept this—to settle for a falsity, to accept the helpless unknown.

Portia's husband was a proud-looking man: handsome, with dark hair and a stern, well-structured face. Its only infirmity—and the one thing that Portia found to be heart-breakingly darling—was his mouth. It was soft and quick to betray what he was feeling. Portia could see so clearly in her mind the way that his lips parted when he was at rest, just enough so that she could see the gap in between his front teeth. Sometimes she felt that she loved him so specifically and microscopically: The way that his eyebrows tapered off, or the place where he was prone to getting a pimple. That one freckle. She knew everything about that one freckle, but she could not figure out why he was upset with her, or why it bothered him so much when she told him that she loved him.

"You say it too much," he told her. "After a while, it starts to sound like a demand. Like you need something from me." This did not make sense to Portia. Having too much love was like having too much fresh air or too many books: the only downside was that you would never have time for all of it.

They had just moved into their first home together, an old Victorian in the same small Vermont town on a street of old Victorians in various stages of renovation or disrepair. Portia's grandfather had given them money—they had sent him photos of the nicest-looking parts of the house, where the paint was not chipping, where the grass was not dead and brittle. There was one shutter that still had all of its slats. They did not want Portia's grandfather to think that he had invested in a dump.

There was an oak tree out front that chose that year to drop a remarkable number of acorns. Portia would wake up to the sound of the acorns popping under the tires of Nathan's car as he left for work. It had become impossible to mow the lawn or to be outside without getting struck on the head. Portia worried that they would fall on her little terrier, Rupert, but continued to watch the dog, with perverse curiosity, whenever she let him out into the yard. There was no getting rid of the acorns. Portia could spend the morning sweeping them away, just for the tree to drop another, larger, load. When she dared to look up into its boughs, she saw that they were full to their capacity, almost frighteningly so, as if the tree were committing a last act of desperation. Maybe it knew something that the rest of the world did not. The squirrels did not know what to do with this unexpected abundance, and they had given up trying to bury the acorns. Portia wondered if they would, in a turn of ironic events, end up starving that winter for lack of preparation.

She was, by then, preparing for the birth of her first child and dealing with her own overflow of belongings. The way that she and Nathan had moved out of their apartment had been hasty and disorganized. They had thrown everything into boxes and garbage bags, like people fleeing the police, and as Portia went through them, she found that most of the objects that they owned were unnecessary but not easy to dispose of. It was far easier, she decided, to keep the broken hangers, the stained pot holders, the lampshade that had been punctured by a pencil, and the tacky gifts given to them on their wedding. There was a white statue, about a foot tall, of two figures embracing—a sentimental thing that she was probably expected to put on the mantelpiece—that Portia spent all of one morning trying to throw away. She did not want it, but she felt responsible for it, the weight of it hitting the trash bag, the fateful thunk of it sinking into the coffee grounds and tinfoil and food wrappers too terrible to ignore. She reached in and pulled it out, lifting and lowering it, like a barbell. Yes, she thought, I will keep it next to the back door, where I will use it to bludgeon intruders.

Portia spent hours sorting through their belongings, trying to decide what to do with them. The house was so big. The walls were so bare. They had some framed pictures, but to hang them, she would need a hammer and a nail. She knew that the tools had not been packed together in the same box, and she feared that she would not be able to find the nails and that the feeling of failure would discourage her so much that she would not accomplish anything else that day. It seemed that all the necessary parts of her life were scattered about. And then, she thought, what if she did find a nail, but then Nathan came home and saw that she had hung the pictures before she had set the clock on the microwave? Or before she had located the toaster oven, like he had asked her to do, days ago? Her priorities were all backward.

"I'm not sure why you are eating processed cheese," Nathan had said to her, one night after they had finished dinner.

"I was craving it," she told him, her hand on her belly. He looked at her, puzzled.

"But do you think that is the best choice?"

Portia knew that this kind of open-ended criticism did not just address the cheese. If he can be worried about something as small as this, she thought, then what else has he noticed? She wondered if he had seen that she had not unpacked the dog leash yet—that she had no idea where the dog leash was—which meant that she had been letting the dog loose in the backyard to relieve itself (with the falling acorns), hoping each time that he would return to her—a great uncertainty. Nathan sometimes wondered if Portia's lack of concern when it came to Rupert reflected her ability to be a parent.

"How do you picture yourself as a mother?" he asked her.

"I don't know," Portia answered him, truthfully. "Motherhood is one of those things. You never know how you are going to be until it happens to you." Nathan had taken this to mean that Portia did not know if she was going to be a *good* mother. He bought her books about parenting. He watched her closely to see how she was behaving around the dog. So the walls were left bare, because somewhere along the way, a series of connections had been made that led her to believe that putting pictures on the wall would mean she was bad at prioritizing, which would make her a negligent mother, when the time came.

Among the boxes, Portia found her wedding dress, lying crumpled at the bottom of its dust bag. It must have fallen off the hanger sometime during the move. She found it in a storage bin that also had in it—to her horror—at least three thank-you cards that she had not yet sent to her wedding guests. It had been a little over a year since the wedding and Portia had forgotten about the dress—not really forgotten it, of course, but had not thought to keep track of it. As a child, she had assumed that weddings and all the precious things that they involved were crystalline and enduring, that they could not be muddled by memory or pushed aside by more immediate things. She had assumed that everyone remembered their wedding and that every new thing that occurred in life could, in some way, be traced back to that beautiful, perfect day. But then her own wedding to Nathan had come and gone. It had been a flash of happiness, a sunny afternoon spent with friends. Afterward, she felt the relief and weariness of having hosted a large party, as well as a new vulnerability, as if the universe were more likely to come crashing down upon her, now that her life had finally fallen into order. She looked at Nathan, as he drove the car toward their hotel, and realized that, in all the excitement, they had spoken very little to each other.

"Hi," she said to him.

"Hi," he said, and searched for her hand with his, his eyes never straying from the road.

It was on a cold Saturday in October that Nathan sliced his finger with a paring knife. He had been using the knife to open a prepackaged bag of salad because he could not find the scissors. The scissors had not been unpacked. Portia found him in the kitchen, clutching his bleeding finger over the sink, his back toward her. She could see the spots of blood on the white floor tiles, how they were spaced farther apart where Nathan must have moved quickly across the room.

"Get the first aid kit," he said. Portia felt something hopeless turn over in her gut. She already knew how this conversation was going to end. She would just have to bear it, beginning with the pain of telling her husband what he already knew.

"We don't have a first aid kit," she said.

Nathan turned his head just enough that she could see his profile. She saw his cheek tic inward. He looked like a man that was doing a good job at staying calm. He was a patient man, she knew, and she admired this about him. She knew that he would stand there and not say a word. He would not blame her or criticize her but instead allow her to get into the car and drive to the drugstore to buy bandages, which would give her just enough time to sit behind the wheel and to think about the lost scissors and the dog leash, the acorns that would not stop falling from the sky, the thank-you letters that she had not sent, and the stack of parenting books beside her bed that she had never opened.

A Young Father

○─○ THEO WAS NOT GETTING MUCH SLEEP. His wife had just given birth to their first son, and the baby woke throughout the night, crying every hour—every two hours, if they were lucky—to be soothed. Theo found that when he did manage to sleep, the expectation of being woken so often allowed him only a half slumber, where dreams were not immersive. Instead, the dreams stuck to him, like spiderwebs draped over his face. He could open his eyes to the sound of his son's whimpers, lift the baby from the bassinet, and fold him over his shoulder, all without removing the sticky dream veil. In this delirium, Theo thought about the child, his son, and wondered where there was time to understand what had happened. Between the baby's crying and needing to be changed and his burrowing search for a nipple where Theo could provide none, how would Theo begin to understand that he was now a father? Would it be when he returned to work and the woman swiveling behind the partition said, "There he is! Hi, Dad"? Would his office be filled with balloons? Would he feel it then?

One night, he woke and discovered that he could not move his body. All he could see was the ceiling of his bedroom, and all he could hear was the soft, moist snoring of his wife beside him. He tried to touch his finger to his thumb, but he did not even know where his hand was, as if it were miles away, deep beneath the blankets, like a frozen carrot in the soil. Slowly, he realized that there was a weight on his chest, some fuzzy planet beneath his chin. It was his son, asleep. He must have dozed off holding the baby. Theo began to feel his hand then, where it had gone numb resting on the baby's diapered bottom. His other hand appeared, just beside it, cold and rigid. In sleep, Theo's body had petrified itself around the baby, so that the baby would not fall. By means of some inconceivable fatherly instinct, he had become stone—just like that—when he was otherwise too tired to shave or to stand when he used the toilet at night.

During the day, he ran errands for his wife. They had one car, so he walked, just in case there was an emergency with the baby and his wife needed to drive somewhere quickly. Despite the constant waking at night, the sticky feeling of exhaustion, and the chatter of dreams that followed him throughout the day, Theo was exhilarated. He walked across town, on his way to the drugstore where you could still get ginger ale in glass bottles (his wife's favorite), and his mind was full of new ideas, for the books that he wanted to write, the movies that he wanted to direct, the scenes he would play, if he were an actor.

What artistic feeling I could express, he thought to himself, if only I could tap into this time. It was a gauzy time of life, where he seemed to exist with his wife as a single, exhausted forest of limbs that passed the baby, who weighed

almost nothing, back and forth. His wife was always wiping a
yawn from her mouth. Theo's eyes always felt as though they
had been crying. He crossed a side street, where the pavement was still striped from the passage of a street cleaner. He
had a new baby, he thought. His wife loved him. A red car
drove by with an open hand stretched out the window. Theo
waved, although he had not seen whose hand it was. His wife
loved him, but, someday, she no longer would. A part of him
already knew this, especially in the sleepy, near-mystic state
that he was in. But it did not matter, because that day was
far off. And he was going to come home with ginger ale, cold,
and in a glass bottle!

At the intersection on Main Street, Theo pressed the
button for the walk signal. He always pressed the button but
then crossed as soon as there was a break in traffic, without
waiting for the light. He had done this since he was a boy
and, although it was such a small act of rebellion, it felt inevitable, as if failing to press the button, or worse, pressing
the button and waiting for the signal to grant him passage,
would certainly bring bad luck. As he was stepping off the
curb, Theo noticed a girl wearing a yellow sundress on the
opposite sidewalk. Theo recognized the girl, who was bent
over to fix her shoe, as Portia Elby, someone he knew only
vaguely, through a familiar circle of acquaintances—artists
and musicians he rarely saw, now that there was the baby.

Still, he felt himself light up, remembering a night, not
long ago, that he had helped her break into her car after a

party. Portia was young—just out of high school—and Theo had watched a pout of naivete play across her features, as she began to comprehend all the things that could go wrong once you got your license, your freedom. She had been impressed by how well he had fashioned a device to pull up the lock— "I'm very forgetful," he had explained—and he could sense that she was perhaps more impressed that he had not offered to drive her home or tried in some way to take advantage of the situation, even casually. Now that she was finished with her shoe, she noticed him coming toward her, and she smiled, involuntarily, it seemed, with expectation and amusement. It buoyed him. He wanted to talk to her, if even for just a moment, to tell her all the things that had been in his mind.

Yellow Dress

PORTIA HAD BEEN PLAYING GUITAR FOR A band called Poor Alice for almost three years. The name had been her idea, based on a misconception that she had long held about the lyrics to the song "White Rabbit," by Grace Slick. The original version of the song opened with a lengthy, serpent-like instrumental that felt to Portia like swimming down, down, through watery light. Slick's voice came in at a low register, at the bottom of this imagined light pool, confident and grave. Portia had seen footage of Slick, standing erect while she sang, not snapping her fingers or swaying or tossing her hair. "Go ask Alice," she commanded. Her presence was a stare-down.

The "Alice" in the song was, of course, Lewis Carroll's Alice—swallowing pills, changing size, caught in a hallucinogenic whirlwind. And the lyrics were not "poor Alice," but, for a long time, that was what Portia heard when she listened to the song. The poor girl, becoming too large and then too small, the telescoping of the character, being used again and again in pop culture. Everybody thought they knew Alice. Everybody thought they knew what to do with her.

Portia had owned her Gibson Les Paul since high school. Her choice in model was guided only by the recommendation of

the Guitar World employee, who had promised that the guitar would make her sound like Billy Corgan, from Smashing
Pumpkins. It was a dream that was quickly abandoned, however; Portia was not adept at playing fast riffs or anything
that required her short fingers to stretch past their limit. But
she felt that she understood the temperament of the electric
guitar, the ways that it wanted to crunch, or complain. Over
the years, she found a way to make its rogue tendencies work
in her favor. That was what she told herself before a show, at
least, when her anxiety was greatest.

It seemed that Portia and Carrie, the band's lead singer
and guitarist, were the most high-strung when it came to
performing and that their drummer, Theo, was more apt
to show up at the last minute, toss down a beer, and start
playing without a fuss. The three of them developed a small
following over the years, mostly playing in the corners of
bars or at outdoor events, where the audience was friendly,
drunk, and mostly indifferent. They practiced every Sunday
at Carrie's house, because Carrie was the most serious about
Poor Alice's development as a band, and because she and
her husband, Gus, did not have dogs or children that would
interfere in the permanent labyrinth of musical equipment
that spanned the living room floor.

Portia looked forward to their practices. She considered
the intimacy between band members to be of a superior nature, where moments of self-doubt and artistic experimentation could be shared and then forgiven. Portia had often

brought ideas to the band that had failed—a lyric or a guitar solo—and Carrie and Theo did not berate her or ask her to explain herself. They themselves suffered occasionally from moments of memory loss, bad performances, bad ideas in general. Maybe it was obvious that this was the way that it should be among friends, but Portia could not think of any other relationship where she could be so at ease. Being in a band seemed to her to be a sacred thing, one that should never be threatened by jealousy or competition and certainly never mixed with romantic feelings.

◆

When Portia was eighteen, she liked to get up early on summer days, before the shops opened, and walk downtown. From there, she would feel the beginning of the day, that hazy, electric sense of morning before the heat arrives. There were joggers and dog walkers at this hour and the scent of pollenating trees and faint whiffs of garbage trucks. Portia knew her town well, and there was no part of it where she felt unsafe. There was an alleyway between the bookstore and the pub that had been painted over by a group of fifth graders to make it look more appealing. They painted children holding hands in a line, with colorful clothing and too many teeth, and the dogs and the drunks still peed in there, but it did not seem like a defeat. More like a compromise, another undeniable truth, along with the brown patch of land where the theater had burned down and would never be rebuilt, the vulgar messages on the stop signs, the man who slept in the vestibule of the library and was polite to the children as they came and went.

Portia wanted so badly to make something of herself during these summers—to finish reading a book without being distracted; to ride her bicycle to another town without becoming tired; to write a song on her guitar all in one sitting. In the early mornings, before she had eaten breakfast or taken a shower, she could sometimes feel the potential of the day building in front of her, like storm clouds—all the things that she could accomplish, all the people that she might become. But then she would find herself walking to the Salvation Army and sliding the hangers aimlessly back and forth.

Who would I be if I started wearing plaid skirts? she would ask herself. Who would I be if I bought that hat? It was easier to think this way—to change her hair, to start a new book without finishing the last one, to throw away all her shoes—than to commit to something deeper and unknown.

There was a morning that she woke up and decided that she could no longer wear pants and that to be completely herself, without pretense, she would have to start wearing dresses. Plain, undramatic dresses—but not ugly, she consoled herself. Ugly could be mistaken for theatrics. She walked to the thrift store and found something that fit the description. It was knee-length and a pale, sun-washed yellow with faint flowers, like an unassuming bit of wallpaper.

She bought the dress and put it on, right there in the store, stripping her jeans and tank top from underneath, ignoring the musty odor of the unwashed fabric.

For the first stretch of her walk home, she felt good, courageously different than who she had been when she started the day. She could feel the softness of her thighs sweeping as she walked and the dampness beginning at her hairline. She had come to the large intersection on Main Street and was leaning over, sticking a finger down the back of her shoe, where there was a blister forming, when she saw Theo crossing the street toward her. Theo existed to Portia the same way the remains of the old theater existed: in a way that was comforting and a little intriguing but easily taken for granted. Sometimes it was hard to remember that in the long weeks that Portia went without running into him, Theo was living a life, that he might be struggling, thriving, and dreaming on his own time. Theo was different from the other men that she knew in this way: he could drop into Portia's day and be completely commanding of her attention and then fly right out of her life once again, terrifically.

"I have an idea for a movie," he said, skipping onto the curb. "About aliens that cause sleep paralysis—or sleep paralysis that causes aliens." He spread his fingers in narrative excitement. "I still haven't decided." Theo was tall and dark-haired and somehow familiar to Portia—his blacker-than-black hair, the freckles on his skin, the color of his lips. She had a notion that they were physically alike, that an outsider, going on only the shallowest references, would probably pair them together. They knew each other only through a casual—and ever-shifting—web of artists and musicians who frequented the bookstores, the college parties, and open mic nights at the coffee shop. They were not the same age, but it was possible that they were unaware of this; it was easy for people in that crowd, who were under thirty, to merge into one category.

Portia took her finger out of her shoe and stood straight. She could not tell if this business about the movie was in earnest or if it was one of those grand ideas that young men liked to talk about: projects that would take years to develop, all for the sake of a gag or a cheap punch line. There was something of a sport in this conniving, of these fantasies that were rarely carried out in full but committed to wholeheartedly in the moment.

She remembered playing along with Theo that day, smiling and walking with him up the sidewalk, while remaining just coy enough to recover her dignity if he wasn't serious in the end. She remembered speaking to him in that certain way that conveyed interest and a cautious level of romantic availability, even though it was clear to her that he was married, a new father, and all the things that made him unattainable to her. It was such a fleeting moment, but it stood out to her, as another one of those subtle, innate decisions that she would make when Theo was around, like a strange pollination that she could barely understand. And just as quickly as he had come, he veered down another street, full of energy, back into his unknown life. Wherever he was going, it comforted her to know that he had seen her that day, in her dingy yellow dress, exactly as she wanted to be seen.

The Rock Star

ALBY PORTER HAD DIED THE SAME YEAR that Portia's son was born. She had been seven months pregnant when her phone began lighting up with messages from friends who wanted to share the news, some who wanted to offer their condolences. He was Portia's favorite musician, after all. *You introduced me to his music,* they texted. *This album always made me think of you.* Her childhood friend, Meredith Leek, called her from Washington: "How are you holding out?" Assuming that she had already heard and that she was devastated.

She was not devastated.

Instead, Portia had been irritated. It was embarrassing how everyone was scrambling to prove how much Alby Porter had meant to them—the songs of his that they associated with youth and girlfriends and breakups. Everyone had something to memorialize on their online profiles in connection to his songs, whether it was a full head of hair, now thinned, or a first cigarette, or maybe the girl who they should have loved in high school but had not. Portia did not blame these people for wanting to be sentimental. It was just that she could not put her finger on how she felt about Alby Porter, and all the noise and chatter about it—the texts and the calls—had been distracting. She was preparing to have a baby. She was already emotional, bewildered, and Alby Porter's death had been like a distant forest fire: you could not conceive of it, could not properly grieve it. But you could see it on the horizon. Everywhere, the headlines and radio hosts lamented it.

Four years later, Portia was in her kitchen, getting ready to make Julian his lunch, when Carrie texted her: *If you haven't already, please listen to this as soon as possible.*

Within the text, Carrie had included a link to a news article about Alby Porter. Apparently, even this long after death, new recordings had been unearthed: a whole album's worth of never-released versions of hit songs. And one new song, recorded in the 1980s, that no one had ever heard before. All Portia had to do was tap a small icon with her finger and she could hear this new song right away. She was still not used to being able to access music so instantly, having spent hours as a child by the radio, waiting for her favorite songs to play. She had almost forgotten how precious music had been to her in her youth, during that time before full autonomy. Listening to a song that you had waited all day to hear was like being aligned, for just three minutes, with the benevolence of the universe.

She played the late Alby Porter's newly released song, and her kitchen filled with that familiar voice, just as alive as it had ever been. She dipped her hands into the sink and began to wash the dishes, listening with as little melodrama as possible. Porter's music had always befuddled her, pleasantly, its message at the same time dark and hopeful, as if the two qualities did not have to conflict. He was an authority on all things gritty and glamorous and countercultural, and she had never wanted to decipher his lyrics or learn them by heart. She was content to let his voice pass through her, unbridled, free from comprehension. She listened this way, until her son ran around the corner and asked about lunch.

"Sure," she said to him. "Let me finish these dishes." But instead she went back to her phone to restart the song.

"E, are we still drowning?" Alby Porter sang in his deep, lusty voice.

Portia scrolled back to hear the chorus again. It had mystery to it. It had the confident delirium of his other work, but there was something unusually occult about it, as in still buried, entombed. Not yet tarnished by the world's ears.

Four years ago, Portia's son, Julian, had been born by cesarean section. She had not been expecting to have surgery and became so panicked that the anesthesiologist slipped something into her IV—something smooth and calming that had made her see things that were not there. There was a blue paper curtain hung in front of her face so that she could not see the doctor and nurses sorting through her insides. She thought: They are like people who have accidentally thrown away something important and now must don gloves and pick through the trash bin. She thought: Oh, what a horrible thing to think during my child's birth.

"It's okay," a voice said to her, and she turned her head.

"Have they tied down my hands?" she asked the man to her left, where her husband should have been.

"You go ahead and think whatever you need to think," the man said, and his surgical mask puffed rapidly, like a heartbeat, with his breath. She did not know who the man was, but she was comforted by him. His voice was deep and familiar, as if she had been hearing it all her life. The man was, she now realized, Alby Porter.

"Don't worry about your hands," he had said. "Your hands will come back to you." Then there had been a sound and he had turned his head and looked toward the foot of the operating table, where they were holding the baby.

"How does he look?" she asked Alby, but he was gone, and it was her husband who said: "He looks like a burrito." They lay the swaddled baby on her chest, and she felt her hands grow back from wherever they had been—cool, like new green plants, like arms floating up from a pool—and they held her son.

"Is lunch ready?" Julian wanted to know. Portia looked down and saw his face, his long black eyelashes that made him look so sincere, the way some animals, like horses or sheep, appear sincere and martyr-like, no matter what they are up to.

"You know," she said to her son, "when I first saw you,

you didn't look like anyone I knew. You looked like someone who had been around for longer than the earth. Have you ever seen the face of a snapping turtle?"

He shook his head.

"Well, babies have a face like that. Older than time." She did not know what had compelled her to say this. She did not know how long she had been standing there, by the counter, where her phone was plugged into the wall, waiting for the song to end so that she could start it again. There was a certain anxiety to it: If I begin making lunch—if I do anything else—then I might not make it back in time to restart the song, she thought.

Why hadn't she realized that it had been him next to her, on the night of her son's birth? Alby Porter had been wearing a surgical mask. She had seen his breath move the mask as he spoke to her, even though, by then, he would have already been two months dead. The breath was proof that he had not been a hallucination due to the anesthesia, as she had suspected all these years.

"E, are we still drowning?"

There was something about the chorus. The E was key—a first initial, perhaps, or a leftover letter. She got out a paper and pen and wrote out the words. Yes, she thought, her hands gripping her head in concentration. Yes, I can figure this out.

"Mom." The boy had appeared in front of her again, and she still had not moved or made any sign of getting his lunch ready. It was almost two o'clock. But her old friend Carrie had brought the song to her attention, and Carrie had not written to her in years.

✦

Carrie and Portia met in tenth-grade health class. The teacher that year was a long-term substitute, who was far too preoccupied with explaining to his female students what type of body they had, of four possibilities. Carrie, he stated with some guarded approval, was a "ruler"—straight up and down. Portia, however, he stated with less guarded approval, was a "pear," which he had better not explain. He believed that each person should follow a high-protein diet dictated by his or her blood type. Everything could be categorized and treated, from oily skin and the softness of tooth enamel to the predisposition to certain chemical addictions. They rarely followed the textbook in class. The health teacher also claimed to have the ability to see auras, especially during first block, before he had polluted his senses with a second cup of coffee. Portia and Carrie were in his first-block class.

"Carrie," the health teacher had uttered one morning from his desk. She looked up. Carrie was less outspoken than Portia, but she had a fierce quality, perhaps owing to the very slight V shape to her forehead and the dramatic crevice above her lip. Portia found it to be intriguing, masculine, and enviable.

"Carrie, your aura is looking very green today," the health teacher told her. "What are you up to?" Before she could speak, he pushed his chair back, which jarred most of the students out of their fog. "And Portia," he said, frowning and shaking his head abruptly. "Yours is brewing something. Like a storm. I don't like it." But, of course, he did like it. He liked whatever metaphysical conspiracy he was concocting.

Portia and Carrie had never planned to take any of this seriously. The attention from their health teacher, linking them, directly or indirectly, should have discouraged them from becoming friends. It did discourage them at first, but as the year progressed, Portia found her eyes drawn to Carrie's more often, whenever their teacher's behavior warranted a look of disbelief, exasperation, or weary amusement. It seemed that the only way to be friends without giving this man exactly what he wanted was to call it something else. They decided that they would teach themselves to play guitar, and they would start a band, just the two of them.

Carrie had been there on the day that Portia was released from the psychiatric hospital. She had brought flowers to the house, which was her way of being sincere without having to address the occasion outright. Some of the flowers still had the roots attached and the gray dust from the roadside. It had been a long time since they had played music, Carrie said. Maybe they could try it. Portia looked at her friend's face, slick with the heat, her fingernails and knees dirty. There was a streaked spot of blood on her ankle, where a bug bite had been scratched too many times. Portia did not want to play her guitar with Carrie. She was overcome by the itch of being back in the world, and she wanted to flex her freedom, like a bird pumping its wings. There was something deeply narcissistic about her desire, as if she had gone unnoticed for too long, locked in the hospital. As if she had to catch up to her own existence, and the most upsetting piece to it was that Carrie's company would not do.

Portia remembered Jerry standing before her, breathing heavily, enraptured. He had flinched at her touch, making a soft sound of surprise. She knew that his nervous energy was neither love nor amazement. But Jerry had ignited something—a craving for the impossible. Intensity. Ecstatic attraction. Things that had no business in normal life.

"I would like to play music," Portia said. "But I'm so tired." She gestured toward her head and blinked slowly.

Carrie nodded. "You should take it easy. Take care of yourself." She placed the flowers on the coffee table, and Portia could see that they had already begun to wilt at the stems, where her friend had been clutching them in her hot hand. It was uncomfortable to see Carrie, who had always been unfailingly tomboyish, attempting tenderness. Portia was grateful, but she also wanted Carrie to go away, if only so she would not have to feel any guiltier for what she was about to do.

She did not want to take it easy. She did not want to take

care of herself. As soon as Carrie left, Portia walked outside, following the sidewalk toward town, until she found what she was looking for: someone new, unblemished, shiny with romantic possibilities. A man who might see her and be excited by her. The man was sitting outside a coffee shop with an espresso, and when she sat across from him and rested her cheek on her hand, displaying the hospital bracelets on her wrist, he merely raised his eyebrows. He had not minded the bracelets and had even toyed with them playfully back at his apartment as they lay together on the couch.

Portia remembered feeling so tired. She had almost forgotten how she had arrived there and who the man was that now had his arm draped over her, so sweetly and possessively. The man—Nathan—would one day be her husband, but for that moment on his couch she could not even recall his name. She sometimes lost track of people in her mind, of how well she knew them. She sometimes introduced people who already knew each other. She had once introduced herself in a restaurant to her family's veterinarian, a man who had known her almost all her life. In her defense, he had been wearing a purple sweater and drinking a beer. Completely out of context. It was not that she was aloof, but that she had no discernment when it came to familiarity: the round face of the boy who worked at the gas station at the end of the street would always be as vivid to her as the face of her best friend.

And so she had experienced a moment of panic, curled

up with the man who would someday be the father of her child. How well did she know him? She had an idea that they had been to many of the same parties together and that they had once had a meaningful conversation in a dark parking lot, after she had locked her keys inside her car. She had the feeling that he had always been around, that he had been a vital part of her young-adult life, springing in and out without warning. He had come to one of her and Carrie's shows, in a friend's basement, and he had said that their music was "surprising," "interesting." Portia had wanted to be interesting to somebody that night, to anyone in the world.

No.

He was not the one who had helped her break into her car. It had been a different man with dark hair, only she could not remember who. She had a habit of letting her associations take over. It was a combination of vague associations, along with an overactive imagination and a dose of insecurity, that led her to these mix-ups. So much of her perception of reality was based on her own secret, wishful logic. Maybe someone else would have been concerned after seeing what she had seen in the operating room, but not her. She had accepted it, nestled it into that place between fantasy and truth, where faces and names were incompatible and memories were kaleidoscopic, beautiful, and untrustworthy— where she had always been most comfortable.

The Bus Game

PORTIA WAS SUPPOSED TO BE RELEASED FROM the psychiatric hospital on a Friday, but Dr. Shay had been called out on an emergency before he could discharge her. The following Monday was a holiday, so that meant that she would have to stay in the hospital for another three days. Portia was not altogether upset by this news. It meant that the length of her stay would be brought to a full three weeks. Three weeks sounded much more serious than two and a half. To say, "I was in a mental hospital for three weeks," was like the difference between telling your classmates that you had broken your arm rather than sprained it. She could not say why she needed to be taken so seriously, but it likely had something to do with the puzzling nature of her illness and the ease with which people—observers—might find room for belittlement. Dr. Shay had come to see her in her room on a morning when she could not compose herself. Her sobs had deteriorated into a hoarse growl; she had torn at her hair, frightened by the way that her face had swollen and sealed with crying.

"Oh, darling," Dr. Shay said as he had taken a chair beside her bed. "You look positively heartbroken." His words had been strong and sincere. He had meant what he had said, this lovely, stray exclamation that could have come from a father to his daughter. But to Portia, it represented a failure on her part to convey her despair so that the world could understand it. There she was, hurling it around, opening herself to the mess of it, crying into the bottomless pit of it, and all that this man—this expert on despair itself—could discern was heartbreak, which was not the same. Other girls, one might say, are polite enough to save their weeping for the bathroom mirror, the dirty dishwater—the moon!—but not Portia. Not our Portia.

When her parents brought her in to see Dr. Shay, he had been concerned, but he had needed a real reason if he was going to admit her. Hospital beds were scarce, he explained to the three of them, and Portia imagined that he might be speaking of a kind of bleak, one-room asylum, laid out like an orphanage, with rows of beds tucked neatly under gray wool blankets. The way that he was talking made the notion of occupying one of these beds sound like a victory.

"If you had a plan—" Dr. Shay caught himself. He was a gray-haired man with shining tortoiseshell spectacles and dark eyebrows. He had been Portia's psychiatrist since she was fifteen years old, and his sophistication, his conceitedness, and his apparent admiration for her had always fixed her in a state of wanting to impress him. There was a balance to be maintained. She needed to remain troubled but also resilient. She could usually tell by his reaction whether she had tipped too far in either direction.

"Portia," he began again. "Many times, when patients

come to me in a *state*, they have a plan. Sometimes they are not sure how to act on this plan, but they have made one all the same." He glanced at Portia's parents, as if to reassure them that all this was almost tortuously commonplace. "Do you understand what I am saying?"

✦

Portia had never truly wanted to die, but the possibility of no longer existing came, every so often, as a comfort. Years later, after the birth of her son, when she was deprived of sleep and alone with the baby for most of the day, she would play, what she liked to call, the "Bus Game." You did not need anyone else to play the Bus Game, but because Julian was there, squirming on his back on the cloth that Portia had laid down for him, and because you were supposed to talk to babies to build their language skills, Portia would play the Bus Game with him.

"I won't be able to take my cell phone or my credit card," she began. The living room carpet was lit only by those lackluster squares of light from the winter sky. Julian swung a naked, wrinkled arm across his chest, willing himself to roll onto his side. His face had plumped in the months since his birth, and he looked less like a root vegetable, less like a shriveled stand-in for a human being, and more like a precious, confused, milk-drunk soul, swinging his limbs around, wanting to succeed at something—anything.

"I'll have to wait till the summer, the day after my period

ends, so I won't be cold or bleeding." She spoke in light, cheerful tones and her baby's eyes glistened, his tongue reaching out in attentiveness.

"I'll buy a bus ticket, going west. To save money, I'll eat very little, and never anything that I would have to cook. Canned beans, beef jerky, candy bars. I'll only ever spend money on a hotel if I have to."

The aim of the Bus Game was to get as far away as possible from her home—her life—as quickly as possible, before her family and Nathan could trace her. To give her enough time to make herself unrecognizable, impossible to rehabilitate. The aim was not to succeed, Portia explained to her baby, but to envision the steps to her ruin, every detail, until she saw herself miles away from home, cast onto the curb, covered in shit and lice. It was comforting to fantasize this way, exhausting all her options, one by one.

◆

And then she would find moments of peace: Julian had gone down for a nap; Portia had a few minutes to stretch her brain, to untether her thoughts from the close-up focus on her baby. She also happened to be staring at the wall.

"What are you doing?" Nathan stepped into the living room, or perhaps he had been there for a while, watching her sit in perfect stillness. "Is this what you do?" His voice was cautious, almost premeditated.

Portia looked up and saw the confusion in his face. She was learning that his accusations came wrapped and shiny in confusion, in schoolboy astuteness.

"I just want to understand," he said to her, stepping forward with his palms pressed together. "I want to give you a chance to defend yourself, before I assume that you are being airheaded, staring at the wall, thinking about nothing."

Portia could feel the weariness closing in again, the anxiety and self-doubt. Some days it followed her, persistent and draining like the shrill whistling of a car window that has been shut improperly. She tried to push it away, but she could not. *Lazy. Not confident enough. Unreliable.*

"I'm only resting," she said. Her voice was already beginning to tremble. Nathan sighed, most likely realizing that an argument was not worth the trouble. He kissed the back of her head.

"I'm sorry," he said. "I only thought that you would want to use your time more wisely." On his way out of the room, he added: "I hope you will not space out like that in front of Julian. What if he needs you?"

◆

Within twenty minutes of examining her, Dr. Shay had extracted from her what he needed to make the call. Portia felt as though she had confessed to a crime that she had performed in her sleep or admitted to a cruel thought that she had had as a child. This version of herself—the one that needed urgent intervention—was unfamiliar, however, she acknowledged, quite probable.

Her parents came back into Dr. Shay's office, and she could see how drawn their faces were, with worry and with the recognition of this probability. She wished that she could take it all back, just as much as she welcomed the relief of not having to make any more decisions that day. There would be a bed for her. A bed. She had never dreamed that such a thing would be available to her: an exit of crisp linens and stainless steel. Sometimes when Portia's family came home from a long vacation, Portia would find her bed made up as neatly as she had left it, and she would slip herself imperceptibly between the sheets, searching for a new feeling, a dormant freshness, like starting over.

Portia hoped that the world would afford her this feeling on the day of her release. It was a Tuesday in late May, and she could see from her window the slow boxing match of the trees outside the hospital, their boughs blowing like great arms.

"What's on your mind?" Her father had come early to the hospital and was sitting beside her in the common area while she finished breakfast.

"I'm watching the trees," she told him. "Sometimes I feel like I have to choose myself again every day. From scratch." She paused. "Like, 'Who am I going to be today?'"

Portia understood that her hospital stay had offered

her a break from this decision. In the hospital, she had been allowed to be a very specific case, shaped by prescriptions, mood charts, and verbal histories. She had also been allowed to be nobody. You could read the tabloids and be no one. You could walk a slow, balmy lap around the grounds, ask for another sedative, and be no one at all.

There was a narrow room lined with metal lockers in the hallway opposite Portia's room, where patients were asked to lock up their valuable belongings. Portia had a portable CD player in there, a diary, and a bottle of perfume that she had forgotten was in the pocket of her bag upon arriving. She left her father at the table with his Styrofoam cup of black coffee to collect these items, and when she came back, slouched beneath her duffle bag, like a college student, she found him standing by the entryway, ready to drive her home.

It lasted an hour, that feeling of wonder upon reentering the world, where Portia could see the houses along the road with their quaintly chipped paint, their open windows with fluttering curtains inside. She saw this holy triptych of depth: the window frame, the patterned curtain, and the interior darkness. She felt the many dimensions of life, the much-longed-for moments where objects held no despair and the summer was still long.

"I met a man named Jerry," her father said, his hands planted on the wheel. "While you were getting your things." Portia turned from the window. She remembered how Jerry had come into her room, fumbling with his pajamas. The memory felt like something that had happened in another time. It came edged with shame.

"He was looking for you," her father continued. "He said, 'I want to say goodbye to that nice girl. She was so nice and so pretty.' I guess you really made an impression."

Theo

THEO HAD FELT THE CHANGE IN HIS HANDS when he was at work, sitting at his desk. The sensations traveled from the tips of his fingers up to his elbows in surges, until he could not rest his hands on the computer keyboard anymore but was compelled to hold them in the air, as if in surrender. His coworkers walked by his open door and caught sight of him like this. They shook their heads. Theo had been on the verge of something outlandish for a while now. No one was surprised.

It had been a difficult year for Theo. His wife had left him, although he never thought of it or described it in that way. It had been a gentle separation—painful, but without cruelty. Theo had felt relief in a heavy, breathless way, like someone sinking to the bottom of a lake. He had watched the air bubbles of his life rise up around him and thought: I will never recover from this, but it is all for the better.

That Christmas, his teenage sons had hung their stockings at his apartment. They were stockings bought at the last minute in the seasonal aisle of the grocery store, because the boys had kept their knitted stockings—the nice stockings, made by Grandma—at their mother's house, where there was an actual fireplace. The supermarket stockings had needed to be attached by an adhesive, because Theo was not sure if he was allowed to put holes in the walls. As he fumbled with the strips of Velcro, he wondered if, by giving his sons two Christmas trees (his and their mother's), as well as double the holiday parties and the holiday treats, he wasn't cheapening the experience in some way. I need to give them a Christmas morning, he had thought, or else I am giving up. I would be giving up on myself. This is just as much about me as it is about them, he thought. And that was the difference: after the divorce, Theo had to make room for selfishness, and it was the loneliest thing that he had ever done. He hung the grocery store stockings. He found an old box of tinsel. *Tinsel!* He threw a clump of it at the tree and watched the silver strands float in a draft from the window. He thought: How does anyone do this?

On the weekends, Theo played drums in a three-piece rock band called Poor Alice. The name had not been his idea, but he had helped design the small white bottle that was their logo. They sometimes sold bumper stickers and pins at their shows: a small white bottle on a black background. Theo thought that it was simple and appealing. He had never thought of himself as a drummer, but his friend, Carrie, had not known this. Before the divorce, Carrie and her husband had been over for drinks and she had spotted the drum kit in the study on her way to use the bathroom. The kit belonged to Theo's oldest son, but the son had lost interest in it by the time Carrie called and asked Theo if he wanted to play in the band. He had been about to say no, that he did not play drums and that his life was falling apart. He and his wife had just started marriage counseling, where they discussed how often they touched each other affectionately or where in their day they might find time to practice compassion. They never spoke about the looks of pity and impatience that Theo's wife gave him whenever he tried to talk about anything out of the ordinary, as if she knew already where he was going with it, as if she had figured him out long ago.

"I'm wondering about that sensation that you get. The sensation of falling when you're trying to sleep," he might say to her, and she would say, "What about it?" with her eyebrows raised.

"I'm wondering if it ever leads somewhere other than sleep. What if—" but she would cut him off.

"I'm sure it's nothing more than what it is," she would say. "You don't have to make everything into something more interesting than it is."

He might say to his wife, "I have this strange feeling in my hands. They feel all lit up, like beacons."

And she would say, "Did you take something for it?"

"It's not a headache."

"Did you call the doctor?"

Theo was about to tell Carrie that she had better ask someone else to be her drummer. He could not imagine taking the kit apart and moving it, piece by piece, into the back of his car, then driving it to her house every weekend. He was tired of everything.

"Do you remember Portia?" she asked him. He was silent. He thought of a humid summer morning, twelve years ago. A sunny Main Street. A girl with short dark hair, who he used to see around town.

Of course he remembered Portia.

Hunger

Ever since Carrie had texted her about Alby Porter's unreleased song, Portia had found herself listening to it on repeat, forgetting to eat breakfast and lunch, nearly forgetting to be at the school on time to walk Julian home. She had not noticed that anything was amiss at first, because it had felt so good and so promising, listening to these songs, as if they had been written just for her. How they moved through her body, like personal triumph, like the thrill of good news, again and again. All she had to do was hit repeat. Hit repeat.

She knew the hills and valleys of Porter's songs, the specific nuances of his voice—where it became gruff, or where it soared, or where it was unguarded and soft—so familiar to her that she could see the shape of his mouth in her mind. Her senses were so ignited that she could not help but feel as though every particle of the world had been designed specifically for her. The grass and spiderwebs in the morning trembling with dew. The air itself, crafted finely to accommodate her body, hugging every eyelash, every goosebump. In this way, she had begun to love the world, through its minutiae and also its laws: Light. Darkness. Gravity. Death. What funny little things, she thought, like Julian with his toys. He could not see that they were much less than he imagined them to be, that their eyes were only buttons, their downy voices his own.

Portia had played guitar when she was young, before she was married and before her son was born. She had been told in college that she was skilled at writing songs, and she wondered, sometimes, how far she would have made it, if she had committed herself. If she had not given up. She could have made it big. She knew this now, hearing Alby Porter's last album, seeing his mouth and the shapes of his lyrics in her mind, understanding that he was somehow reaching for her through the lyrics.

"Did any part of you step back from this," Dr. Shay wanted to know, "and question what was going on?" Portia had been seeing Dr. Shay again. He was nearing retirement and had already begun referring his patients to other doctors. However, he had made an exception for Portia. After all, they had known each other for so long.

"No," Portia answered. "I kept it to myself, so that no one could take it from me, tell me it wasn't real."

"So part of you, deep down, knew that it was a delusion?" Dr. Shay lowered his voice. In all the years that Portia had known him, he had never used that word. She had not come to him because she suspected that she was delusional. It was only that she had been losing sleep over the matter and it was making her irritable. She had shouted at Julian one morning, for scraping his cup along the tabletop. She was not a mother who shouted.

Portia looked hard at Dr. Shay. "Do you know that you are going bald?" she asked him. "Right on top, where you think people can't see." Part of this new sense of daring sometimes meant that she was not afraid to be blunt—even rude.

Dr. Shay tilted his head, incredulously but fondly. She could see that he was deflecting the insult by looking at her this way, as if he knew her so well, as if she were a young lover acting unreasonably and he found it adorable.

◆

She had become aloof toward Nathan during the day and clingy at night. The days were full of things to do and music to listen to. The days filled her with gratification—when the sun shone through the windowpane, she could see the specks of dust churning through the wedge of light, and it changed, and it was endlessly brilliant. At night, however, the activity of the day—the lights and the music—disappeared and she was left alone with a cavernous ache inside her chest. She lay in bed and wanted to pull the world into her, to gather it up around her and press it to her. She pushed her face into Nathan's hair and breathed in the dull, oily scent. The desire that she felt for him was like nothing that she had ever experienced, like being engulfed in flames, looking desperately for someone to drag into the fire. Her hand found the elastic to his boxers. She tasted his neck, bit him, right behind his ear. She wanted something from him—something explosive and annihilating—but he swatted at her.

"What's wrong with you?" he asked.

She eventually dreamed that she climbed a mountain and found the castle of God and that the castle of God was so unfathomably large that she required a special kind of goggles to be able to see it. The angels fitted her with the goggles, which looked more like a heavy, transparent helmet that magnified the light shining into her head. The result was overwhelming. She experienced the feeling of being very high up and important, having climbed all that way, to the highest point in the universe. She could sense the angels dancing around her, all creamy and fair, trailing their bright auras. That was when she realized that what she had been looking at—the immense house of God, this impossibly large building, balanced on the peak of everything—was not a castle at all, but only the very first brick of the foundation of something even larger, something that she would never be able to understand.

When Portia woke the next morning, things were better. She was hungry again, so she made herself an egg in the frying pan, watched the white skirt of it sizzle and snap in the butter, and she began to feel the pain in her stomach, just under her ribs. It felt like the pain of coming back to life. She had heard accounts of people regaining consciousness after having been pronounced dead, how to some, it had felt as if they were being dragged back into the world against their will, the agony of their nerves rekindling, like a million tiny fires.

Root

PORTIA LIKED TO WATCH FOR THE ROOF OF
her husband's car before she washed the dishes. She would
look out the window above the kitchen sink, waiting for it
impatiently, but nervously, as one might wait to catch the
dorsal of a sea creature passing by. Once it appeared, she
had two minutes to make sure that the water was flowing
and hot, the suds thick and dripping. It was a mistake to
start the dishes too early and then to be left with empty
hands when Nathan walked in, to be caught standing stu-
pidly in the kitchen, without a purpose. She liked to be at
the sink so she could have her back turned and her hands
moving when he arrived, so that the moment would not be
idle and raw. She never knew how he was going to be when
he came home.

Nathan was not a cruel man, but his demeanor was severe, which was why it was so miraculous to Portia when
he laughed at one of her jokes or closed his eyes and sighed
upon receiving good news. When she made him happy, she
felt that she could breathe again and she forgot that anything had ever been wrong. It was like winning at gambling,
the way she became euphoric when she had something for
him—a good report card from Julian's school, a bit of extra
money from her mother—and she forgot for a moment all

the times that she had fallen short and his disappointment had become palpable.

◆

"How does he look?" she had asked her father on the day of her wedding. They were standing in the small corridor of the church, about to walk down the aisle. It was a hot day in July, and Portia could almost see the wood swelling in the old banisters and floorboards. She suspected that the women who had worn short dresses would stick to the pews when they stood to watch them enter. Her father glanced around the corner.

"He looks happy," he said, and she heard the gravity of these words. Portia's father knew what it meant for Nathan to be happy. She felt that everyone in the church that day knew it too, that all eyes were turned to the man at the altar, who had such a heavy soul. The wedding was not so much a symbol of their love, she decided, but a day where the conditions had come together just right, like an eclipse, to allow this poor man a moment of hope.

Portia remembered the early days, after she had gone home with Nathan with the hospital bracelets still on. She had expected their time together to be fleeting—the cuddling on his couch, which led to another night together, and finally to sex—but there was a pull to Nathan, like the electricity in the air before a storm or the weight in your lungs before you begin to cry.

"Why are you with me?" he had asked her in a moment of insecurity. They had drunk too much wine, just the two of them, in an act of personal rebellion, after friends had canceled that evening's plans at the last minute. "Why do you love me?" he asked. He was sitting on the bedroom floor, trailing his finger down the grate of a box fan. It was summer. The room smelled of wine and the laundry-pile mustiness that fills a space when it is humid. Through the open window, they could hear peepers and distant traffic, the electric eruption of cats fighting. Portia knelt beside him, not knowing how to say it. She lay her head against his chest and heard his heart thudding, and it sounded like a sad timekeeper, like someone made to play a drum at gunpoint. The thought of not loving Nathan was unthinkable, because it was clear to her that he required so much love. And it was not that she pitied him, but that she longed to be the person he reached for in the night when he felt alone. The person he went to when he needed to know, "Why?"

✦

"How does he look?" Portia asked the man in the operating room.

"He looks like a burrito," said the man. It was Nathan, sitting there, dressed in scrubs, looking like an imposter in his puffy hairnet. He had a baby in his arms, swaddled so tightly that he was only the size of an eggplant.

Later, after the visitors had gone home, she would be left for hours lying in her own blood due to an error in scheduling, the sheets soaked red up to her neck. Her body was still numb from the surgery, so she had only noticed when she turned her head and saw the creeping edges of the stain. No one had told her that she would bleed from her vagina, even though her baby had not been born from there. No one had told her that it was not acceptable to be upset by the emergency surgery.

"Some women don't get a healthy baby in the end," the nurse who had finally come in to change her sheets had said. "You should be grateful that everyone is alive." She leaned over the bassinet, where Portia's son was sleeping, his brow pressed down by the cap on his head. "Besides, C-section babies always have such round skulls. They look like pretty little dolls." It seemed that the prettiness of her baby should outweigh the shock and indignity of having been rummaged through like a handbag.

Portia's baby looked like no one that she had ever seen—like a little root child, dug up from the earth. The way that he had been folded inside her, facing the wrong way, with his legs pointed straight up, made him lie in the bassinet like a frog on its back, his hip joints springy and loose. They swaddled him tighter to keep his body in place.

The next night, she woke to find that the bassinet was no longer in the room with her. The sensation had returned to her legs, and she discovered that she could walk again. They found her pushing her IV pole through the hallway, dripping blood from beneath her gown.

"I'm looking for the baby," she said, and the doctors wanted to know why she had not said "*my* baby." They watched her closely for the rest of her stay, in case she did, or said, anything else that was alarming.

The Light

THEO AND PORTIA WERE LYING IN BED, FACing each other, in a bedroom with a peaked ceiling. It reminded Theo of a cabin, but a nice cabin, with skylights and clean quilts and neatly stacked firewood. He had the feeling that the cabin was in the woods and that they had come there to be alone, to sort something out in the remoteness and quiet of the place. They were pulling away from each other, as if they had just kissed—what else would they have been doing, in bed together like that? Surely there had been times that he had thought about kissing her, had fantasized about her. It would seem natural to dream of this woman that he knew, to allow his imagination a little freedom. But this particular dream had a different feel, as if Theo had been dropped, uninvited, into a version of his own life that he did not recognize or understand. It was not like a fantasy at all. There was light in the dream, light that filled the bedroom from a window on the slanted ceiling that opened with a tiny crank—and Theo wondered: How was the mind such a good painter? How was it that the crudest human brain, in dreams, could fill itself with such elegant and accurate light? He saw the way that the light fell onto the side of Portia's face, how it caught the auburn threads in her hair. Had he ever noticed the color of her hair in waking? Had she ever looked at him like that? No.

"What do we do now?" she asked him, and he did not know how to respond, so he reached out his hand to touch her shoulder. It was bare. He had not been aware of the rest of her body, whether she was wearing clothes or not or whether they were both naked underneath the blankets. He did not have time to look, because the moment that he touched her skin, his hand burned so terribly from the heat of it that he had to pull away.

Animal

Of all the instruments that she could play, Portia was most intimidated by the drums. Every time she got behind Theo's kit—even for fun—she froze. To choose a rhythm out of thin air was to reveal that awkward animal that had been bumbling around inside you. Like being caught dancing in your kitchen, like blushing. Like showing the world your secret heart and realizing that it was a 1990s pop cliché.

◆

And there was the time that Portia found herself kneeling over the thrashing body of her five-year-old son, as he fought against having a vaccination at his doctor's appointment.

"I can't believe this!" he had screamed at her, twisting to escape her hold. Portia had pressed down with apportioned strength—too much force and she would hurt him, too little force and he would hurt himself—while the pediatrician prepared the syringe. Portia thought: Let's get this over with and then I can wonder where I have gone wrong in my parenting.

That morning, there had been a terrible fight with Nathan.

"Portia," Nathan had sighed. He was sitting in bed,

coffee mug gripped in his hand. "I believe that Julian is capable of more than he is demonstrating in school. That's all." Portia knew that, to Nathan, the most unforgivable sin was to be mediocre. In Nathan's world, mediocre people often became criminals or fat jurors dozing in his courtroom, waiting for a chance to take a piss or buy peanuts from the vending machine. Mediocre was the receptionist in his office, who ate slimy salads at her desk and filed everything backward. Once, she worked an entire day with a glob of mayonnaise on her cheek. An entire day. He continued:

"If people think that Julian is stupid, then they will treat him like he's stupid."

"It's not fair, but it's the truth, Portia. Reality can be inconvenient."

"If only you could be more structured, more assertive with him."

"Studies show—" But he could not finish, because Portia had cut him off.

"I don't care if Julian is mediocre for the rest of his life."

There. She must have said it aloud, by the look on Nathan's face. He had the covers tucked neatly around his waist and an arm laid out over the blanket. He was seated in the direct center of the bed, where their two pillows touched. It seemed absurd to Portia that he should be conducting such an argument from the dead center of the bed, to look as appalled at her as he did now, with his toes making little tents. She felt sorry, almost immediately. She regretted aggravating a man who was sitting so prominently and securely in his bed like that, to watch his face redden, his torso pitch forward as he spat the words: "That is the most fucked-up thing you have ever said."

And just as the needle met Julian's thigh, he ripped his arm free and scratched her hard across the face. Portia saw, through her own pain, Julian's bright eyes and how they could not see her—even though she was right in front of him—for the brilliance of his will to remain unharmed. In that moment, her worries about motherhood ceased and she was proud of her son. From the pit of her stomach, she loved the animal in him that would not be broken.

◆

The day after Julian was born, a nurse admonished Portia for crying over the cesarean birth of her baby.

"You should be grateful," she said, gazing into the bassinet where Julian was sleeping. Portia reached for her giant cup of ice cubes and lemonade and dumped it on the floor. It was the most aggressive act that she could muster with all the IV tubes and tape and her gown hanging open in the front. The nurse looked at the floor in shock.

"Yeah, well I'm still fucking angry about it," Portia said. The sharpness of her voice caused Nathan, who had been half dozing in the recliner by the window, to stand and approach the bed.

"Portia, what's wrong?" he asked, placing his hand beside her head on the pillow. The nurse's face returned to its previous state of placid righteousness. She said to Nathan, "The pain meds will make some women moodier than others." She left to find a mop.

The Letters of Alby Porter

⟲──⟳ PORTIA HAD BEEN WALKING JULIAN HOME from school when it began to rain heavily. They took cover in the bookstore and Portia found herself drawn to a shelf in the section for biographies and memoirs. It was the face on the cover that caught her eye, peering at her from the book's haphazard placement on the shelf. Someone had not pushed it in all the way or had abandoned it before pulling it out. As if they had left it for her to find.

"I knew who it was, of course," Portia told Dr. Shay a week later. "But there was something else. This time I *recognized* his face like I would a picture of myself. With a little embarrassment but also affection."

"Alby Porter's face. On the book jacket?" Dr. Shay had already gotten out his notebook and pen. Here was another episode, he must have thought. Months prior, Portia had spent all their sessions discussing the dead rock star and now it seemed her obsession was evolving. He scratched at the notebook paper commandingly, then looked to Portia for more.

They were in Dr. Shay's office, the one where they had been meeting since she was fifteen. He had another office in Moulton, about an hour east, over the mountain. Soon, he said, as he was seeing fewer patients, he would be available only in Moulton; Portia would have to drive there to see him. But for now the office was as it had always been: friendly, with potted plants and a pretty piece of stained glass in the window, which Portia had taken to admiring over her doctor's head when she spoke or when she did not want to make eye contact. The stained glass filled with rosy sunlight and then was drained, as a cloud passed overhead. Portia liked to think of the glass as a little beacon of encouragement, swelling with light, the way she imagined her eardrum might look when the doctor shined an otoscope at it. *Yes*, it seemed to say. *I am listening.*

"Yes, Alby Porter," she said. "It was a book of his letters, from the 1960s through the mid '80s. It took me three hours to read." In truth, it may have taken even less time. Portia had started the book on the walk home from the bookstore, holding it open in one hand, Julian's hand clasped in the other. She had laid it open on the countertop while she buttered Julian's toast, had let the rain fleck the pages when she brought the dog into the backyard.

From Alby Porter's letters Portia learned that the musician suffered a great deal from creative blocks and from the fear that these blocks might return, crushing his ability to write music when he needed it the most. He wondered during these spells: Would the magic of his creativity ever return? Had his powers run dry for good this time?

His dread soon turned to compulsive superstition. He threw away expensive clothing and jewelry, believing these items to hold some kind of supernatural properties for stifling ideas. He refused to meet with friends or family members. And he once famously left his Porsche 356 in neutral and watched it roll into a lake, because he associated the car with a devastating six-month period where he could not pick up his guitar or touch the keys of his piano without bursting into tears.

◆

Nathan wanted to know if Portia had read any articles on the subject. Who had she talked to? Had she met with the kindergarten teacher?

"No," Portia said. She found it difficult to look him in the eye. They were in the bedroom, speaking in low voices so that they would not wake Julian in the next room.

"It's only that he is still so young," Portia added. "Children learn to read at their own pace." She had not seen this last statement in any article or parenting book, but it had been on a colorful, hand-painted sign in the elementary school's lobby. She wondered if that counted as expert advice. Lately, it seemed that Nathan could not trust her judgment when it came to making decisions about their son, unless it had been backed by a reliable source. That source could even be Portia's mother, who had, at one time, studied early childhood psychology. Just as long as it was not Portia herself, with her lazy intellect and her burning list of "gut feelings."

Their most recent disagreement had been about how to address what Nathan perceived to be a lull in Julian's reading ability. On his kindergarten report card, he had barely met the standard and had fallen short of the statewide average on his letter sounds. Ms. Annabelle had not been alarmed. She had told Portia and Nathan that Julian was a quiet student who liked to see that his classmates were being treated fairly.

"He's so obviously bright," she had said, smiling and dimpled. "The kindest little soul." But Nathan had been nervous. He had no evidence of this brightness and kindness, and, in his hands, he had a sheet of paper with a bar graph that only reached into a grainy dark area.

Portia knew that she was not a perfect mother, but she believed that she knew her own son. She knew that Julian's soul was already aching to be good. Even his moments of defiance were filled with experimental exuberance. And regardless of all that, he was just a little boy. He had plenty of time to learn how to read.

"I know that he will catch up in his own time," she said to Nathan.

"How? How do you know?"

"I see it in him."

But it was not good enough.

Portia had not spoken to Ms. Annabelle about Nathan's concerns because the thought of it made her squirm—sitting in a tiny blue chair, explaining to the young, bubbly teacher that she was worried that her five-year-old son (the youngest in his class) was not on a "college track." Nathan had asked her to set up a meeting with Ms. Annabelle weeks ago, but every time Portia picked up the phone to dial the school, she was overcome with anxiety. She tried to make Nathan understand how uncomfortable she was, but he only looked at her, like a professor about to pose a tough question.

"Is your comfort more important than our son's future?"

Portia left the room and walked down the stairs, her hand shaking on the banister. Rupert, who had been sitting silently at her feet throughout the conversation, followed at her heels, taking the steps sideways so he could keep his eye on her. Maybe he was afraid that she would stumble, or maybe he was merely hoping, with all his expectant, trembling heart, that she would walk toward the kitchen cupboard, where the treats were kept. She pulled the dog leash from the wooden peg by the door and hooked it to Rupert's collar. Sometimes when she was feeling flustered, she liked to walk outside without her shoes, hoping that the cold beaded grass or the slimy stones on the walkway would shock her back to her senses.

That evening, the rain had stopped falling, but dampness clung to the air, especially toward the end of the yard at the tree line. She watched a crumpled mushroom spring back to life where she had walked, while Rupert lifted his leg over another patch of mushrooms and released a carefully allotted stream—there was no use wasting an entire pee on one pile of mushrooms.

The problem was not necessarily in Nathan's words, Portia thought. She could not contradict him and say that her comfort was, indeed, more important than their son's future, because that was not the truth. However, it was not completely untrue either—she *was* uncomfortable. It seemed to her more of a red herring, as if Nathan could toss out an accusation like that because he knew that it would knock the breath out of her. Yes, she thought, once Nathan started to suspect that an argument was not going as he had planned, he would do anything to stop it in its tracks.

Rupert strained against his leash toward a stick that had fallen in the grass; any and all deviations from what was standard and flat must be peed on. Portia followed him. Nathan knew that if he raised any doubt in Portia's suitability as a mother, then she would retreat, weigh his words carefully, wring herself out to find the places where she could do better. By the time she was done, he would have another complaint handy—if she ignored the dust bunnies, Julian might get asthma; if she slept in Julian's bed, he would grow up a coward—and thus created a never-ending mountain that Portia would have to scale before she had any grounds to criticize him. Portia and the dog had almost reached the tree line when something from inside the wall of wet brush caught her attention. There was a pair of eyes looking out. Portia and the dog had interrupted a grazing doe, the doe now staring at Portia, one hoof raised in caution, as if wondering what Portia's next move might be.

When she got back to the house, Portia had lost her resolve. What she might say to Nathan, even if she knew exactly what to say, how to deliver it perfectly, would be too colossal. She might tell him: "These are all the things you do to disarm me. These are the tactics you use to keep me second-guessing myself!" And he might smile at her, as if she were a child, disproportionally angry about something trivial, like an uneven lace on her shoe. He might wait for her to finish, nodding sympathetically, and then say, "It's all right, Portia. I will handle Julian's teachers. I will go to the school and take care of it." His voice would be sincere and helpful, because he could see now that it was all too much for her. He carried the bulk of the responsibilities, and he would carry this too.

◆

Portia did not tell Nathan about Alby Porter's book of letters or how she had read it a second and third time. How she revisited her favorite letters, soaking in the words, as she had done with the lyrics of his songs. She read the letters while she pushed Julian on the swing, tucked the book under Julian's pillow, then read by the light of her phone while she lay with him, waiting for him to fall asleep.

Her favorite letter was about the joke Alby played on his friends. In the late 1970s, he threw a party at his home in Los Angeles, having promised his guests that there would be a spectacle. An escape artist would be there, he told them. "Better than Houdini," the invitations had claimed. Later, in a remorseful letter to his lover, the painter Emile Berne, Alby confessed that he had not had a plan for how to resolve the spectacle and was surprised he didn't die at the end.

"And what if I had died, E?" Alby wrote. "If I were dead, would you hear my voice inside your dreams? Would you find it to be more accurate than what was left of me, spinning on your stereo? I know what I want, E. I want you to feel the difference inside you. My soul entering yours. All my unsung, unrealized dreams hitching a ride with you, like rats deserting a sinking ship for another stronger vessel. Would you let them in?"

At the party, Alby's guests were met by only the catering staff, who had not seen Alby since that morning and who were not invested at all in answering questions about where he might be. The guests had settled into entertaining themselves when Alby walked onto the patio with heavy chains around his wrists and ankles.

"Please follow me," he said, the long ash on his cigarette breaking as he spoke. Beside the patio, there was a modestly sized swimming pool, around which the guests soon found themselves standing. Some said later that the unspoken consensus was that the chains binding their host were part of an elaborate distraction. Either he was going to introduce them to the real escape artist, or something bizarre, whimsical, and unrelated was going to surprise them, making the whole thing obsolete. Alby was known by his friends to love embellishment and sometimes to push a joke a little too far, and when he asked for a volunteer to take his cigarette, which he delivered cleverly with his tongue, revealing the key to his chains behind it, and then dropped backward into the pool, no one came forward to stop him. No one jumped in to save him. He was Alby Porter, who wore tight nylon bodysuits, doll-like red lipstick, Alby Porter who painted a shimmering third eye in the middle of his forehead. Who writhed and pranced like a centaur. They were all too afraid to be the one to ruin the show.

✦

Portia watched the piece of stained glass above her doctor's head flush with color. She appreciated Dr. Shay's willingness to hear the full story, to twiddle his pen and not interrupt, while Portia struggled to get it right.

When Alby was not crippled by creative blocks, he could be incredibly creative and manic, and his mania was captured in the verbose, handwritten letters, which covered the page in ink, his sentences creeping around the margins, bending upside down. One of his crazier notions was that creative talent could be passed around, like a sexually transmitted disease.

"I believe that you can be in power of this transmission, choosing who to share your artistic energy with. Or you can be at the mercy of it, if some creative vampire of a person wanted to drain you, until you were as uninspired and ordinary as a muskrat. It is my intention, as always, E, to be generous with my talent and fame, but—heaven help me—I am not ready to lose it all."

"He was right, you know," Portia said to Dr. Shay. "About the transmission of talent."

She was conscious of the tremor in her voice, the growing note of desperation as she explained herself. It was such a private feeling that she was trying to express, this feeling of seeing Alby's photograph and recognizing it as her own face, although not literally her own face, but with the same flash of discomfort that comes with stumbling upon a picture of yourself.

He had visited her when she was on the operating table, while her body was literally spread open. The doctors had removed the baby, but the spirit of Alby Porter had been there to replace it with something else. Maybe a piece of his talent had broken off and been transferred to her, just as he wrote about in his letters.

"I am trying to understand, Portia, how this is possible," Dr. Shay said. His tone was cautionary but friendly and faintly impressed. It reminded Portia of something that he had said to her when she was younger, when he would lend her books, treating her as if she were a beautiful specimen: "If only I could have a grain of that manic spark," he would groan, as though he saw in her something that he could not have.

"Maybe you can't understand it. Maybe it's not for you to understand," Portia said, shaking her head. She was always caught between her desire to be understood and the hollow desperation that followed when she sensed that the people around her, especially Dr. Shay, were getting close. To be misinterpreted was torture, but to be *figured out* was a kind of death.

Being

    AND THEN ONE MORNING, TWO YEARS LATER, Portia was leaning over the bathroom sink with her eyes wide, drawing a dark line along her bottom eyelid. She was doing this for Theo, the drummer in her band. She knew that much, but she did not know why, or how it had started. The nub of black eyeliner in her hand she had found at the back of the medicine cabinet, behind the old prescriptions and a box of bandages. Its pigment took coaxing, and her eyes welled in irritation as she retraced the line. Poor Alice was rehearsing at Carrie's later that day, and Portia wanted Theo to see her at her best, which, in that moment, meant wearing makeup, but not too much of it. It should not be so obvious that she was trying to look good. She did not want to appear to be trying at anything at all. Yet there she was, practically seething over the bathroom sink, the engine inside her revving a brand-new motto: *be, be, be*. Portia did not want Theo's attention the way a woman would normally seek out a man. She wanted to become her real self, her deepest self—the one Alby Porter had seen in the hospital—and she wanted Theo to be her audience.

After she was dressed, she made a sandwich for Julian and kissed him on the head.

"You look different," he told her. He was kneeling on the

kitchen floor, his palms laid flat. Around him were toy cars, a stone from the garden, and a toilet paper tube with some kind of code scribbled across it in marker. Julian was always trailing the debris of his world. He was only ever halfway present. "Can I eat my sandwich on the floor?" he asked.

"I'm going to band practice," Portia said, placing the plate under the table for him. She knew that she would hear about it later from Nathan, who was in the next room, waiting for her to leave. Even though he was the boy's father, Portia still felt indebted to him because he watched Julian for her every Sunday morning while she was at Carrie's. Nathan had read an article about how lapses in routine (such as eating under the table, she imagined) led to childhood anxiety and possibly other disorders. Julian took the toilet paper tube and army crawled toward the sandwich.

"Is it the kind of band that is a famous band?" he asked, studying the sandwich through the tube.

"No," she said. "It's not that kind of band."

Portia felt a sense of excitement as she drove across town. She felt that she was waking up all over, as if she could not remember where she had been her whole life and suddenly she had been applying eyeliner in front of the mirror and then, just as suddenly, she was in her car, waiting at the intersection for the light to change. The streetlight swayed in the wind—red, with one faulty pixel, where a white light escaped, full of rebellion.

Carrie's house was set back from the road behind a row of towering pines. A slate walkway led to the front door, the wooden steps stippled with moss. Beside it, a board lay broken beneath the porch, where stray cats squeezed their elastic bodies through, coming and going. Carrie was tuning her guitar inside, kneeling on the floor. She had perfect pitch, which meant that she could pull an A out of nowhere, without hearing it first.

"The thing is," she said, "I don't actually find the note in my head. I can whistle it, like this"—and she would send a sharp squeal through her teeth. "The note lives in my teeth." Her living room had been cleared of most furniture and converted into a practice space, the cords from their guitar pedals, amps, and microphones duct-taped along the floor in a permanent circuit board of black lines.

Carrie liked to work on making her guitar sound precisely how she wanted it to—from various gravelly distortions to sonar-like echoes—and Portia knew that she spent hours turning the knobs this way and that, tracking the different combinations of settings and marking them down. It must have pleased Carrie to see her own system of musical shorthand fill her notebooks, like equations. Portia herself did not have the patience for this kind of experimentation. She suspected that it was because, although she considered herself a musician, it was not actually sound that she was chasing. It was something else, something elusive, like one of Julian's marbles when it rolled beneath the refrigerator. She set her guitar case against the wall and felt someone standing beside her.

"It's good to see you," Theo said. Theo sometimes placed his hand on Portia's shoulder when they saw each other. He would hold it there and look at her and ask, "How are you?" waiting for her to respond before pulling away. This gesture always surprised Portia. It felt good to be met in this way, to be looked at so steadily, to feel the warmth of his hand through her shirt. Also, she could not trace his eyes back to anything other than what he said and what he meant. Sometimes men flirted with her, harmlessly. Other times their sincerity was potent—a hard glance across a room—like a payment made, secured for the future, just in case. As if to say: *Remember how I have always noticed you.* She found that people, even the monogamous, liked to check in with what could have been or what still could be.

Theo was different. She had grown used to him in a certain context: she could be vulnerable in front of him. She could play him a new song on her guitar, wondering what he thought of it and if he wanted to come in on the second measure or count off and start together. She could slap out a rhythm for him on her knee or play air drums, blushing and asking him if he understood what she meant. He might tease her for this, but always gently.

Theo did not lay his hand on her shoulder that day. He walked past her to the drums, rolling his sleeves to the elbow. He sat, pushed up his glasses, keeping his eyes lowered.

As Portia watched him, she began to feel a sense of dread. It was clear to her that, somehow, in the depth of her being, she had always been in love with this man and now the world, in a sweeping act of cruelty, was making it known to her. There was nothing that she could do. She would have to wait it out—this instant and agonizing love—and watch her hope stumble around in the dark, groping and coming up with nothing, until it gave up.

Carrie was in a rush to start playing. Her amplifier was warmed up, and she had already calibrated her effects pedals on the floor. That day she wore fitted slippers on her feet, the kind that curled into a kind of black husk when they were removed. Portia watched her slippered toe hop lightly over the buttons of the pedals, carefully setting the tone for their first song. There had always been something intimidating about Carrie. In high school, she had walked the halls with a dangerous independence, as if she were not stuck there, like the rest of the students, but attending each stage of her life by the power of her own will. Their health teacher may have called Carrie a "ruler" based on a very superficial—and inherently lecherous—means of classification, but there was some truth to it; she seemed unbreakable, driven, and matter-of-fact when it came to the things that she was good at or the risks that she took in life. In turn, Portia had, since high school, reluctantly accepted her "pearishness," the bottom-heavy, womanly injury to her intellect.

They began to play, Carrie picking a melody while Portia

found her way into it, strumming her own tune, feeling the two parts size each other up. She and Carrie had always had the ability to create music from nothing, knowing nothing about time signatures or keys except of course for the accuracy of what Carrie could whistle through her teeth. Portia sometimes felt like they were children building an island from sticks and mud and bits of grass, not caring who was watching. She had been pleased when Theo joined and had no trouble fitting in. He was not a passive member of the band; he added his own style, but he also did not try to change the two women or correct their playing, like so many men had tried in Portia's life, thinking that they could fix her technical problems and maybe somehow save her from some helpless feminine condition while they were at it. Theo did not offer his opinions. He was quiet when Carrie stopped everything to fuss with the knobs of her guitar pedal. Sometimes, while she was doing this, Theo would look up from his drum kit, across the room at Portia.

+

In just three weeks, Portia and Theo would be standing in the alleyway of a bar downtown, sometime after midnight, waiting for a police car to pass by. Hiding in the alley would seem like an overreaction, but Portia knew that there were cops in town who owed her husband favors. Nathan was often up late at night, instructing them how to conduct a traffic stop or advising them on how to justify a drug search when they could find no reasonable excuse.

"It's technically a crime," she had heard him say over the phone. "It's probably enough to get him." She did not know to what lengths the police would go to bring her home or what they would do to Theo, what tricks Nathan might have up his sleeve. In the alley, Portia would wonder, wildly and briefly, if she and Theo might escape it all together, ride a bus out of town, into nowhere. But the Bus Game, at least the way that it unfolded when she described it to Julian on those long lonely days, worked only when the relief of hopelessness was better than the pain of hoping. If loving Theo was painful, it was because she was not ready to give up. Not yet. With this thought, she would reach for Theo's hands, because she was cold and because she was afraid, but he would step away, shaking his head. Even in the blackness of night, he would not touch her, or hold her, or do any of the things that she wished he would do.

The Woman in the Blue Dress

◯━━◯ LIKE MANY CHILDREN, THERE WERE BOOKS that Julian insisted his mother read to him, every night. Portia did as she was told. She did not question why her son needed to see the scruffy bird find his mother or why he needed the dump truck to do its job, dumping loads of perfect black dirt all day, until it closed its eyes and said goodnight to the world. He liked Portia to make sound effects. She soon learned that if she made the car screech to a halt in *Go, Dog, Go!*, then she was destined to make the same car screech to a halt in all the subsequent readings of *Go, Dog, Go!* Sometimes the repetition was maddening. Why couldn't Julian make the screeching sound, for once, in his head? But she knew that this was also inevitable, in the same way the scruffy bird and the dump truck had to accept their lot in life.

There was one book, a large picture book of French origin, that defied these rules. The book depicted large illustrated scenes of an imaginary European town, the houses and schools and stores in cross section, so you could see how the people were living, what they were up to, even if they were in the shower or on the toilet. The book had no words, and so Portia was free to make up her own stories, even if they were short and simple:

"The little boy is looking at the dog, and the dog is looking at the turtle."

"The window in the toy shop is about to be broken by a baseball."

Julian did not mind if the book was different every time or if they spent long moments in silence, examining the page. They might notice that the man with the green suitcase from the apartment building on page one was, two pages later, waiting at the train station. Where was he going?

She often chose this book, so that Nathan, skulking around in the hallway, could not correct her. It was surprising how many words there were in children's books for her to mispronounce, how many concepts Julian asked her to explain that she got wrong. The moon, for example. She knew so little about the moon, why it never faces away from Earth. Is it a caring moon? A suspicious moon? These were the conversations that she wished she could have with her little boy. She did not even know how a vacuum cleaner worked. Maybe there is a very hungry tornado inside, she said to Julian. And then Nathan was beside the bed, his phone in hand with the correct information loading on the screen.

More than once, Portia found herself lingering on the sixth page of the French picture book, where it was springtime in the town square and the marketplace was open. Children played in the fountain and a mischievous magpie had stolen a girl's earring. A man with his nose buried in a book was about to walk into a tree. Some of the windows of the apartments above the shops were open so that wives could drape blankets over the sills or pull in a line of laundry. But there was one young woman, in a blue dress, who stood in the window and seemed to gaze over the square, with no apparent purpose at all.

"That's Portia," Portia said to Julian one night, pointing to the woman in the illustration. "She lives in that apartment, all by herself. She is a copyeditor and reads books at home for a living. And when she is done with those books, she reads her favorite books, over and over, until they are so worn they come apart in her hands. Then she sews them back together and reads them again. Every Saturday, she takes the train to the science museum, where there is a giant artificial heart. She likes to stand inside the heart, closing her eyes and listening to the beating sound it makes. Every Sunday, she takes the train in the opposite direction to the zoo and watches the zebras. There is a man there who would be in love with her if he met her, but he is always watching the giraffes."

"Which page is the zoo?" Julian asked her.

One night she dreamed about the woman in the blue dress, in the apartment above the square, who lived by herself and did not have to answer to anyone. The woman in the blue dress watched the marketplace on the weekend, the vendors selling flowers, little molded cheeses, and curly mushrooms. In real life, Portia would have loved to be a woman who walks to the market to buy mushrooms, because it would suggest a certain folkloric knowledge and necessity. Boiling them into risotto and soup, breathing in the steam. She remembered the gifts that family members brought Julian when he was born, the plastic rabbits, the plastic kaleidoscopic monstrosity that was supposed to clip to the side of his crib, the harsh woman's voice that sang the nursery rhymes while the lights flashed in her baby's face. It was never supposed to be like that. But in rejecting these gifts, she would have risked becoming the kind of woman that rejects kindness.

Suddenly, the woman in the blue dress was no longer alone but was instead a young mother, living above the square with her son. Mother and son could go entire days without speaking a word, drawing pictures instead with their fingers in the flour dust on the table. She allowed the boy to eat his lunch under the table, if that was what he felt like doing. They liked to go for long walks in the countryside, letting the hours get swallowed up by the sky and the mountains. Once, the child fell and a rock split his knee. He cupped the blood in his hands and asked his mother why the blood was red, and she said that it was red to balance out the big blue sky. He liked that explanation and it stopped him from crying.

Dreams of Other Women

◠─◡ THROUGHOUT THEO'S LIFE, THERE HAD BEEN dreams of other women. There had been fevered dreams where attraction bloomed in dark corners, then developed into stolen kisses or awkward groping, fears of being caught. Most disturbing to Theo was that his most erotic dreams usually involved women who did not interest him at all: coworkers, for example, or his ex-sister-in-law, or—and it shamed him to admit this—older women, whom he had not considered an option for their age. And it was never reliable, straightforward sex presented in these dreams with women whom he did not desire but hot and shameful acts of lust that perhaps did not even resemble sex but were presented as such because they were ruled by his subconscious mind. A woman could show you her belly button in a dream and it would be sex. She might put your foot in her mouth, spit on you, smear her lipstick across your face—things that in waking life would be unappealing and confusing but in the context of the dream were exciting or at least deeply meaningful. So, when Theo awoke from his dream about Portia, where he had reached out to touch her shoulder and burned his hand, he did not know what to make of it; it did not seem to fit the pattern of the other dreams, and, besides, it had not felt like a dream at all. Waking up did not feel like waking up but like being struck over the head, opening your eyes in a white daze. He lay for a long time in the darkness of his room, opening and closing his fingers, which tingled and ached. He did not know if he had enough coordination to work the switch on the bedside lamp or if his hands would fail him, knocking it onto the floor. He was glad for once that he was alone, feeling as exposed as he did, as if the dream had played out not just within the privacy of his own mind but also on the side of his apartment building, or pinned to the underside of the clouds, by means of a giant projector.

When Theo joined Poor Alice, there had been a part of him that wondered if spending so much time with two young women would make his wife suspicious, if maybe she would become jealous enough—consciously or subconsciously—to want him again. This he hoped for, secretly and pessimistically, without ever allowing the possibility full access to his thoughts. Meanwhile, he did his best to enjoy himself, learning Carrie's songs and following her instruction. Often, he stayed after practice to have a coffee with Gus, who liked aimless scheming as much as Theo did. Gus was not shy about discussing his personal life, and he took Theo's marriage troubles as an invitation to disclose his own frustrations with Carrie. In this way, Theo became more closely acquainted with Carrie through her husband's sheepish portrayal, as a woman who was to be discussed with fondness, utter confusion, and fear, which eliminated her as a candidate for any sort of fantasy.

Portia was different. Disregarding the fact that she was married, Portia having represented the last dark hope between Theo's marriage ending or surviving placed her in a certain realm of her own. Theo had fantasized briefly about Portia—kissing, sex, even just gaining her approval—but only in connection to what his wife might suspect was possible. It was as if he had been concocting these scenarios for his wife's sake, hoping that she would catch wind of them somehow, so that she might see how desirable he was, how talented and interesting, and question her motives for leaving him. When at last it was final and Theo was divorced, Portia remained for him in that separate world—married, of course, but also a reminder of her own unattainability and his own failure.

But now that wall had broken down. She had appeared to him in a dream that was not like a dream but rather like a small cross section of time. Her eyes had been asking him something: *What happens now?* As if they had been through something harrowing together—harrowing in the way that love can be harrowing. Theo sat up, cradling his aching hands in his lap, feeling that they were as useless as a set of paws or hooves. He remembered the night that Portia had locked herself out of her car and the small, heroic part that he had played, bending a coat hanger through the half-inch crack of the car window. How wonderful he had felt that night, clearheaded and full of purpose. Sometimes, during band practice, Portia would sit at his drum kit, sticks poised as if about to play, but fall into a state of blushing so deeply that she could not continue. Sometimes, when Carrie was crouched over her effects pedals, concentrating on turning the knobs like someone disarming a bomb, Theo would catch Portia's eye across the room, and she would smile patiently, sympathetically. He loved her. He knew that now.

Child

◎──◌ WHEN PORTIA WAS LITTLE, SHE CLIMBED TO
the top of her bookshelf and could not climb down. Her parents
had taken care to bolt the shelf to the wall so that she could not
pull it down upon herself, but they could do nothing to keep her
from climbing if she wanted to. She remembered sitting at the
top and looking over her bedroom from this great height, a ma-
ture feeling of complacency coming over her, as if she had driven
herself into a ditch and come out thinking: Well, now you've
gone and done it. Except she was not even two years old. Portia
had called out for her father and he had come. She remembered
him coming in, arms outstretched, ready to save her. He did not
say to her, "Do not do that again." He did not laugh at her look of
helpless outrage. He just came in, arms outstretched, and set her
right again, as if she were a wind-up toy that had gone off track.

When Portia was between the ages of six and eleven,
she and her father would go on long outings together. They
would go to flea markets and estate sales, following handwritten signs along the back roads of Vermont. They were not
looking for anything in particular, and they were never sentimental about this time spent together. But sometimes they
would have a good laugh about something—they thought
that the windmills on the mountain were monstrous and
that the 1960s Christmas decorations at the garage sale were

corny—and Portia's father would look at her and say, "This might be as good as life gets and that's okay." It was his way of being absolving, of embracing the absurdity of this little life that they were living together, rattling around in his car on these dirt roads with the dusty grass growing along the side.

"Who would we become if we bought this lamp?" he asked her in the aisle of an antique shop. The lamp was purple, with ceramic purple balls that stuck out, like a child's drawing of a bunch of grapes—or maybe a child's drawing of a friendly alien, depending on the child.

"I don't know," Portia said.

"I don't know either," her father said.

As she got older, Portia became aware of an increasing sense of nervousness. She had always been self-conscious and prone to embarrassment when an adult had any opinion of her. A hairdresser told Portia, when she was seven, that her cheeks were very plump and beautiful, and Portia had fallen silent for the rest of the day, dragged down by the injustice of having a feature that could be commented on. As she passed the age of thirteen, however, she found that she could not escape into herself as she once could. School became a problem. Suddenly, she was aware that she was in a classroom, in the world, in the universe, shrink-wrapped in skin and bone, her lips fitting over her teeth the way that they did. *Did* her lips fit over her teeth? If she thought about it for long enough, then she could no longer be sure. She did not know how to hold her mouth so that it looked and felt normal, while her tongue just lay there, thickly. She felt that she could not breathe. She felt that she was idiotic—for getting worked up over such a thing.

When Portia's teacher pulled her out of the classroom and explained to her that she was having a panic attack, Portia nodded and dried her tears with a damp tissue, but, privately, she rejected the notion. She was not having a panic attack any more than she was having a stroke or an allergic reaction. Panic attacks happened to innocent people who did not ask for them—people who were just trying to go about their lives. She was not innocent. She had invited the thoughts into her head, with the same selfish curiosity as someone who does not break up a dog fight, even though they should.

The school called Portia's father and he found her in the administrative office, holding a paper cup of cold water, her eyelashes pinched with tears. She had been dreading her father's arrival, worried about how he might react. Perhaps he would want to make light of the situation, joking with the secretary, or maybe he would be sober and concerned, his palm on her forehead, as if she were a sick child. But Portia's father marched into the administrative office just as he had when she was a little girl, stranded on top of her bookshelf. He walked in there, neither alarmed nor uncaring, slung her backpack over his shoulder, and got her out of there.

It was Portia's father's fault that she was like this. It was because her father loved her when she was little. It was because her parents said things like, "You're the best thing to ever happen to us," and curled up with her in her toddler bed to help her sleep, even if it gave them backaches. It was because her father brought her with him on outings that he enjoyed and included her in his decisions, even when she was too young to have an opinion.

"I like this photograph," he would tell her, and show her an old portrait of a family with starched collars and high, Victorian hair, standing in front of a house.

"I like this photograph because you can see how muddy and unfinished the yard was. The hoofprints and the cart tracks. Everything was so new and muddy back then. You forget about that."

It was Portia's father's fault that she expected to be treated as if her opinion mattered, as if her happiness was a worthy investment.

✦

"I don't get it," Portia's husband said to her. "I don't get why you can't just get out of the way when I'm walking. You always stand there, looking blank." Portia was taken aback by this. She had thought that her husband was coming to see her when he walked in her direction, or, at the very least, that he would want to acknowledge her as he passed by. She was a person who liked to give and receive small signs of affection throughout the day.

"I thought that I might get a little kiss," she said to her husband. It was the truth, but as she heard the words spoken, she realized how entitled they sounded.

"It seems like such a simple concept to grasp," he said. He was smiling now. He was not angry with her, only perplexed. "To move when you see someone coming toward you." He gestured with his hand, as if showing her how to do it. "To move . . ."

Portia heard this and knew that she had been wrong to assume that attention would be lavished upon her. She had learned earlier that year to never hold out her arms when she was sitting on the couch and to call his name.

"You're the one asking for the hug," her husband had said. "But for some reason, I'm the one who has to walk all the way over there. If you really wanted to hug me, then you wouldn't make me work for it."

Portia hated herself for acting spoiled. When had she become like this? she wondered. So smiling and expectant and foolishly in love? She wore silly shoes, she was too loud during sex, and sometimes she read the map backward. A stupid, child of a woman.

◆

The Bus Game was just a fantasy. It was comforting to envision your own demise, to have it in your own hands. She would get on a bus and go all the way to the end. She would take the book of Alby Porter's letters with her, the only thing that made any sense to her.

On the days that she argued with Nathan, the idea couldn't save her. Nathan was inside her mind. She fantasized about divorce, if only to wonder about how she would raise her son by herself. But there were always details that got in the way, like how she would earn a living, and she got caught up in thinking about the demands of surviving her imaginary independence and rarely arrived at the point. She could work as a waitress, she often thought, like she had done before Julian was born. She could wait tables again at the large restaurant at the edge of town that overlooked the mountains, where the colors of the leaves in autumn made the restaurant's patrons hostile. The patrons there always wanted the best view. They always wanted the most private table along with the best view. They wanted pasta made with flour that had not been bleached, to know if the fish was farmed or pole-caught. They wanted to know if Portia was from the area and why she had never left. Then, feeling a little sad for her, they told her that her home state was beautiful, that they always made sure to visit.

Portia remembered how the stress and the exhaustion of the job made her love these fussy, often overdressed people. She brought them their plates of food and asked them if they needed anything else. Sometimes they gave her a look of gratitude—sometimes gratitude and pity—and she wanted to throw down her heart, much like how she would untie and throw down her apron at the end of the night. Tired. Fed up. But also strangely prostrate and humble—ready to give more, if only someone would ask.

Yes, may I have some more ice?

I don't mean to be a pain, but could you get me a dry potato?

I think I'll go for the soup after all.

Yes. Yes, she thought. I'll give you everything. And after they left the restaurant, she worried about them—the man who had dripped cream sauce on his tie and tried to hide it with his napkin. The woman with the fake eyelashes and the poorly blended concealer, who had been overcome by a fit of coughing and turned splotchy. The people of the world were fragile. They had been driving all day and all they wanted was a table by the window, where they could see the leaves on the mountain, and a bottle of red wine served in the correct manner. Portia understood this. She understood better than the other waitresses, who complained behind their stations and wiped away tears. It was always much too hot where they huddled together, behind the salad bar, next to the kitchen. The makeup on their foreheads bubbled with sweat. But complaining was a way to catch their breath amid the chaos. Portia understood this too.

She remembered a night in autumn that had been particularly busy with diners—reservations were full, and there was a growing line of walk-ins at the door. Portia's manager had been away, and the front of the house had been short-staffed. The bussers were running the food and fetching drinks from the bar. The hostess had unplugged the phone and was nursing a bloody palm wrapped in a cloth napkin, scratched from picking up shards of a broken wineglass. And then, to add to the chaos, a waitress named Corrina had taken a cigarette break and not returned. When Corrina's tables complained, Portia had to pick them up in addition to her own, and there was no time to even speculate or care about what had happened to Corrina.

At one of these tables was an older man who came in to eat by himself. He was pleased with the seat that he was given but hoped that he was not depriving someone else from sitting there, perhaps someone who was not alone. Portia poured his water and introduced herself.

"You don't hear that name every day," he said. No, Portia said. You really don't. Later, when he told her what he wanted to order, he handed her the menu and looked so sincerely at her—a little self-conscious, she thought, as if he shouldn't be ordering the beef Stroganoff but he wanted it too badly to resist. The look—boyish, relenting—reminded Portia of her father, of how he was always ready to forgive the things that no one else would think to forgive.

Another man snapped his fingers at her from the next table.

"We're still waiting on that refill," he said.

"I'm sorry," Portia said, and she quickly took his empty glass.

At that moment, Corrina showed up in the dining room

holding a pitcher of water. She stopped to fill a woman's glass, and Portia could see her face in profile. It was flushed, and there was a large red spot on her neck. A hickey. It was obvious what it was. Corrina turned her eyes and saw Portia watching. There was guilt but also freedom in her expression, as if she knew that what she had done—abandoning her co-workers to screw around with a line cook named Darren in the dry storage pantry—had been a terrible and selfish decision, but the thrill of it had left her incapable of remorse. Portia did not know how to feel. She knew that she should be angry, but her curiosity was too intense—and not about what had happened in the dry storage pantry between her coworkers but about Corrina herself and her new badge of irreverence.

"I'm keeping your tips," she said to Corrina as they crossed paths in the dining room. Corrina dumped a cluster of ice from the pitcher into the drinking glass.

"Take them all," she said, and her upper lip, which was buoyant and independent from the rest of her face, lifted, showing her teeth. It was not a smile—it was more involuntary—as if she knew, and also did not know, that she was radiant. Unstoppable.

Pills

It was late. Portia knew that it was late as she dug through her purse, searching for her key to the back door. For whatever reason, the motion-detection light above the garage had not come on and she had to feel for the key in the dark. She thrust her hand in, pushing around the Tylenol bottle, the mascara, and all that loose change, afraid suddenly that she had left the keys at the bar, in the crevice of the booth where she and Theo had huddled under the neon lighting. If it came to defending herself to Nathan, she could say that they had not kissed, their knees had not touched, and she had paid for her own drink. It had only gone wrong toward the end, when a loud group of women came in and played the jukebox and she could no longer hear Theo's voice above the noise. He had leaned in to say something, slipping a little on the vinyl seat, and she had felt his breath beneath her ear. Portia replayed the moment in her head, on the back porch, crouching now to look hopelessly into the bottom of her purse. How could something so slight, she wondered, undo her so completely? She had never been one to admit to total infatuation. She had tried her whole life to keep herself above a certain mark of foolishness when it came to love, but now she wanted to dive in. She wanted to stay awake the rest of the night, just to remember the feeling of his breath on her neck. She was like a tree, guilty of having its leaves blown off by the wind.

A light came on. Portia could see her keys, lying on the welcome mat where they must have fallen when she first began looking for them. Nathan stood outlined in the doorway. Portia, in her state of stupid, ecstatic confusion, had not considered that he might have waited up for her. She thought that he would ask her where she had been or how much she had had to drink, but he was silent. He backed away, slowly, down the hall as she entered the house. He was calm. He was dressed. Portia took off her shoes and saw, as she passed the kitchen, that it was two in the morning. She had not meant to be out that long. It worried her, for an instant, how easily she had been swept away, forgetting about time and all the other moving parts of her life. Someone might say that she was losing her grip. But she and Theo had only the two drinks, in the dark booth by the corner. From there they had watched the group of women come in. The one with the ill-fitted pink dress had danced with the pool cue, upsetting the couple trying to play.

"When did you stop taking your pills?" Nathan asked her. The woman in the tight pink dress danced slowly in the back of her mind, wrapping her plump leg around the cue, as if it were a pole.

"What pills?" Portia asked. Nathan knew about Theo. She had confessed to him already, told him he had better sit down and listen. She had never been so direct in her life, and, thinking back to it, she remembered the conversation as if someone else had been sitting behind her eyes, relaying the message through her mouth. Since that night, Nathan had kept his feelings concealed from her, going about his routines with only a sharper curve to them, the way actors must articulate their movements so that those farthest from the stage can understand what they are doing. Quite simply, Portia could tell that the news had hit a nerve in Nathan; she just could not tell which one. She wondered if she was going to see his anger now.

"You know what pills." He had the bottle in his hand already: small, orange, with a bulky white cap. Portia took the bottle and peered through the translucent bottom.

"I don't know what you mean," she said, shaking it. "I'm almost out of these." She was about to hand it back to him when he produced another bottle. It must have been in his pocket. Portia knew what this was leading to, but she continued to play ignorant.

"That's an old prescription," she told him. Her face and fingers felt numb. "I don't have to take those anymore." Nathan's mouth twitched. He was upset, but he could not control his satisfaction.

"What about these?" There was another bottle, this one slightly fatter, but orange and generic like the first two. "It's strange," he said, twisting the cap.

"Those are antibiotics—" Portia lied.

"It's strange," Nathan cut her off. He was trembling

now, his mouth twitching again—smiling then frowning. Portia could see that his hand was unsteady as he poured the contents of the bottle onto the floor. The little white pills spread out on the rug. He dumped the other bottle, shaking it, and another shower of white pills clattered softly over the first pile.

◆

Portia had been prescribed the pills two years ago by Dr. Shay. Within the first week of taking them, she noticed that the bottom of her sink was getting whiter. She had been scrubbing it every afternoon with a pasty bleach solution. She was content to scrub it, and the sight of the whiteness appearing from beneath the years' worth of residue was not unmoving, but it was not exactly exhilarating either. She was pleased by the cleanness in the same way her hand would be pleased by the roundness of a stone, something satisfying and with just enough heft to it. It was simple. It was as it should be. After the sink was done, Portia moved on to the crisper in her refrigerator. Why on earth, she wondered, had she never addressed the stickiness at the bottom of the drawer? It had always been there, and all she had to do was spray it and watch the stains dissolve. This was how the changes in her mind unfolded after the pills took effect: her life broke apart into smaller portions and she began to manage them.

"If you were not a mother," Dr. Shay had begun

regretfully, "then perhaps I would let you become as quirky as you wanted to be." Portia had just finished describing how some of Alby's potential had been transferred to her when he died, just as he had believed was possible. But she was realizing that potential was not purely potential, that, without imagination, it was only a form of accuracy. Carrie, for example, could whistle a perfect A through her teeth, but what made her special was what she did with that A. What made Alby special was his madness, which, when looked at through the lens of his genius, could be considered not madness at all but bravery.

"What if," she had asked Dr. Shay, "the only thing keeping me from reaching my highest potential is my lack of bravery? What if I am wasting Alby's gift to me? I could live more fiercely. I could wake up one morning and leave it all behind. I could get on a bus. Fake my own death."

"Yes, well," Dr. Shay said. "I'm worried about the day that you are no longer able to come back to reality." And he wrote out the prescription. It was a new drug, he explained, but so far, studies had shown no evidence of weight gain or fatal rashes or liver failure.

Portia should have resisted the pills—she opened her mouth to say, "No, I don't want them," but the words did not come. Instead, she thought: Here is something that explains why you feel different from everyone else. And it excuses you for being the way that you are. Now, Nathan might understand why you sometimes stare at the wall. Why simple things—like maps—confuse you. There was a part of her that desperately wanted to be acknowledged, even if it was in a negative light. She remembered her time in the psychiatric hospital in Moulton, how peaceful it was to live inside the confines of her diagnosis. For those three weeks, she had been able to stop wondering what—if anything—she was doing wrong or if she was overreacting when she became upset. She did not ask herself if she was spoiled or selfish or lazy for not handling life as well as other people seemed to.

And at first, being medicated did feel novel; her house was clean all the time, and her patience and energy were unshakable. She went for walks around the neighborhood, she watched television and read books, and when she closed her eyes at night, she fell asleep instantly, as if she could pull the curtains closed, black out her mind, and then open the curtains anew in the morning. But then Carrie had invited her to a show in Massachusetts to watch a band called Anxiety Marathon, and something had changed. She and Carrie had developed a friendship with the lead vocalist of the band, a woman named Sasha, and they liked to attend her gigs whenever Anxiety Marathon toured close enough. Carrie and her husband, Gus, had offered to drive, while Portia sat in the back seat, listening to Gus talk about music theory. He was interested in something called counterpoint, which Portia knew to be a kind of harmonization. Gus's voice was passionate, as he seemed to enjoy, overall, the experience of appearing nerdy in front of his wife and her friend. It was dark, and when they pulled into the crowded parking lot of the bar where the band was playing, Portia felt as though they had already been on a long outing and that they should be returning home by now. Gus brought over their drinks just as Sasha was taking the stage. Sasha had long straight hair. Her appearance reminded Portia of a young Grace Slick or Joan Baez. When she sang, her eyes rolled up and her mouth hung open and twisted. She knew how to be a queen and something possessed all at once. It was always a terrific show.

The lighting in the bar was low and violet hued. There were people standing around high-top tables, mingling in front of the stage, respectful of their surroundings and somewhat unkempt in appearance: the way you would want your fans to be. Portia had ordered something in a tall-stemmed glass that claimed to be mixed with blood orange. She removed the crescent of lemon rind from the surface and bit into it, experimentally, tasting nothing. She usually left Sasha's shows feeling energized, motivated to become a better musician, as if Sasha's talent and strangeness gave Portia permission to make bolder music. As an amateur performer, it was all she could really hope for. But that night, Portia was not inspired. Instead, she was irritated. She watched the band's guitarist hop onto a folding chair, teetering precariously as he pushed out a raucous solo. Except, to Portia's ears, it was merely a prolonged moment of fuzz threaded with feedback. The music was gone from it. The music had detached and fled the scene, like birds scattering from a statue.

Sasha, her long hair flung over her face, moved back to the microphone and wrenched out a note. She looked clownish and demonic. Perhaps Anxiety Marathon had lost its flair. Portia did not understand what she had once found intriguing in this mess of a band.

◆

"It's been months." Portia said to Nathan. She looked at the pills on the floor. Months of pills that she should have flushed down the toilet to hide them better but had instead taken from the bottle and tucked away in an older bottle at the back of the cabinet, so she could keep track of when the prescription needed to be refilled. She went through the motions every day, transferring the pill into another container instead of swallowing it. In all other parts of her life, she pretended that she was still taking them. At the dentist, she still listed the name of the medication on her medical history forms. She still reported to Dr. Shay how she was feeling, how well the dosage was working. It was too painful for her to tell him the truth: that all the years that they had spent trying to understand Portia's problems had been a waste. Portia knew that Dr. Shay had worked hard to take her seriously, to listen to her long-winded accounts of what was troubling her. Her doctor, who listened to her when she spoke and sat upright with his pen and paper beneath a glowing pink eardrum in the window. Perhaps Portia had mistaken this for friendship.

Nathan took a pill from the pile and, between his finger and thumb, held it out to Portia.

"I want you to take this," he said to her, placing the pill between her own fingers, like she was a doll. "I want to watch you swallow it." He grabbed her by the wrist and led her to the kitchen. The green digits on the microwave read 2:05. It had only been five minutes since she had walked through the back door. Nathan kept his hand around her wrist while he ran the tap, filling a glass with water. The stream reached the brim of the glass, then spilled over the edge, over his hand. Portia could sense the speed of his mind firing, so intensely that he must not have seen what he was doing. He raised the hand that was around her wrist so that her own hand, which was clenching the pill, rose to her mouth.

"Take it," he said.

"I won't." She wondered how he failed to understand that swallowing one pill would be pointless. She could not possibly catch up all the months that she had missed with one pill, and to take them all at once was out of the question. It would kill her.

"Take it, or I am going to have to make a phone call," he said. Portia did not like the sound of this. She could see the back door from where she stood, her crumpled purse where she had dropped it on the doormat. She thought that she could escape this awful moment, make a dash for the purse, for the keys that were still lying on the porch, and drive away. But she knew that Julian was upstairs, asleep in his bed. Sometimes he still slid two of his fingers into his mouth for comfort, like a baby. Sometimes he still wet the bed and waddled into her room with sleepiness and shock across his face, needing her to tell him that it was okay. She imagined Julian waking up and looking for her, asking for her. For seven years, without fail, she had been there, every morning.

Nathan was still talking, lit only halfway by the light above the stove. Her husband had become an ashen, shadowy figure. The threat he posed was linked closely to Portia's own conscience. He was powerful, not because he was larger and stronger, and not even because he had the force of the law on his side, but because he had been present for all her shortcomings. He had a mind like a filing cabinet, packed meticulously with all the mistakes she had ever made; all he had to do was reach in and start pulling them out.

"You're a diagnosed bipolar case," he was saying, "who has gone off your medication without your doctor's consent." This was not a situation that she had ever rehearsed in her head, this sense of panic and sudden loss of control. There had only ever been the Bus Game, the woman in the blue dress from the storybook, fantasies that went nowhere.

"What would you do if I left right now?" she asked Nathan.

"I would call the police," he said. He had not hesitated. It made Portia wonder if he had already talked to someone about this, if he had asked his connections at the police department what rights he had over her. She and Theo had watched the police cruisers drive slowly by from the cover of the bar's alleyway. Portia had known that they were looking for her. She, Nathan's wife. His lying, cheating, unmedicated wife.

Daydreaming

She liked to be at the kitchen sink when she was waiting for Nathan to return from work, so that her hands could be busy when he walked in. She could not say why, only that it felt safer this way, not knowing how he was going to be. The stiff soap bubbles clung to her arms; the steam surrounded her. She tested the water with the back of her hand. It had been three days since she had woken up thinking of Theo, and she had been thinking about him ever since. She plugged the sink, aiming a squirt of soap so that the basin erupted into white froth, and sunk her arms in. She imagined Theo in the kitchen with her, having appeared for some impulsive reason. He had forgotten a cymbal in the back of her car. He had been on a walk and it had started to thunder, just as he was passing by her house, and he had appeared on her doorstep, sorry to come to her in such a sorry state, eyeglasses fogged, clothing soaked through. Here, she said. Let me make you a coffee while you dry off. And then he was standing behind her, sweeping aside her hair, so he could kiss her where her neck met her shoulder. All this thinking was just an experiment, she told herself. She tried a different scenario: Nathan was out of town and she was frightened by something in the yard—the garbage cans knocked over, the dog growling into the darkness. She called Theo, her most trusted male friend. He was surprised by her need for him, and he arrived quickly at her door. *What's this all about, Portia?* And then he would understand when she kissed him on the threshold. Her mouth grew wet as she imagined this, which shocked her, like a slice of lemon squeezed onto her tongue. And something else was felt, down in the central seam of her jeans, a reaching pain, like the one she sometimes felt in her lungs when the air was too fresh.

All these ideas were reliant on the promise that Theo wanted her as well. It was difficult to believe that he would respond how she wanted him to, even in the safety of her dreams. Still, she kept at it, exercising this part of her mind that she rarely allowed full range. She was about to allow Theo to loosen the strings that crisscrossed up the length of her dress (she owned no such dress in real life, but mom jeans felt insufficient for a fantasy of this kind) when the door closed loudly behind her, followed by the sound of Rupert's claws on the stairs, his short, dutiful barks, alerting her that Nathan was home. By now, the sink was filled with sudsy hot water. Portia dried her hands against her pants and went to the back door, where Nathan was untying his shoes.

"Let me get my work clothes off," he said. He did not like to be touched until he had rid himself of the signs of his workday. He had explained to her in the past that he often pretended that she and Julian did not exist when he was at the office. He did not keep a picture of her on his desk or a rock painted by his son as a paperweight. Nathan said that there were always criminals nearby, wandering the halls of the state building, slouching in the courtrooms in their dusty boots and cheap neckties. He did not want to introduce his family, even in theory, to this debased environment. Nathan was a smart man with a disciplined mind. It made sense, somehow, that he did not want a good part of his life to encounter a bad one. Portia, on the other hand, could not segregate her thoughts in the way that her husband described. The people in her life, the ones that she loved, were always in her head, intermingled with the rest—a conflicting bundle of feelings and memories. It was for this reason that it was so difficult for her to stay angry at Nathan when he said something that hurt her; there was already a garish heap of self-loathing in her head. Any criticism that Nathan tossed her way risked colliding with some of her own shame.

Nathan went upstairs and Portia went back to the sink, slipping the dishes beneath the white foam.

◆

In the early days, when she and Nathan lived above the attorney's office, Portia had suffered from mood swings. How, she had wondered, could she go to bed tired and content, then wake up the next morning despondent, ravaged by senseless worries and doubts, nothing left to live for? She became overwhelmed by tasks that had been easy the previous day, such as moving the wet laundry into the dryer. She could think about that mass of wet laundry all day, be haunted by it, her inaction creating a monster in the washing machine. The least that she could do was go into the alcove off the kitchen and open the washer door, so that the clothes would not mildew, which could happen quickly, especially in summertime. Somedays, however, even that was too much pressure. She might open the door and, in that dripping cave, see proof of her negligence in soggy twisted lumps. It was horrible.

"What's *really* wrong?" Nathan asked her, trying his best to be helpful. Or sometimes: "Why don't you take a deep breath and force yourself to do it?" It was clear that he did not want to see her suffer, but what she could not express to him, as she was pressing her wet face into her tearstained pillowcase, was that she wanted him to hold her, to assure her that he loved her whether she did the laundry or not. It seemed too complex to require love in this form. It was too advanced of her to expect another person to be able to have the solution ready. And if she could not bring herself to even look at the washing machine in those moments, then how could she demand someone else to put the effort into loving her, to lift her hair and find beauty in her pitiful, bloated face? She could not figure out how to make it fair.

One night, after she and Nathan had eaten dinner, she became upset again. She did not want to admit to Nathan that she was nervous about reapplying to college because it had been the only task that she had given herself that day and it was, therefore, the one task that she had avoided doing since getting out of bed. Nathan had stayed late at work, waiting for a jury to come to a decision. There were crimes being committed every second of the day, every time that he blinked, and the poorly ironed, beer-bellied jury was a slow ooze of indecision. Still, he picked himself out of this languor in one last effort to help his girlfriend, who was the kind of girl who left notes on the fridge telling herself to stay away from the chocolate cake. Who sat around all day, making problems for herself to avoid.

"What's wrong, Portia?"

"I can't explain it," she told him. "I want to break something." She reached for an empty wineglass on the coffee table and held it at arm's length to demonstrate her point. "I want to throw this glass." She made a small motion, swinging the glass but not letting go.

"Why don't you just do it then?" Nathan said. He did not sound angry or sarcastic. Portia saw a flash of sincerity there, as if he was giving her permission, for once, to be frustrated. She brought the wineglass above her head and hurled it toward the front hallway. It crashed, scattering shards across the wood floor. Portia was immediately relieved. The pop of the exploding glass had startled her out of her darkness. She turned to Nathan, hoping to smile, to assure him that she was better and would clean it up now, but he had moved away from her. He was standing on the other side of the room, his hands held out in astonishment.

"I didn't think that you would actually do it," he said.

He seemed shaken. It occurred to Portia that Nathan was under a lot of stress, that she had not asked him how his day had been, even though he did not like talking about his day. Regardless, she should have asked, just to show him that she was thinking of him.

"I'm sorry," she said.

"It's just that throwing things like that," Nathan said. His voice was solemn, apocalyptic. "Some would consider it a form of abuse."

Ten years later, she would remember the wineglass as they stood at the top of the stairway sometime before sunrise, Nathan's cell phone lying at the bottom of the stairs.

"I could hit you right now," she would tell him, and Nathan would remove his glasses, close his eyes, and say to her: "Go ahead."

Moulton

PORTIA HAD AN APPOINTMENT IN MOULTON with Dr. Shay. He hardly saw patients anymore and had closed his office in Portia's town, but he made the exception for her. Moulton was an hour's drive east, on the other side of a mountain that was known for devastating car accidents in the winter. Because of it, Portia would forever associate the word *jackknife* with tractor trailers, ice, and death. But in the summer, the drive was pleasant. The trees were wizened at that altitude, almost mythical. And there were marshes up there where moss-type plants grew in yellows and reds. At this time of year, Portia was tempted to pull the car over and walk into the forest, breathing the mountain air. There had always been this urge, but she could not figure out what she would do, should she give in to it. Would she keep walking until her legs gave out and the grass grew all around her? Would she curl up on a bed of moss and disappear in a little puff of mushroom spores? Her daydreams had a way of being fatalistic, just as her desires had a way of being incomplete, obstructed by her own fear or an inability to decide what was possible. Dr. Shay's office was in the hospital, the one where she had been admitted all those years ago. It was a giant brick building with netted balconies. There were old, unused courtyards with cracked tennis courts, and she remembered a steep, littered path that led to a lake, where the patients could go on supervised walks. Returning to Moulton was comforting. It felt morbidly precious, like returning to the scene of a childhood trauma—a terrible little niche in your life that was all yours, that no one could take away from you. It felt like lighting up a cigarette, years after quitting: *Oh, how awful. But yes, I remember how it was.*

Portia was able to attend these long appointments because she was still out of work. It had been her intention to look for a job two years ago, when Julian entered kindergarten, but then something had changed. Nathan didn't want her to anymore. Portia had had to tend to her mental health, and that took time. She might have been ashamed of this, but sometimes it was nice to feel cared for and to have a mountain to drive over, regardless of context.

As she continued up the winding highway, however, Portia became uneasy. There was a tug to turn around, like the dread of running headlong into a storm. She had been fighting the notion—it was such a foolish notion—that the reason for this sense of dread was the awareness that she was moving farther away from her hometown and therefore farther away from Theo. For the last week, since they had parted ways at Carrie's house, Portia had been content to run errands nearby, for the slim likelihood that she and Theo would cross paths. Everyone in town shopped at the same grocery store, drove through one of three ATM machines, waved to each other while throwing cardboard boxes into the dumpster at the transfer station. But to see Theo outside that scope—the synchronicity that would be required for a chance meeting over the mountain—would be monumental. The pressure in Portia's ears popped as she reached the highest point of her drive. She passed an abandoned restaurant with large vacant windows painted with the dark silhouettes of birds, so that real birds would not crash blindly into the glass. Some people still pulled over for a closer look at the green bowl of wilderness below, dropping a quarter into the metal tower viewers posted along the cliff's edge. Portia had always thought that the tower viewers were a scam, like paying to look through a magnifying glass at a carpet. There was nothing but trees and sky; the thrill was in the vastness, not the details. She held her foot on the brake, taking the turns carefully, as she began the descent. Sometimes, she felt as though her car would slingshot right off the side of the mountain, into a ravine, if she did not take extreme care. In the same way, she had to keep her thoughts controlled, her desires within the realm of reason and integrity, or else they might spin away indefinitely, like how she used to imagine trapeze artists would, if they were not caught by their partners. At the bottom, she drove past a one-pump gas station, a car mechanic's shop, and, not long after, a two-story house that flashed FORTUNE TELLER in neon in the corner of a dingy downstairs window. During her hospitalization, Portia had romanticized the town of Moulton. Its atmosphere was gritty, but friendly, and comfortably impoverished, as if a town could have the personality of a street artist. There was power to that type of living: mending your own fences with wire, growing cabbages and peas in narrow strips of soil, and smoking weed on the back porch with your neighbors, not giving a damn. Portia had imagined that after her release, she would find an apartment above one of the shops downtown, where the buildings were three stories high, which was tall for a small town. It would be hot up there in the summertime, and she would have a big box fan in the window. She saw herself, young, sweaty, and perhaps in her underwear, sitting on a mattress on the floor in front of the fan, picking notes on her guitar. Up there she would be hidden from the world. No one below would think to look up and wonder what was behind the window. She used to dream that she could be successful in this solitary, restrained kind of life. There would be a faulty knob in her shower, doors that stuck, stains on the wallpaper, but these details would become the hallmarks of her newfound sense of durability. She would find that incorruptible identity that she was always searching for, much like the promise of the thrift-store dresses from her high school days; she could not wait to be herself without distraction, and she was relying on her release from the hospital to be her grand send-off.

There were many heavy granite entryways to the hospital, most of which led to waiting rooms where receptionists rolled around, captive inside oddly partitioned glass islands. When you were called out of the waiting room, you were then directed down one of many spidery hallways lined with fake trees. Dr. Shay's office was at the end of one such hall-way, and it looked from the inside as if it had been sectioned off from a larger room. The antique molding near the ceiling cut off abruptly at one wall, and there was a white door with a glass handle that was bolted shut, the keyhole smothered in white paint. Portia lowered herself into a chair with thread-bare arms.

"How was the drive?" Dr. Shay asked her while he thumbed through a pile of forms. One of his shirt buttons was undone. Here, in this office over the mountain, he seemed slightly more befuddled, less potent with his questioning, his admiration, and his *maleness*, if such a thing could be said of her psychiatrist. He went over his usual checklist: Was Portia having thoughts of self-harm? Thoughts of grandiosity? Was she sleeping too little or too much? Portia recited her answers, which were humble and levelheaded. She had been pretending to be on her medication for over six months now and had learned that credibility was never glamorous. For example, you could not fool someone into believing that you were following your diet if you said, "Oh, yes. It is easy. I only eat lettuce." No, for it to seem real, you would have to say something like: "I licked the frosting off my son's cupcake, but other than that, I have been good."

Dr. Shay seemed pleased with Portia for being articu-late, as always. As she explained to him that she was sleeping well but that she sometimes missed the excitement of being a little crazy, he got up to unlock a narrow closet behind his desk. The closet was deeper than Portia had expected, considering that she had entered the room from that direction. By her senses of space and depth, there should have been a hallway directly on the other side of that wall and nothing else. She had not meant to say any more. Perhaps it was the unexpected nature of the closet that made Portia want to confide in him.

"There is one more thing," she added.

Like Dr. Shay's office, Portia's room in the Moulton hospital thirteen years ago had been noticeably off-kilter, the bathroom sink chopped at the corner so that it would fit around a pipe, the baseboard not lining up properly with the wall. Portia, with nothing better to do, had tried to use the gap behind the baseboard as a place to store contraband—not that she had anything to hide, but she had a phone card that she slipped inside, because it was comforting to have a secret, even if it was a meaningless one. The phone card fell deep into the crack, and she could not get her finger inside to retrieve it. Later, she created a pair of tongs using a plastic straw from lunch, chewed flat and folded in half. After some attempts, she was able to get the phone card out. But there was something else in there too. Something that looked as if it had been in there a long time.

Dr. Shay was tracing his finger along a shelf of free medication samples in his closet, each box about the size of a box of granola bars. He pulled out a stack of six and ripped through the plastic film that held them together, and the boxes, now free, toppled to the floor. They were purple, with white and green lettering—the colors of a sneaker from the eighties. The name of the drug itself sounded like it should have been an aerobic fad or a planet from a cheesy sci-fi series. Dr. Shay bent down, gingerly, to gather up the dropped samples from underneath his desk.

"I can't hear music anymore," Portia said. At this, Dr. Shay paused. He stood up, his face flushed, the gap where his shirt was undone revealing an eye of hairy pale skin.

"What's that?" he asked her.

"Ever since I started the medicine," she said, "I can't hear music the same way. My head hears it, but not the rest of me."

Dr. Shay placed his palm over the small tower of boxes to keep it steady. He frowned thoughtfully.

"You know," he said, lowering his voice. "Some people might not know what you mean, but *I* know what you mean." There was a small red clock on the edge of his desk that had been facing Portia since she sat down. She had always supposed that when a clock like that was positioned at eye level, the doctor was putting his faith in her ability to manage time wisely. She saw now that there were only a few minutes left to their session. Dr. Shay had taken his chair again. He seemed very thoughtful, almost wistful, as he buttoned his shirt and lightly touched the rest of the buttons to make sure that they were not also undone.

"Have you been writing music?" he asked. He looked as if he were settling down, ready to dedicate another hour to this new problem.

"No." Portia could feel her face becoming warm. She pulled her bag out from where it had been crushed between her thigh and the chair cushion, gathering the straps in her hands. It had been a while since Dr. Shay had spoken to her of brilliant writers and misunderstood rock and roll stars who had perished, tragic geniuses.

"Perhaps the medication is stifling your brilliance," he said. "There have been many great songwriters with your affliction." There it was. And it did make her ego swell to hear him say this, just a little, until she remembered that she was only an average songwriter, moderately talented. There were times when she did feel inspired, when she dreamed of the peaks and pillars of the universe and believed that she could be brilliant, that she could open the valve between her soul and the world's secret voice. During these times, she would sometimes rip into her guitar, as if she could find it there— in her bleeding fingers and bending strings—but the next day she would forget what she had played and be left with only a muffled sense that something authentic had taken place. Their time was up, but Dr. Shay had not made any signs of hurrying the conversation along. Portia believed that he wanted to help her, but her patience was shutting down. She was not ready to be taken seriously in this way, to sit by modestly while he glamorized the idea of her—young, manic, diabolical in her way. She had no stomach for it.

"It's not a problem, actually," she said, sliding the pill samples into her bag, shaking the doctor's hand.

Outside the sky was clean and blue. On the steps of the hospital, Portia faced a long front lawn crossed by brick walkways. At the far end, where the property ended and the town began, there was a stone fountain. It could feel so classical being ill, inside these courtyards, the plaques, the statues, and the tennis courts. She walked across the grass to the fountain: a large granite sphere with a hole in the top that spurted water weakly, a little glossy stream over veins of discoloration. Beyond the fountain was Moulton's downtown, where shoppers carried their bags and their lattes, where lanes of traffic stretched downward and out of sight. And there he was, a small figure across the road, waiting for the light to change. Portia could make out his height, his clean haircut and black-rimmed glasses. The slight nod of his head while he crossed the street, as if deferential to his own right of way. Portia could not accept this. She could not decide if it was an enormous coincidence or if it was ordinary or if it was a sign—a wonderous, benevolent sign—to see Theo in Moulton, on the same day, at the same time.

Doll

⌒⌒ IT WAS LATE WHEN CARRIE AND GUS dropped Portia off after the Anxiety Marathon concert. Rupert greeted her at the back door, cowering and whimpering with pleasure, as dogs do. She took off her shoes and patted the dog, and when she lifted her head, Julian was standing in the hall, in his crumpled pajamas.

"You're awake," she said, lifting him, her warm, sleepy child, and carrying him to his room. She lowered Julian into his bed and untangled his sweaty fingers from her hair.

"Stay," he said.

Portia got into bed with her son, pushing her knees behind his so that they would both fit. His hair smelled faintly of candy from his shampoo. She could feel his body soften, his breath change. She felt a mixture of guilt and relief—the guilt of coddling him, but also of having been away, and the relief of being with him again—lulling her, along with the feeling of completion that comes with exhaustion.

"You smell like a wet fire," Julian said, yawning.

Portia wondered why she had traveled two hours to a smokey bar just to see a band called Anxiety Marathon. She used to think that the name was clever, but now she wondered what separated that name from any other haphazard idea. Ever since starting the medication, there had been a rift opening inside her mind, separating her from the things that she used to care about. From across the rift, she could still see the bands that she had liked, the music, art, and ideas, but they were vague now and strangely sterile. It reminded her of a bad case of the flu that caused her to lose her sense of taste for a week. How the red, gleaming apple had looked in her hand and how it had fallen apart in her mouth, like cardboard, like biting into a bar of flavorless soap. As she drifted to sleep, she tried to envision the next day and the moments that she would look forward to. She thought of the next morning's coffee and how good that first sip was going to be before Julian woke up. She thought about taking the dog outside, coffee mug in hand, looking for deer along the tree line. She looked for the deer in her mind—the light-footed does that appeared to be gray in the early hours but were really a deep golden color, if you caught sight of one in the sun. Portia could not imagine them. She felt as if her thoughts had come up against a wall, that familiar backyard dissolving around the edges, the deer in the shadows withering into something like a child's drawing, a stick figure, and then just a pair of round dots. She turned over, untwisted the blanket from her ankles. That night she had ridden in the back of Carrie and Gus's car, listening to Gus speak of topics that interested him. He had talked about counterpoint and a small instrument called a Stylophone that he had ordered in the mail, a type of handheld organ that you played using a stylus. He was excited about the prospect of using such a novel device; maybe Carrie would consider letting him play it for one of her songs, he implored. Portia had concentrated on the Stylophone that Gus had been talking about as she watched him reach his arm over to stroke the fine blonde hairs behind Carrie's ears that had escaped her ponytail. Portia heard the word Stylophone in Gus's nasally voice and then could not stop her mind from saying Stylophone, pestering her with the word, like Julian might when he was trying to exasperate her. *Stylophone.* It was an indigestible bit of information. She turned over again in the tiny bed, agitated now. It was an absurd problem to have, this uninvited word rattling around, like a pick fallen through the sound hole of an acoustic guitar. Finally, she went downstairs. She saw the blinking red dot of the wireless router at the top of the bookshelf. A sheer fringe of light traveling over the wall as a car passed. On her way to the bathroom, she tried to remember the Anxiety Marathon performance, Sasha, the singer with the long hair, but all Portia could see was the hair, disembodied in front of a microphone, like a wig on a string. There was something wrong with her mind. She folded herself over the toilet, holding her hair away from her face with one hand and using the other to touch the back of her throat, which felt like a giant, unexplored world. She would vomit, she thought, and it would release the plug from her head. Whatever it was that was blocking her would come out and she would be able to think and feel like she used to. She retched. Her stomach pulled tight, and a thin stream of something mucous-like and cloudy slipped into the bowl. She tried again and some solid thing made progress, rising slowly toward her mouth. She spat and it hit the water in the toilet: a small, triangular yellow island, drifting. The lemon peel from her drink.

Portia had done this before, while she was in the hospital at Moulton. When she first arrived, the staff had watched her closely, interrupting her sleep every thirty minutes to sweep a flashlight beam across the room. During those first nights, her dreams were ruled by images of crime scenes, deep-sea divers scanning the dark ocean floor. She was allowed some privacy, however. Her room, for example, had its own bathroom, which, although doorless, was generously L-shaped, so that she did not have to be staring out into the open room while she sat on the toilet. The shower had a curtain, and she could stay in there for as long as she liked, or until the water turned cold. When it came time for medication, there was a frosted window in the common area that slid open with a nurse behind it. Portia had seen depictions of such a thing in a movie once, complete with overdramatized zombies waiting in line for their drugs. The cliché moment where a nurse asks you to stick out your tongue and show your tonsils to prove that you were not tucking the pills behind your molars. And suddenly there she was, in such a line, a woman standing behind her asking her to "cheek a clonazepam," in other words, to hide a pill in her mouth and pass it along when the staff were not looking.

"Meet me in the laundry room," the woman said. "We'll pretend like we're making out." She scratched her hairline. Portia suspected that the woman had lice. She turned around and heard the woman propose the same thing to the man standing behind her. When it was Portia's turn at the window, she inspected the three pills that she had been given. Yesterday there had been only two, but she had a vague memory of a doctor making a note on her folder after she showed him her bloody nailbeds and the inside of her mouth, how raw it had become from chewing at it. She tipped her head back and swallowed all three. No one asked her to prove that she was not faking.

The effects hit her while she was watching television. Someone had fed the VCR an unlabeled tape, and a group of them had plopped down on the carpet, like schoolchildren, in anticipation. The movie turned out to be *Lawrence of Arabia*, which no one was particularly thrilled about, but they accepted it, because agreeing on something else would be a colossal responsibility. Ten minutes into the film, Portia felt the shade come down over her brow. She had felt like this before, after smoking pot at a party, this inexplicable need to tilt her head upward when she spoke, as if looking out from under an oversized hat. At the party it had been amusing to her, but not this time. She was drowsy, seized by an urgent need to retreat to her room while she could still move. She reached the corner of the carpet, where the floor became speckled vinyl. Sleep was there, in the grain of the floor, but she could feel how bottomless it was, or would be, if she allowed it. It frightened her. She followed the hallway, keeping her hand against the wall for balance. She would go to her room, to the bathroom, and make herself throw up, so she could get the pills out of her system. Her panic was such a slow, disarming panic. A wet flutter in her stomach, warning her of danger. Wet butterflies. Baby animals mucked up in an oil spill. Then a pain in her armpits, like the time her daddy held her up to see inside a hollow tree, where there was a nest. Someone was lifting her off the floor. She could have opened her eyes, but, instead, she allowed this person to hold her, to drag her slightly. It was wonderful in a way, to be pliable beneath a stranger's hands. The man who held her was talking to another man, in a commanding but unconcerned voice. He had found her here, on the floor of the bathroom. They were going to move her to her bed and get a doctor round, at a convenient time. She was lulled by the guilt of being a burden to these men, and yet there was such pleasure in it, in the possibility of being moved about like a doll, her actions, for once, not her own.

We Are Still Wondering

〇——〇 For days now, Portia had been on high alert. She might be brushing mascara across her eyelashes, picking a slug out of the garden, or tying Julian's shoe—at any moment, it could all unfold, the miracle that she was waiting for. She was certain that Theo's presence in Moulton had been a miracle, although she was not sure what kind. At the same time—and perhaps unrelated—she had the notion that her life, up until that point, was finally showing its shape to her, the way a large aquatic animal humps the water before it breaks the surface. There were events that had never made sense: her vision of Alby Porter sitting beside the operating table, telling her that her hands were not tied down; how she cut up her legs in the hospital when she was twenty; or, when Jerry dropped his pants in her room, how Portia had kissed him gently on his eyebrow and said to him, "I know you too," before the nurses came in and hauled him away. And of course, meeting Nathan, tossing herself into his life, as if she could fold herself up and slip discreetly into his mail slot. She and Nathan had been newly married when Alby Porter died, and it had been Alby's newly released song, years later, that brought Carrie back into the picture. She had written: *listen to this as soon as possible*. Soon after, they had gone out for a beer downtown, managing to grab the last two barstools at a grungy, subterranean bar that they had always assumed was going out of business. They had not known that there would be live music that night, a band that they had never heard of, called Anxiety Marathon.

"Remember when we thought we were going to be rock stars?" Carrie asked, nodding at the band setting up in the corner. A woman with straight waist-length hair adjusted the microphone.

Carrie had only recently moved back to town after spending the better part of her twenties roaming the country. It had started out as a vagabond type of thing. She had in her possession a van, a mandolin, and a pit bull named Roxie, as well as some pins on the map, where she knew she could stay if she needed to make extra cash. There had been a lot of waitressing and busking in vacant storefronts. She had spent an icy winter as a ranch hand on a wild-horse conservatory in North Dakota, had been a paid guinea pig for a drug company. She had confessed to trying her luck with a sugar daddy but complained that the guy did not even want sex, just blurry photographs and a lot of pairs of her socks. She had broken it off after a month. The way she saw it, she could have gone to med school like her parents wanted her to and found herself selling her sweaty athletic wear to the same sad man. The motivation for most of Carrie's decisions was fearlessness, which was why it was so dumbfounding when she came back to Vermont married to Gus.

"Is that what we wanted?" Portia asked, still watching the

stage. It seemed to her that all she and Carrie had wanted back in high school was to be friends, but their health teacher's teasing had made friendship unappealing; there was a sense that by being friends, they would also be abetting him in his tireless goading, his winking and smirking. This was what Portia had always assumed, of course. It could have been that Carrie had seen it a different way.

"Yeah," said Carrie. "We thought we were hot shit." When she smiled, the V shape in her forehead turned pale. When she laughed, it turned slightly blue, especially in the neon haze of the bar.

It had been only a few months since Carrie had texted her Alby's song. Portia must have listened to it hundreds of times—"E, are we still drowning?"—uncovering anagrams that were tantalizing but meaningless, like *A wintered owl lingers*; *We are still wondering*; and even *I wrestled wrong alien*. All leading her nowhere.

The PA system crackled as the long-haired singer pulled the mic closer and pressed her lips to it, humming at first, like a locust. A band sat behind her at their instruments, gazing out across the room, more like props than musicians. And they might have appeared this way because they knew that once the long-haired woman stopped her humming and began to sing, no one in the bar would be looking at anyone else but her. She hurled out a note, her lips peeled back, eating the sky. She looked like she had forgotten that she was human. Portia admired the commitment: even at the seediest nowhere bar, this woman was not going to sell herself short.

"Do you want to try it again?" Portia asked Carrie after the first song had ended.

"Try what?"

"Play music again."

◆

Theo was already at Carrie's house when Portia arrived for band practice. Portia spotted him before he saw her, through the top half of the open Dutch doorway. Gus and Carrie's house was relentlessly eclectic—a Dutch front door, a purple stained glass window on the landing, and a pair of hieroglyphics carved into the shed out back that Gus argued were symbols burned into the boards by hobos. They collected records and art, and their sense of décor was irreverent but also somewhat oblivious: an antique bedpan used to hold flowers, a framed nineteenth-century portrait of a dead baby, propped up by its unsmiling, but living, siblings. Theo was coming around from the kitchen. He held a mason jar filled with a murky brown liquid.

"This is supposed to make me feel better?" he asked, not addressing Portia but someone behind him who was out of Portia's line of vision. He sniffed it and made a face. There were spider plants hanging around his head, and bright sun was coming in from the kitchen windows, making the plants hairy with light. He noticed Portia with her guitar case and her bag of guitar cables, and he set the mason jar down on a portion of the kitchen doorway that jutted out like a shelf (there could not just be a straightforward doorway, not in that house).

"Let me move this stuff," he said. He cleared the tangle of extension cords and cables on the ground with a sweeping motion of his foot so Portia could put her things down. He moved swiftly, and Portia caught a glimpse of what it would be like from now on, to see Theo in this light: every action, every word, would be a new opportunity for him to be unattainable to her. She wanted to go home, bury her face into her pillow, like a teenage girl. Gus came into view, cradling an identical mason jar in his hands, his red hair brushed upward from his forehead. There was a patch of small holes on the front of his shirt, exposing the vague pattern of a tattoo on his chest. Gus had a way of looking disheveled and convincing, like a famous person with a hangover.

"I'm telling you," he said to Theo, "you can feel it stripping away the junk. It's all the junk that's keeping you up at night." He sipped the liquid in his glass and swallowed, gritting his teeth, then held the jar to the light to inspect it. Portia could see some dark floating debris settling at the bottom. "It tastes like burnt Christmas," Gus said.

"I'll wait to see what happens to you first." Theo went to

his drum kit, and Portia saw that the back of his neck and the tops of his arms were rosy. Somehow, this made him even more astonishing; he had been existing in Portia's head so persistently that it surprised her to see proof that he had also been existing in the world, getting sun on his skin, maybe throwing a ball around with his sons, hanging his arm out the window while driving. She popped open the latches of her guitar case, watching him.

"You don't want to see what it does to me, trust me," Gus said, taking another cautious sip. He winked at Portia. "But it feels amazing."

The brown liquid, Gus explained to Portia, was a concoction that he had put together himself, finely tuned to fit his particular set of ailments, which included sleep apnea and joint pain.

"It mostly involves boiling pinecones," he admitted.

Carrie had come in from outside while Gus was speaking, her shins wet from where she had been kneeling in the garden.

"It smells like shit Christmas in here," she said, and went straight for her guitar. Carrie had purchased the powder-green Reverend from a guy in a van behind a Pet Center in New Hampshire. She had wanted that Reverend so badly. She loved the religious implications of the name, how she might fall into a place of worship when it came to her music—rough, creative worship, she imagined. And she had changed in that year after the purchase of the guitar, but not excessively. She bleached her hair, wore less makeup. Sometimes Portia could tell by the way Carrie spoke that her taste in music had become less about pleasure and more of a kind of self-assigned homework. There was sophistication in this approach to art, something controlled but also courageous and slightly unhealthy, and therefore enviable.

"You good?" Carrie asked Portia, and lifted open the window, the guitar slung expertly round her back. There was a breeze, the honeyed earth smell of the first days of summer. Crows cawing from somewhere up high. By then, Gus had already gone upstairs so that he could be close to the bathroom, ready for his pinecone concoction to take effect. For a moment there was only the dim pinging of Carrie's unplugged Reverend as she tested the strings again. Theo tapped his leg with his sticks and looked at the floor.

"I went to Moulton this week," Portia said, although it did not exactly answer Carrie's question. She wanted to see if Theo would react.

"I love it there," Carrie said. She turned on her amplifier so the tubes inside it could warm up. "I haven't been for a long time, but Gus and I looked at a house in Moulton before we bought this one. Sometimes I wish we had gone for it." A pipe shuddered from somewhere inside the walls. "But it was really out in the woods," she added. She lifted her eyes toward the ceiling. "We might have killed each other by now."

"Where?" Theo stopped his stick tapping.

"Moulton," Carrie said. She flicked the standby switch on her amplifier, and a low distorted hum filled the room.

"I was just there," Theo said. His face was expressionless. Portia stared. She wanted to march across the room and grab his sticks in her hand, holding them hostage while she demanded an answer: *Why were you in Moulton? What were you doing there?* But her back remained against the wall. Her fingers worked silently along the strings of her guitar, tuning. Her other hand turned the pegs.

They started into their first song. Portia waited for her cue, then began a series of sustained notes that would repeat in the background. Theo came in on cymbals, a low crash that he achieved by using a mallet. The kick followed, throbbing. Carrie sang this one. She sang, picked something intricate on her guitar, and clicked her pedals with her feet, all at the same time, and never admitted that she was brilliant.

As they played, Portia began to feel uneasy. Most likely she was looking too far into it, but there had been a drop in Theo's voice that she did not like. *I was just there*, he had said. Behind those four words was something ominous, or secret, as if he would not have spoken had there not been something else that he wanted them to know but could not tell them. Theo seemed to be the kind of man who liked his privacy, or at least did not consider his personal life to be a subject of interest among two married women. He would not, for example, feel compelled to brag to them about a date that had gone well. It would embarrass him. But there might be a part of him—a very human part—that would try to drop a hint in such a way, to remind those two married women that their bachelor drummer was not completely undesirable. It hit Portia like a wave. For even if Theo had not been in Moulton that day to meet a woman, it would not be long until he did meet someone. Imaginary Theo might show up at her doorstep at three in the morning, yielding and impressionable and filled with longing, but real-life, self-interested Theo did not operate this way. If Portia could have lighted a bundle of sticks on fire and smoked out her feelings right then and there, she would have, watching them crash back into the wilderness, like foxes forced from a den.

✦

Back at Skip's trailer, all those years ago, Skip had liked to make it clear to Portia that she was a poor replacement for his ex-girlfriend, a woman who had broken his heart. Portia had seen a picture of the ex—beautiful, slim, and smiling wide with a hunting rifle slung over her shoulder—and the few times that she had been naked in front of Skip, he had pointed out the places on her body that were lacking in comparison. Portia was nineteen, in college. She had a small chest, and her buttocks did not disappear seamlessly into her thighs—her thighs, which needed to be waxed.

"But it doesn't matter beforehand. I don't see these things beforehand," he said, meaning before sex, before he was finished with her and she became unappealing to him once again—which was why, she imagined, she and Skip rarely had *real* sex and mostly talked dirty over the phone or messed around on his couch, Portia allowing him to degrade her, humiliate her. Somehow, maybe because of Skip, or a combination of many things, Portia began to accept that she would never be as desirable as other women, that whoever she ended up with would have to be grateful for her in some way, due to their own deficiency. Older men, or sad men, like Skip, she assumed, might think that she was the best that they could get, and they would worship her for that. They would worship her for loving them but not for her own merits. She had seen signs of this in Nathan, who was eleven years her senior and who seemed to be already defeated when they met. His drinking was erratic but always heavy and emotional. She saw his bleak face in the morning, his readiness for the day to go wrong in all possible ways. She loved him best in the moments where she could get in front of this malaise, show him that she was determined to make it all better.

♦

Portia did not want to stay at Carrie's any longer. She told Carrie and Theo that she had a headache. She told them that Julian had not been well, that Nathan had somewhere to be that day. She did not know what she told them. On her way down the slate walkway, she could hear the crows carrying on, far up in the pine trees that shaded the house. She had once read in a scientific article that crows could recognize human faces, and, ever since, she could not pass a crow without wondering what it thought of her. *Watch out*, they might croak to each other. *Here comes the pathetic one. Fat cheeks. Weak chin. Caw, caw.*

She had already thrown her guitar case into the back seat of her car and walked round to the driver's side. Her hand was on the door handle when she heard him behind her. She turned.

"Portia," Theo said. His voice was soft, measured. He looked at her when he spoke. He looked straight at her when he told her that he had dreamed of her, that it was the most intense dream that he had ever had.

"We were in bed—in a bed together." He held his hands vertically, side by side, to demonstrate how close they had been in the dream. He seemed utterly unembarrassed at the implications. Yet he was neither impassioned nor even confessional. He conducted himself sincerely, like a close friend who wanted to get to the bottom of something.

Mercy

◦──◦ WHEN PORTIA FOUND THE RUSTED RAZOR blade behind the baseboard of her hospital room, she knew that she should turn it in to the front desk. Tell them that it was not hers. If they did not believe her, if they took it as some kind of confession or cry for help, then at worst she would have to endure the sweeping flashlight of the orderly over her bed for another three nights. They might not let her take walks with the other patients, down to the lake, where the litter from the highway collected in the reeds. She might have thought about it as a responsibility instead of a personal choice: giving the razor up could save another, more desperate patient from finding it in the future. But she did not turn it in or even slip it back into the wall. She brought the razor with her into the shower and placed it on the narrow ledge beneath the showerhead, where it fit perfectly. She kept her eye on it as she washed her hair, working the water into her roots, making them clean and pliable again. She wondered if keeping the razor nearby was her way of holding on to a small piece of power. A small but devastating decision.

In college she had majored in traditional music be- cause she thought that it would help her become a singer- songwriter. It may have been an idealistic pursuit, but it was something that could be done at that school. Others were studying German fairy tales and silent films and the democratization of rivers, all in the same day. Portia took instruction in violin, fiddle, and piano and had just signed up for classical guitar for the spring. Because she was expected to expand her range of study, she added classes on political economy, religious history, and small-town government. Throw in a poetry class and she had everything: the music, the grassroots edge, and the words. But what she liked best were the practice rooms in the music building, how you could sign up for an hour-long slot for 2:00 a.m. on a Monday, set your alarm, and walk across campus in the dark with your cup of coffee from the vending machine. It felt like true freedom, to occupy that room, sometimes in a completely empty building, by your own force of will. To be still on the verge of sleep, playing the piano with a piece of the moon framed in the window. Portia's acceptance to the semi-prestigious school had not been for her extraordinary academic skills—her SAT scores were an embarrassment—but she slipped through admissions because the woman who interviewed her had been impressed by Portia's homemade demo tape. She confessed to having played it in her car on repeat, singing along to the choruses during her commute. Portia showed *promise*, which was a word that made Portia's stomach hurt. It suggested that there was achievement on the horizon, a solid identity gilded in all the subjects that she would have to master. Sitting in the admissions office in her yellow dress from the Salvation Army, she imagined herself on a stage, playing for an audience who, like the admissions counselor, knew the words to her songs. The people in the crowd knew her name: Portia Elby. Portia Elby was her music, not her face, her body, her clothing, or how she laughed or behaved at parties. It was perhaps her only real desire, and this woman was going to allow her to pursue it. Portia had gripped the cushioned arms of the chair, looking beyond the counselor through the window of the admissions building. There was a lilac tree outside, nodding against the glass, and, behind it, a stream of students walking across the lawn. They walked and swung their arms easily, wearing sandals and skirts and paint-splattered denim, so much closer to reaching their potential than Portia, who had not even started. She wished that she could fast-forward to the end. She wished that she did not have to struggle through the next four years to finally begin to like herself.

The first year was not so hard. Portia stayed up late reading her books. She could hammer out a few easy pieces on the piano, which was a real accomplishment for her short, stiff fingers. Her professors and instructors seemed to like her, for her enthusiasm but also for situations that were beyond her control: she was local, from a working-class family, and she sometimes arrived at her lectures sweaty and tired from one of her many part-time jobs, like the dog boarding facility, where she used a high-pressure hose to roll dog shit across a concrete floor. The man who taught American poetry told her that it was nice to see someone who came from the "real world." The way that he looked at her, with a wistful tilt of the head, reminded her of Dr. Shay, how he used to praise her for traits that were involuntary. She accepted this. It made her want to push herself even harder: *Someday,* she thought, *these men will admire me for something that I have worked for.* When spring came around again, she picked the lilacs outside the admissions building and arranged them in a coffee mug on the windowsill of her dorm room. There were only three more years to go.

Portia wondered what had gone wrong. Soap ran down her face, between her eyes. The hospital soap was yellow. It came from a dispenser attached to the shower wall and smelled like soap from a Kmart restroom. It made her fingers almost too slippery to grip the blade, which she held experimentally to her throat, then against her breast, then to the small hollow beneath her ribs. Every part of her felt arbitrary until it was in danger of being cut, and then, for a brilliant second, that inch of skin was beautiful and important. The temperature of the water began to drop. Portia put the razor on top of the soap dispenser and stood in the stream as it got colder. Portia Elby was supposed to be the name on a poster, a name tagged on a guitar case, printed on a ticket. Portia Elby was now a name written in red dry-erase marker on a whiteboard behind the nurses' station. A file stuffed into the desk of her shrink.

The first night she was there, she had called Skip from one of the pay phones next to the vending machines.

"I wanted you to know where I am," Portia said into the phone. A nurse sat about six feet behind her, flipping through a fly-fishing magazine. Skip did not say anything at first. She could hear a dog barking in the background, the television blaring.

"I'm not surprised," he said at last. "You'll be back. You always come back, Kitty Cat." Somehow, between Portia's withdrawal from school and her admission to the hospital, she had developed a persona, where this kind of talk and its implications were encouraged.

Skip lived in his dead grandmother's trailer in one of the more remote mobile home parks in town. It was quiet out there, at the foot of the state forest. June bugs collected on the screen door, and his grandmother's lawn ornaments remained innocently outside, as if waiting for her to return. Inside, on a TV tray next to the couch, there was a reddish photo of a baby in a quilted frame, a white orb, or photographic defect, appearing to hover above the baby's head. It was the ugliest baby that Portia had ever seen, but it must have been a beautiful baby to someone, once upon a time. She sometimes wondered if the baby was Skip himself, while she lay prostrate on his couch, waiting for him to slap her on the ass.

"Your *mom* goes to college," he once said to her, and spanked her so hard her eyes watered. Whatever that meant. He liked to accuse Portia of slumming it. Privileged college student, he said, getting off on her cheap bad-girl fantasy. There was almost nothing that she wouldn't consent to, just to prove to him that she was for real, that she enjoyed the insults, that she was comfortable wearing his girlfriend's

Valentine nighty, her face pressed into his threadbare couch. Yellow foam bulged through the woven cushions. There was a spot on it that always smelled like cat food.

"You don't fill it out in the front like she did," Skip said of the nighty and tore it off her, taking a pair of his grandmother's fabric shears from a jar on the TV tray and cutting it into scraps, to punish Portia for being flat-chested and to punish the ex-girlfriend for being somewhere else, with someone else. He smiled maniacally while he did this because it was clearly an overreaction. This was all a game, like the phone calls that they would have, that Portia's father would be unfortunate enough to overhear. They were both in on it, pretending to be degenerate, when, in fact, Skip liked to read about Buddhist rituals and Portia was on her way to becoming a folk singer.

"Tell me you're Daddy's dirty slut," Skip said over the phone. Portia turned to the nurse behind her, thumbing through his magazine. She turned back to the wall, cupping the receiver.

"What the hell?"

"Do it."

Portia heard the slap of the fly-fishing magazine hitting the pile, the creaking of the nurse's chair as he stood and stretched. "That's just about time," he said, showing her the digital watch on his wrist.

The woman in the lime-green dress from the dean's office had not liked saying "drop out." Her office was in the same admissions building with the lilacs but in a smaller room upstairs. The interior of the building had been painted white but not quite white. It was an academic white, like manuscript paper. Not farmhouse white, not whole-milk white. The furniture was modest but chic, with colors that seemed to Portia to be deliberate, to match the understated, minimalist branding of the institution. She thought that she might miss all the dark grays and serious blues, the flyers for silent meditation in the cafeteria, the view of the stone music building from her room. She had liked how the windows were shrunk with vines. She figured that without these hallmarks of good taste and intellectualism, her mind might regress, soften into something round and stupid, like the kitschy laughing-onion figurine her parents kept on the shelf with the spices.

"Once you *withdraw*," the lime-green woman was saying, "your credits from your work study will be dropped. You will not be able to transfer them should you reapply." She was friendly, that woman, with her pink lipstick, her sharply cut bangs that stopped a centimeter above her eyebrows. No one in town looked like that. No one in town wore lime-green dresses with matching heels and had tattoos that did not look as though they came from a horny teenage boy's sketchbook. But maybe Portia was being moody, remorseful. Portia told the woman that she understood. Her required work study had been a five-week apprenticeship for a guitar maker in northern Vermont, a seventy-six-year-old man who had been less interested in showing her how to make guitars and more intent on having her transcribe notes for a novel that he was writing. He said he enjoyed having someone around to shovel the walkway.

Portia drove away from campus with only her acoustic guitar and a box she had packed with belongings from her dorm room: some framed pictures; a soft, worn copy of *Cannery Row*; and a potted cactus. The rest—her clothing, her jewelry, the bedside lamp, the whole nightstand with whatever notes and letters she had forgotten in the drawer—she left in a free pile in the common room. She had done so well during her first year. She had learned all the piano pieces and written all the essays.

Portia remembered fragments of what happened after that. In her version of it, she drove from the college to Skip's, without even calling him first, and waited in her car outside his trailer until he got home. Before that night, they had been on only one failed date, where Skip tried to bribe the waiter at a nice restaurant to serve Portia, who had just turned nineteen, a glass of wine. When the waiter refused, Skip became embarrassed, having expected the gesture to go over smoothly. He scoffed in the waiter's direction as he walked away.

"He's just giving me a hard time," he told Portia, and he drank straight from the wine bottle. When that did not seem enough to recover his dignity, he excused himself from the table and headed toward the door, the bottle still in his hand.

"What?" he shouted at the hostess, shaking the bottle with his thumb over the mouth. "If you can't serve her, how can you trust her not to drink it while I'm having a fucking smoke?"

Portia had waited in her car in front of Skip's trailer until the headlights from his pickup blinded her rearview mirror. Suddenly this move of hers—the spontaneity, the boldness of showing up unannounced with all her belongings—felt desperate and a little frightening. She stayed where she was, sitting behind the wheel, waiting for Skip to appear in her window.

"You," was all Skip said, walking past her. He was carrying a ten-pound bag of dry cat food.

What Portia did not want was to end up there again. She imagined that it must be like having an addiction, the way that she wanted to be around Skip only when she was at her lowest. He made her feel worse than she was already feeling, which sometimes managed to convince her that none of it was her fault.

Portia turned off the shower and let her body drip. She knew that she was not going to use the razor blade for anything other than dramatics. It was too easy, not to mention corrupt, wicked. As she toweled off, she found herself picturing her mother. There was a photograph that she had seen of her mother, her mother as a fat baby, sitting on top of a table and clutching a cat a little too hard but smiling because of it. The baby in the photograph was pleased with the world around her, the things that she could touch and grasp. Behind her, on the table, lay a little spoon. Somewhere in Portia's heart there was a kind of reverse love for that baby, as if that baby were not her mother but her own hypothetical daughter—or possibly herself—as if she could find a loophole in time in which to love herself, to show herself mercy.

Ant Poison

A CAT HAD LET HERSELF INTO THEO'S APART-
ment, a small tortoiseshell cat with large amber eyes. She
came in through the second-floor window, just followed a
path from the sky and slid in where the screen did not close
properly. It wasn't a path through the sky, of course, but in
the dim light of the evening, that was how the cat had appeared, the two eyes moving closer, until they were at the
foot of the bed. The paws walking over his legs, like hard
pegs. Purring. The cat did not want to be touched or petted,
so she hopped onto his bookshelf and swatted at everything
there: a bottle of sleeping pills, a three-day-old glass of water,
a framed picture of his sons, a birthday card signed "Mom
and Dad."

"Hey, stop that." Theo propped himself up on his elbows
and found himself staring into the cat's eyes, the exceptional
feathery depth of them, an aerial depth, the way a forest appears from high above. *Let me do this*, he heard the cat say.
It was a woman's voice, deep and woolly in his head, like a
beautiful kindergarten teacher or a fairy godmother.

"Okay," Theo said aloud, and lay back down. The cat
walked over his face to the nightstand, where it continued to
paw at the objects there, lightly, but deliberately, as if trying
to make a point that Theo was too exhausted to figure out.

He fell asleep, the water from the tipped-over glass dribbling slowly over his books.

When he woke up the next morning, he had forgotten about the cat and wondered why his room was in disarray. A wind must have blown through, he said to himself, but he did not close the window. If that was the worst of it, he thought, a water stain down the spines of my books, then so be it. In the kitchen, he held his coffee mug and stood in front of the sliding glass door, looking at the tough yellow weeds growing up through the patio. All his life, he had known there to be reasons for change. If the change was painful, he had learned, then it meant that its reason—its purpose—would be worth it, in some way, eventually. Sometimes, he could not fully recall the moment that his ex-wife left him. When he pictured her, she is leaving on foot, her hair long like it was in high school. It is sadder to be abandoned by a long-haired woman, he thought. She is walking barefoot, holding a box with her belongings, packed messily, trailing necklaces and the tendrils of houseplants. The box shudders. She adjusts her hold on it, still walking. A paw appears from inside the box, followed by a pair of round amber eyes.

"She took the cat with her." It was what Theo might say to a bartender after tipping some fiery drink into his mouth. "I think I miss the cat more than I miss her." The bartender nods because he hears this all the time, all these lonely men, missing the dog, the cat, the woman: the chimera of loss.

Theo sipped his coffee and frowned. The coffee was

bitter. He had thrown out the sugar two days ago, after a line of ants found their way into the bag.

He had thrown away three bags of sugar that month. He kept going to the store with the intent to buy ant poison and coming back home with another bag of sugar, as if the ants had gotten hold of his mind and were controlling him. Just the other day, he got into his car and started driving to the store again, the letters *A* and *P* written in ballpoint pen across his palm: *Ant Poison*. When he got to the intersection downtown, where he should have taken a right, he felt that he needed to turn left instead. It was not a feeling of foreboding about the right turn, or a magnetic pull to go the other direction, but something more like a blind spot that removed the right turn as an option altogether.

It looks like I will have to go shopping in another town, he thought. Since the divorce, it was not completely unlike him to do this. Some days, to be spotted in the grocery store, walking the aisles alone, was too much to bear. Someone might misinterpret the stubble on his face or the single roll of toilet paper in his basket as a sign of unraveling. It was a relief to stroll through another store, where the chances of running into someone he knew were much slimmer. He put on his left blinker and began driving east. He would drive over the mountain, for no reason at all. There was nothing stopping him.

Crazy Bitch

It was sometime after midnight, and Portia was knocking on Carrie's front door with the side of her fist. Poor Alice was still in its infancy, and Portia and Carrie had not yet officially added Theo as their drummer—they may not have even been called Poor Alice yet. They were going to hold a kind of audition next week, not knowing what they would say to Theo if they found that he was not a suitable fit—most likely they would just keep practicing until he was.

Dr. Shay had not yet prescribed her the pills.

Nathan had not yet confronted her about failing to take them.

Portia was underdressed for the weather, the cuffs of her boots gaping, her ankles burning as more snow slid inside. She had been walking for so long that the snow no longer melted when it touched her skin but just clumped and sunk further around her feet. Her guitar, slung over her back, was probably frozen. She should have put it in its case, but there had not been time for that because she had written a new song and she wanted Carrie to hear it. The melody that had come to her in her sleep had been already on her lips when she threw off the covers and padded down the stairs, into her drafty living room. The writing and playing of the song had happened all at once, and it was so glorious that it was painful. When she arrived at the chorus, she had felt so helplessly excited that she wanted to run back upstairs and shake Nathan awake. Shake him and tell him that she had discovered a spark of genius, this thing that was so much bigger than a song, as if she had stomped on the ground and felt the shockwave shudder the entire earth.

And now, with each knock against Carrie's door, she could feel the impact deep inside her fist, which was numb but for a sensation in her bones, as if crystals had grown there and were shattering. She had not woken Nathan, of course, because Nathan understood nothing about music. The few bands that he listened to sounded like depressed men muttering into their pillows. Nathan did not appreciate showmanship, did not like it when singers opened their mouths wide to sing, the obsceneness of their molars, the flesh flapping in their throat. She had not even woken Nathan to tell him that she was leaving, which he would be angry about, but the threat of his anger was gone, like a tiny voice calling to her from underneath the snow as she walked away from her house, leaving her car buried in the driveway.

Carrie opened the door. Her jeans were unbuttoned around her hips, like she had pulled them on in a rush. Her bleached hair was twisted from sleep, and there was a deep rut of concern in her forehead. Portia, for a moment, felt bad about disturbing Carrie, but that was forgotten as soon as she stepped inside, her fervor boiling again. She felt it in the tips of her fingers and toes, burning with the revving of her blood.

"I have to show you something," Portia said, and she swung her guitar around to the front of her body. She searched in the dark for Carrie's amplifier, forgetting that there was a light switch. It was Gus who turned on the lights from the bottom of the stairs. He blinked in confusion. His face was pasty, and Portia could see how white his thighs were, the irregular nub in the center of his briefs. By then, Gus was probably used to seeing Portia in his home, although she could see that he was struggling to make sense of what she was doing there at that hour, with a guitar around her neck.

"We're fine, babe," Carrie said to Gus. "You can go back to bed." Carrie's voice was so steady and assured that Portia wondered if somehow Carrie already knew the purpose of her visit and just how important it was. She nudged the end of the cable into the port at the base of her guitar, clicking it into place, hearing the connection crackle through the amplifier. It would be such a relief to know that Carrie understood what she had brought to her. But Carrie did not understand. When Gus had gone back upstairs, Carrie's tone changed. She walked toward Portia, buttoning her jeans.

"Did you walk here?" she asked.

"Just listen." Portia started playing the first few bars, her fingers stiff on the neck of the guitar. She worried that she would not be able to convey the perfect collision of notes that had formed an hour earlier in her head, that Carrie would not give her enough time to finish, and that she would be forced to leave while Carrie's understanding remained fragmented. It was a thing that needed to be experienced from beginning to end, and, as Portia played, she almost forgot that it was only a melody that she was conveying—that it was not absolute meaning expressed with angelic precision, accompanied by the sickest rock and roll hook that had ever been wrenched from an electric guitar.

Sometimes Portia felt so helpless in the unfolding of certain ideas. It could take such a long time—a lifetime, on some occasions—to create something worth creating, and then even longer for the world to accept it. All she wanted was to be able to translate the enormous, godlike buzzing in her head into something that other people could see, hear, or touch. She wanted to be recognized by others in the sense that she wanted to be *recognizable*: as herself, which was at the same time lowly and miraculous. She had felt this way with Jerry, when he had come to her in her hospital room. Here was a man at rock bottom, but from this place of destitution he had seen Portia and had claimed to know her, and this had seemed to her as powerful as if he were a king, picking her out from a crowd.

Carrie was silent as Portia let the last note fade out. She walked into the kitchen, and Portia could hear the soft thump of cupboards opening and closing in the dark. Some dishes knocking dully together and the clicking of the gas stove.

"What do you think?" Portia asked. Carrie came back into the living room and unplugged the amplifier. There was a hollow sound, like the deep pressure of a bathtub beginning to drain, and Portia's guitar deadened in her hands.

"What do you think?" she asked again. Carrie rolled her neck and sat with her legs crossed on the hardwood floor. The perfectly round moon of her middle toe poked through a hole in her sock.

"I'm going to make you a cup of tea, and then I am going to drive you home," Carrie said. There were brass light fixtures around them: two for the long wall, where the amplifiers were stacked, and one between the entrance to the stairway and the archway that led to the kitchen. In each of these three light fixtures, there was a bare bulb that grew brighter and somehow more naked as Portia looked around, as if some protective layer were being peeled away. She wondered if perhaps she needed to do something more heroic. She began to loosen the wet laces of her shoes, not knowing why, only that it seemed like the beginning of a more realized act of protest: she would not go home until Carrie understood. Her socks came off next, withered from the melted snow, and her feet were red and puffy underneath. She stood, looking down at Carrie, powerful and resolute. What she did next would remain in Portia's memory as one of her greatest humiliations.

It began with the tea water boiling. Carrie left the room once again to move the kettle from the burner, and Portia, seeing this as an opening, plugged the amp back in and turned up the sound. The amplifier was a powerful piece of equipment, with a Master Volume knob that Portia had never had to position past the first notch, so turning it up at all—which she did, although only to the third notch—made the floorboards vibrate, the loose screws in the light fixtures buzz. Portia began her song again, standing with her legs wide, her thawing feet throbbing along with the floor. She pitched her head back and sang, like she had seen Sasha from Anxiety Marathon do, which was more of a howling, and she felt that there was music flowing up from her belly, up from the soles of her feet. Carrie might have rushed back in to stop her or to yank the plug once again from the wall, but she reappeared calmly, a veteran look on her face that suggested that she had been in similar situations before and that the way to deal with them was to move slowly and speak only when necessary. She held her cell phone, extended in her hand, and kept it poised like that as Portia ripped through the song for a second time. The noise brought Gus downstairs again, still without his pants, and Portia remembered him, if only in the periphery, as a white figure framed in the shadowed archway of the landing.

Later, Portia could not imagine how she had appeared to Gus or to Carrie. It would be too painful for her to imagine, considering how unguarded her behavior had been, which she might have forgiven herself for, ironically, if her actions had been more impressive. She might have climbed the railing of a large bridge or parking garage and threatened to jump to her death, or she might have stolen a car or walked naked through town. In a way, these deeds would have been excusable in their detachment from her—they could be seen as separate from her identity, like a demonic possession. But instead, she had become too closely obsessed with her own inflated sense of talent and worth. She had curled inward, become a loop of self-congratulatory feedback, and it was awful to think about. When she remembered that night in Carrie's living room, she dug her nails into her palms. She called herself a "stupid woman," under her breath.

Carrie had not needed to unplug Portia for a second time. When Portia was finished playing, Carrie flipped the phone around to show Portia on the screen that she had recorded everything. She helped lift the guitar over her head, then ushered her to the kitchen table. Gus sauntered over as well, sleepy and obedient and still not sure what he had walked into. They listened for a long time to the sound on Carrie's phone, the three of them stooped over the table, resting their heads in their hands. It was not a pleasant sound— something like an alarm going off in irregular intervals—and Portia wondered what the importance of it was.

"I don't get it," she said to Carrie, but Carrie only moved the phone closer and played it again.

"That's you, Portia," she said. Portia saw the pale V in her friend's forehead, full of tired sympathy. Carrie tapped the screen and the recording stopped. It was quiet in the kitchen, except for the *crr, crr* of the Formica wall clock. Gus sniffed.

"Okay," Portia said. She remembered looking at her hands, which she expected to find laid flat on the table, and seeing instead that they were holding a mug of ginger tea. Perhaps, she thought, Carrie was jealous of her talent and the recording was meant to sabotage her. It seemed unlikely, but at the moment, it was the only reality that Portia could make sense of.

Gus had dressed and gone outside to start his car and clear the snow. From where they were seated at the kitchen table, Portia could hear the scraping of Gus's shovel as he walked it down the length of the driveway. It occurred to her that he was doing this for her, so she would not have to walk home. She imagined the car idling, heating vents aimed upward, the growing mouth of thawing ice on the windshield. At some point, unbeknownst to her, someone—either Carrie or Gus—had laid her wet socks over the tall iron radiator by the window. At the sight of these rumpled socks, Portia's confidence began to come undone. It often happened like this: some small thing came along and knocked her ego aside just enough for her to see what was really going on. She yawned. She put both her hands over her face because she could not stop yawning, and then she was covering not just her gaping mouth but also her tears.

"I'm so sorry, Carrie," she gasped.

Gus had come inside and was stomping his boots on the mat. He must have seen how Carrie was standing behind Portia's chair, draping her arms around her. Carrie might have looked up over Portia's head and signaled to him with her eyes, because he stood quietly in front of the closed door.

"Do you remember the day you got out of the hospital?" Carrie was asking her. "I brought you flowers?"

Portia did remember, vaguely. Carrie had arrived at Portia's house in frayed shorts, cut so high on her leg that the blue pockets poked through the hem. One of her ankles was bloody, and her shoes were dusty from where she had picked the flowers by the roadside. It had been thoughtful of Carrie to come and somewhat surprising; Portia had always considered their friendship as strong but unyielding, where deeply private ideas could be shared with the thoroughness of scientists but never to the point of vulnerability. If a beautiful song made them want to weep, they would tear their hair, claw their eyes, exaggerating the urge to cry into oblivion.

"I'm *dying*," they said.

"That *killed* me," they said. This way they could speak of feelings, hold them up, like signs written on cardboard, without acknowledging them. Not really.

And so, when Carrie came with the flowers, Portia took it as a way to sidestep the rules of their friendship, just enough. A safe gesture of love, picked from the dust and indifference of the shoulder of the road.

"I remember," Portia said.

Carrie moved around to the front of Portia's chair and moved her hands, gently, away from her face. "You're one crazy bitch, you know that?" Her voice was softer now. Loving.

On the drive home, Portia watched the windshield wipers pin large snowflakes to the glass. Gus gripped the wheel with oversize gloves, taking the turns slowly, using his blinker, braking well before the stop signs, while Carrie sat behind them, bent forward in the center seat, so that she could feel the blowing heat from the dash. They did not speak because the roar of the heat was turned up so high and because it was clear that Gus was concentrating on getting them safely through the snow. Portia thought about what Carrie had said to her in the kitchen, astounded by the tact with which she had handled everything. She had called Portia a "crazy bitch" because in that moment, it was the truth. But there had also been such pride in her voice, looking up at Portia with the annoyance and compassion of a mother scolding a spirited child. It was clear now to Portia that waking her friend in the middle of the night had been a mistake, but, through her humiliation, she could see that she was accepted and that her pride would not have to pay dearly for it. When they reached her house, Nathan met them at the door, smiling and gentle. He held open a blanket and hugged it around Portia's shoulders, then shook Gus's hand and thanked Carrie for taking care of his wife. He was not angry, like Portia had expected him to be. He was not weary from worry or responsibility, and Portia found that she was so grateful. All she could do was sink into his embrace, close her eyes, and sleep.

Ask Portia

꩜ THEO ARRIVED IN MOULTON ABOUT AN hour after leaving his apartment in search of ant poison. He parked his car in the public lot at the center of town, thumbing into the meter enough quarters and dimes for about five hours of parking (which was an arbitrary and unnecessary amount of time). It was a sunny day, there was a breeze, and a woman on a bench was wearing a sun hat. He figured that he would start walking and see if he found a store along the way. After placing the paid ticket on his dashboard, he stood by his car and studied the letters on his palm. *Abundant Person. Abandoned Panda. Apple Pie.* The ink had bled into the tiny lines in his skin. *Arrogant Prince.* There was a dreadful moment of disorientation, where he no longer knew what he had intended the letters to mean, a vertiginous feeling of forgetting what day it was and what he was doing there. He had not told anyone that about three weeks ago, he had quit his job, not his friends or his family. His ex-wife would soon find out when her monthly alimony did not appear in her bank account, but that day was still far off, if he was careful. He found a side street and started down it, enjoying the back view of the stores, the second- and third-story apartments. One window had a batik curtain printed in yellow and red dye, another a sheer lilac fabric. He had always wanted to live above the street. Somehow, he reasoned, it would make his solitude feel more important, like someone living in the city, only without the city. At the end of the side street, he came upon a large brick building surrounded by lawns and neatly laid brick paths. The paths met in the middle of the lawn in a circle of spiraled bricks, with two benches on either side. It looked shady over there and peaceful. Theo liked the idea of sitting on one of the benches, alone, in this town that he had picked at random, without a purpose. It made him feel like he was shrinking, in a pleasant way. When he was a boy, it was common for him to lie in bed with his eyes closed and the lights out, waiting for sleep, and to feel as though the room were shrinking rapidly around him, collapsing in on itself in a kind of loop. A black hole. Except it was soothing, like being rocked to sleep by a shockwave or a magnetic field. He took his wallet out of his back pocket so he could sit, placing it beside him on the bench, and he experimented with scooting away from it, seeing how far he could sit from the brown leather lump before he started to worry. Someone might not know it was his and take it. A fat man could sit on it. A bird could shit on it. He did not know how long he sat there, edging farther and farther away from the wallet, but, eventually, he found himself looking at the letters on his hand again. *Anxious Pigeon*. He searched his mind for the right words but could not find them. In a flash it occurred to him that he was sitting on the grounds of a giant psychiatric hospital. He was probably losing his mind, but his subconscious, in a last-ditch effort to save him, had landed him here, at the gates of the biggest loony bin in the state. He wondered if people were allowed to stroll right through the doors and ask to be locked up, like walking into a police station with your wrists forward, waiting to be cuffed. There was a steady stream of outpatients, visitors, and staff coming and going from the three main entryways, walking to the bus stop, or searching for their keys on the way to their cars. Sunlight flashed and shimmered off the nearest line of cars in the parking lot. Theo squinted at the cars, trying to focus his mind. It would not be right to say that this kind of distractedness was unusual for him, but it had never interrupted his life like this. For the last three weeks, he had been going about his business as best as he could, not entirely sure what was real and what was a memory from something he had dreamed, or imagined, or heard secondhand. There was a vague memory of a cat jumping out his window last night, how silently she had come and gone. He stood, put his wallet back in his pocket, and rubbed his face, hard, with his hands. When he opened his eyes, he was looking at a black-and-white sticker on the bumper of a car parked in front of the hospital. A little white bottle on a black square. He had designed that little white bottle. That was his band. It was Portia's car.

Fangs

◌─○NATHAN HAD SOMEONE ON THE PHONE. IT was three in the morning and Nathan was saying into the phone that Portia was having an emergency, that he needed someone to come over, right away. She had been out late. She had been out late with another man. She had been out drinking, had dropped her keys coming in, was behaving erratically. There was a pile of pills on the living room floor that had never made it into her stomach.

"—against medical advice," he was saying. The way that he was speaking to the person on the other line suggested that he had not called 911, that it was not an unknown, unbiased person of authority. Portia swatted at the phone, but Nathan held it high above his head and looked at her sternly.

"I have put up with more than any other man would," he whispered hoarsely to her. The phone back to his ear: "Yeah, she is threatening to leave."

Nathan's tone was resolute, businesslike, but also apologetic. It was frightening for Portia to hear her husband talk like this, like she had already been shut out, a difficult decision already made, only Portia did not know what exactly the decision was. She could not imagine who he was talking to. She found then that she was begging, sinking to the floor.

"Please don't do this," she was saying. "We can talk in the

morning. Please. What if Julian wakes up?" Nathan turned his back to her.

"I'm so sorry to trouble you like this," he said into the phone. Portia rushed out of the kitchen, up the stairs, and into Julian's room. She found the bed empty, stripped of pillows and blankets, Julian's books stacked neatly on his bookshelf, his stuffed lion on the floor. He had been asleep when she left. She had piled the books beside the bed; one, she was sure, had been forgotten facedown under the blankets. Before she could form an explanation, she heard Nathan's footsteps on the stairs. He stopped in the doorway of the bedroom.

"He is at your parents'," he said. "I was wondering when you were going to realize that your son wasn't here." Portia whipped around to face him.

"Fuck you," she hissed. She walked toward him. "Fuck you," she said louder. Nathan's expression did not change. He brought the phone again to his ear.

"I think she is about to attack me," he said, like he was speaking around a lump of fear but also hurt, disbelief. Like any husband would sound who was worried about his wife, a tired husband who just wanted everything to be right again. His eyes were fixed on Portia, like pins, like he wanted to see what she would really do. Portia moved forward, grabbing for the phone, but the phone was gone. She had knocked it away from Nathan's hand and it fell onto the floor, bouncing, tumbling to the bottom of the stairs.

Nathan had Portia by the wrist again, or it might have been her arms, up by her shoulders. It was strange how quickly the details were lost to her. Her mind was working too frantically to figure out what was really going on. Nathan must be serious if he took Julian away, she thought. His actions likely did not stem from the shock of finding her hoard of pills in the cabinet. This was calculated. And now he was holding her and saying that she was in the middle of an *emergency* when all she wanted was to have her son back home, to go to bed. Portia realized suddenly that she had not seen Rupert either. He was a small dog, protective of his owner to a fault. He did not like to see people approach Portia in ways that he did not understand. Once, the dog had darted at the heels of a man who was trying to give Portia a balloon at a flea market. The gesture, along with the large, looming red ball, had seemed criminal to the dog, and he had tried to save her. Sometimes Rupert would not even tolerate Nathan leaning in toward Portia for a kiss and would growl a low, distrustful growl from the back of his chair. *How dare that man kiss my girl*, he must have thought. Portia's dog would not have liked to see her like this, Nathan taking her by the wrist and raising his voice. He would have run at Nathan and barked and yipped. He might have bitten.

"I'm so angry," Portia said, but her voice did not sound angry. Instead, it sounded as if she was confiding in him. As if he might help her with this problem after all, instead of holding her there, against her will. "I could hit you right now," she whispered into his face.

At this, Nathan released her. He stepped back and, closing his eyes, removed his glasses and folded them.

"Go ahead," he said to her.

✦

"What is your marriage like?" Theo had asked her in the empty parking lot of the old Catholic church. They were sitting, hidden partially by a thicket of Japanese knotweed, on a ridge of broken blacktop above a river. A chunk of blacktop had fallen down the bank, about twenty feet below them. It was large enough that someone had fashioned a narrow tent around it using a tarp, the craggy height acting as a boundary between the occupant and the river. It was difficult to say whether the tent was still in use. A very white and new-looking sneaker lay in the leaves beside it. Portia used to come here when she was young, an experimental smoker of cigarettes who wanted to be alone but not completely invisible. The church parking lot overlooked a community of homeless men, who existed quietly during the day, who had only ever nodded respectfully at Portia when she appeared at the top of their bank, sniffling and struggling to light a cigarette. She would sit there and smoke and let her tears fall silently, wiping her nose on her sleeve, more grateful than anyone would ever know for the men, sitting with their eyes closed or washing their pocketknives in the water, pretending not to notice her.

"There is nothing wrong with my marriage," Portia said.

She liked Theo's candidness, the way he had not waited for an opportune moment to ask about Nathan, the way he dealt with what she had said to him moments earlier—the reason that they had come to the river in the first place. He sat there, next to her, like a man open to learning all that he can, not worried at all if the information would be bad or good. It put Portia at ease.

"I have . . ." She did not know how to say it, but she felt as though Theo deserved a warning. She wanted to tell him that sometimes she believed things—outrageous things— with all her heart. How did she know that this was not just another one of those outrageous things?

"I see a lot of doctors," she said. With her finger, she loosened a rock from the broken earth and watched it tumble, picking up speed. She worried at first that it would strike the makeshift tent below them—someone might be sleeping inside after all—but it rolled safely into the river, without even a splash. Theo was silent, so she went on: "Please don't take offense to this," she faltered again. She could not look at him. Something broke loose inside her, plummeting, like the rock had just done. Remorse. She stood up, brushing the sharp bits of gravel from her hands. What she was doing was cruel. She had brought Theo here, to this secluded place, and told him that she was falling in love with him and that there was absolutely nothing that could be done about it.

◆

She was dreaming of him already. Already he was appearing, unremarkably, as if he belonged to her mind, her life. She had crawled underneath a barbed wire fence into a field. It was difficult because, as she discovered, she was pregnant, her round belly dragging along the ground. She had come into the field early in the morning to have her baby, alone, like an animal that leaves the herd in the night to give birth. Her body rang with pain, a bell being struck violently, and all around her, the grass began to turn red. She wondered where she had left Julian, where she had left the baby. But wasn't she having the baby, right there, bloodying the ground? And then she was standing outside a small one-room house, in the same field. The house was blue, a single white door left open, a single square window reflecting the sun. Theo was in the house, she knew. He was huddled in the corner, afraid to look at her. That was when she knew that she had not been crawling away to give birth but instead to die, which is also something that animals do.

Next, she was in line at the airport, about to have her luggage scanned. It was her turn to put her suitcase on the conveyor belt, her suitcase that she had forgotten to pack. It still had the things in it from when she was hospitalized, more than a decade ago. Shirts that probably did not fit anymore, underwear that had never been washed. The broken phone card that she had used to slice up her legs, the confiscated shoelaces, the underwire bra.

"Wait," she said to the security agent, and she tried to

get her suitcase back from the belt, but there was suddenly a hand over her mouth.

"Leave it and walk away," said a voice. It was Theo. He was dressed in doctor scrubs, shaking his head at her, as if warning her of some danger. He moved his hand away, and she saw that it was bleeding.

"This is what I was trying to tell you," he said, and she saw, without a mirror but by way of the dream, that a pair of sharp fangs had grown in her mouth.

◆

Portia did not hit her husband. The desire to do so had died as soon as she had spoken. Still, he waited for the blow to come. Almost hopeful, like a man waiting for a miracle to save him. Even though she was still confused, disoriented, Portia understood that Nathan was looking for ammunition because that kind of thinking was ingrained in him from his work with the police department. If you are not certain that you can lock up a man for selling drugs, then find something else—belligerence, obstruction of justice, alcohol on his breath. Anything. If you are not certain that you can lock up your wife for not taking her pills, then make sure she leaves a bruise. She heard the door opening downstairs, and Nathan opened his eyes.

Alby Porter

It was in a letter to his lover, Emile, where Alby Porter first began to question the soundness of his mind. He had known that not one of his guests would dive into the swimming pool to rescue him after he dropped backward into the water bound in chains. He had known this because he had seen how competitive they all were—this blend of writers, musicians, artists, and producers—when it came to their image. They had been told to prepare for a spectacle, and now their dear host was writhing in an explosion of bubbles at the bottom of his pool, surely drowning but, then again, surely up to something that no one had planned for. So they stood around the edge, martini glasses alert in their hands, and did nothing. It had occurred to Alby, as he felt the last small pearl of air slip through his lips, that not only would he die, but he was also going to miss his guests' reaction to his stunt: their confusion, their shock, the dark blossoming of guilt when they realized that Alby could have been saved if it were not for their pride. "I understood, and my understanding was as heavy as my chains," he wrote to Emile, "that my reasoning had failed me, and that I had neglected to plan for the most obvious mishap: death."

It was a woman who saved him finally, a young nobody

who had been abandoned by her date and, knowing no one at the party, should have been the last person to act in the face of social uncertainty. She herself was not strong enough to lift Alby to the surface, but once she broke through, diving in wearing her minidress, others followed. They dragged him out and slapped his pale face. He was loaded into an ambulance with his hands still bound, for he had swallowed the key. "I am the world's biggest fool," he wrote. "Please don't leave me."

But Emile did leave him, and Alby, in his devastation, sought out a psychoanalyst.

Since the swimming pool incident, as you might know from my previous letters—if those first letters were read at all, which I still hold out hope that they were—I began seeing many doctors. Shrinks. None of them were right, of course, until I found a man who practiced good old-fashioned psychoanalysis, his office all dark wood, long couch, leather armchair. Emile! The man smokes cigarettes at his desk and wears a tweed jacket! It's the wildest thing you've ever seen. And his demeanor is perfectly frigid and bored, gaunt and bearded like a goat—not one of these big, dapple-eyed women in shoulder pads, patting you on the knee, telling you that it is okay to cry. I see him up to four times a week, which is excessive, I know, but I realize that I am ill, and my illness needs an audience or else it will destroy me.

At first, Alby's desire to fix his apparent mania was in earnest.

"I can feel that my blood is hotter now," he said to the therapist. "I don't sleep. Instead, I shut my eyes and the dead hold soirees in my mind." But it soon became clear, through the letters, that Alby's obsession with psychotherapy was tied to his heartbreak over Emile. Around this time in the book's chronology, Alby stopped writing to his other regular correspondents altogether. He wrote to Emile every day, recounting the therapy sessions, as if his confessions on the doctor's couch were a direct line of communication to his ex-lover. There was no evidence that Emile ever wrote back.

It seemed obvious to Portia, from the moment she bought the book of letters, that Alby Porter's mind was a mirror of her own. Not a perfect mirror, but that was not the point. Although Porter's life was not in any way similar to hers, she felt that they had a connection beyond what was linear, beyond what could be understood chronologically and factually. She read his letters from front to back and then from back to front. She saw meaning in the manic run-on sentences, in the bizarre and imperfect patterns of Alby's language and his reasoning. It made sense to her that reincarnation would not be a full stop, a complete cycle, but rather that lives could overlap, minds could collide. Energy was transferable in more ways than death and rebirth.

"When Porter says, 'E, are we still drowning?' he is referring to the swimming pool. He is asking his lover if what he has done is irreparable," Portia explained to Dr. Shay. "Even years later, when the song was written, he is still wondering if he ever left the pool. In a sense, he is asking me the same thing, but kaleidoscopically. Because he knows I still have a chance to pull myself out of the water. To be *better*."

Dr. Shay smiled.

"That is an interesting coincidence about the name," he said, lowering his eyes. He bent down to straighten the cuff of his pant leg. "There are some hallmarks that we professionals are taught to look out for." He seemed to make sure that the word *professionals* had a hint of disparity to it. "They are not condemning by any means, but still, something to look out for." Portia looked to the piece of stained glass in the window behind Dr. Shay's chair. It hung dully, with no sunlight shining through, as if letting Portia know not to take any of his advice seriously. Not today.

"There is a tendency for some to look for clues, to find words that sound or look similar, rhyme, or fit together in interesting ways. Sometimes these similarities are so striking that we might forget that logically, they are unrelated."

"Like what?" Portia asked.

Dr. Shay seemed to struggle for a moment. "I don't know," he said. "Like *brain* and *Brian*, I suppose. Or *do not* versus *doughnut*." He tilted his head, apologetically.

"You mean like Alby Porter and Portia Elby?"

Dr. Shay inhaled slowly and lowered his chin into his palm, in a gesture of satisfaction but also modesty, pleased that Portia had figured it out but too proud to say as much. He let out his breath, as if counting the seconds, before speaking again. "All I am saying is to approach these ideas with caution."

◆

They had gathered in the living room. Portia sat alone on the couch, facing Carrie and Gus, who had brought chairs in from the kitchen, while Nathan tended to the mess of pills that he had made on the rug. He knelt with his sleeves rolled up and his collar crooked, sweeping the pills into a dustpan with quick, dispassionate strokes. It was three thirty in the morning.

Carrie and Gus said that they wanted Portia to go to the hospital, where the doctors could get her back on her medication. They had long, worried faces, like spirits come to give her a warning. They were dressed. They wanted her to get into the car.

Portia did not know why Nathan had called Carrie and Gus, of all people. When they had let themselves in, she had almost expected it to be the police, or a horde of men in white coats with their syringes drawn. She would not have been surprised to see Dr. Shay, in his slippers, gazing at her sharply but dotingly. Moreover, she was surprised that Carrie had listened to Nathan in the first place. Carrie had always been a bit cold toward Nathan (and Gus did not know him at all). She had been in New Mexico on the day of Portia and

Nathan's wedding, living in an RV without electricity. For a wedding gift, she had sent them a small basket about the size of a hummingbird's nest, woven by candlelight. Portia would have expected Carrie to question whatever Nathan had to say, or to have insisted on speaking to Portia herself, before barging into her house.

"You're not yourself," Carrie was saying. "This isn't you." She looked pained. The V on her forehead was white with concern.

"I'm fine," Portia told them. She was not sure what was keeping her from telling them to go home, from laughing in their faces. It was going to be humiliating for her friends once they realized their mistake, and as much as Portia wanted to put an end to the whole misunderstanding, she had already decided that she would do so gently.

"You're not fine," Gus said. His voice was deep with resolve. Portia had never known Gus to be anything but exuberant, or at least comically somber. He could be like a sad clown when things did not go his way. He had never addressed Portia like this. "We don't want you making the same mistakes," he said. This was Gus talking—Gus, who had known her for only three years, who boiled pinecones on Sunday mornings. He was wearing a striped gray shirt, without holes in it, buttoned to the second-to-last button. His pants were not wrinkled. He did not look like someone who had been called out of his bed at three in the morning, made to dress in a hurry. Behind him, Nathan was shining a small flashlight across the carpet. Portia was confused. She did not know what mistakes Gus was referring to.

"What are you doing?" she asked Nathan, rising. In an instant, Carrie and Gus had laid their hands on her shoulders and pushed her back onto the couch. Not forcefully, but in a way that implied that they were waiting for her to snap, perhaps lash out violently toward her own husband.

"I think she is going to attack me," he had said over the phone.

"He is trying to do the right thing," Carrie said. But Portia had been asking about the flashlight. She wanted to know why Nathan was now crouched so low that he was almost lying on his stomach, staring down the beam.

◆

Dear Emile,

I have noticed that my doctor, our nineteenth-century goat, always sits in perfect stillness at his desk while I talk. Every day, his typewriter is there, with the date written at the top of the page, and yet, every day, he does not lay a finger on the keys. What does he do with all those dated blank pages? I wonder. Does he cram them into his desk drawer, in a file labeled "Porter"? Does my madness amount to a stack of carefully organized white space? And most importantly: Is he listening to a damn word that I say?

Today I decided to test him. I said: "Doctor, I have been thinking about what I told you three weeks ago. About pheromones." Without missing a beat, he drew a cigarette from his breast pocket and said, "Oh yes. You were concerned about the pheromones produced by live audiences." He placed the cigarette between his lips and then seemed unable to find a match to light it with. He bent over his desk, opening drawers and shuffling a pile of notes. "I believe you used the word *effluvia* to describe it." I watched an ashtray of emerald-green glass vibrate with the force of the doctor's rummaging, inching dangerously close to the edge of the desk, until the jarring of one final drawer sent it toppling to the floor. The green glass shattered.

"Yes," I said to him, trying to hide the surprise in my voice, upset by the broken ashtray. "I believe that sweat sends signals. Like herd animals, the performer sends out 'fight' responses since he certainly cannot flee. It's the performer's job to be onstage, after all, as terrifying as it is." At this, I received no reply, just the quiet snapping of glass beneath the doctor's shoes as he went to his office door, calling into the hallway for his housekeeper to come quickly with a broom. I continued:

"I only wonder—and it is more curiosity than fear,

mind you—with all the chemical output in the theater, does the body think that we are at war?" Finally, I turned my head, only to find our goat crouched beside his chair, aiming his desk lamp at the floorboards.

"What on earth are you doing?" I asked him.

"Casting shadows," he said. And I realized that that was exactly what he was doing. Searching for the tiny pieces of broken glass by shining a light at the floor, looking for the shadows to reveal what the naked eye could not see.

Isn't it brilliant, E?

If your shadows could speak, what would they say to me?

Your broken ashtray,
Alby

Inkblot

August 18, 1982

Dear Emile,

Have you ever seen an inkblot test? What do you think
would be the most damning thing to see in an inkblot
test? For me, it would be my own face, and to know
for sure that I am a narcissist. You would probably say
it would be worse to see nothing recognizable, to stare
and stare and feel no images reaching for you from the
other side. Emile, I will tell you what I saw in the doctor's ink, but first I had the most wonderful idea: What
if you never write back to me, but we send each other
inkblots in the mail? Big, smeary alien shapes folded into
envelopes. Then I will never know for sure what you are
or aren't saying to me, but I will know what I want to
hear from you, deep down. It will be the most magical
correspondence. Please send a blot in reply. I will read
much too far into it. I will see in it your lion's hair, your
towering confidence, your Beethoven fury.

The thing is that I lied to the doctor when he showed
me the first framed splotch of ink. I told him that I saw two
sphynxes, because wouldn't that be regal and impressive?

Who wouldn't want to see two sphynxes? But for a very brief moment, I saw a pair of terrible-looking fetuses, curled up with too many limbs, connected to each other at the navel by a spiky, electrified cord, feeding off each other, giving life to each other. I thought: They are identical, but one of them must be stronger, or else they will both die. One twin must consume the other for there to be life, or else there is only death.

I miss you. You were right.

Yours,
Alby

Ferns

⌒◯ SHE KNEW THAT HE WOULD CALL HER, so
she was not surprised to see the unknown number blink onto
her phone. The phone buzzed in her hand as she walked out
the back door, down the porch steps, into the yard, which was
laid out like a long green rectangle. Flat and glossy green, still
shining from the house's previous owner, who put a great deal
of care into maintaining it. All the neighbors had said so when
she and Nathan moved in. The phone felt like a giant insect in
her hand as she walked. There was no one at home, so there
was no need to hide herself or to be discreet. She could have
taken the call in her kitchen. She could have answered it from
under the table, as Julian liked to when he was taking his birthday calls from family. But she kept moving, feeling the grass
beneath her feet turn to moss, then grow softer and colder still
as she reached the spongy ground near the tree line. This was
where she sometimes found the tapered prints of deer, inches
deep in the mud, sometimes deeper, like a bore hole, but still
with two neatly pointed crescent moons at the bottom. There
was no fear in her that he would grow impatient and hang up.
If her phone went to voicemail, then he would ignore it and call
again. Once he had given in to dialing her number and expecting to hear her voice, he would not back down until she had answered. She knew this because she would have been the same

way. She crossed into the woods, her feet sinking now, into the mud. It was cold between her toes. She tapped the screen.

"Hello?"

There was a rock in front of her, dimpled with small wet craters. She stepped over it, finding herself waist-deep in a cluster of ferns. The ground was firmer and covered with leaves, mulch, and shining crawling bugs that sprang to life when she cleared a place with her hand. She set the phone onto the spot that she had cleared and got down low, until her body was hidden by the ferns. There, she lay down on her side, aligning her ear with the phone, which was only a thin slab of electricity between her head and the earth. She curled her knees to her chest and listened to his voice come up out of the ground.

"Portia," said the ground. "I've been thinking."

"I know."

"I can't stop thinking." The ground had Theo's voice. She felt that his voice was as safe and solid as the forest floor.

There was a moth pressed tightly to the underside of one of the ferns, sleeping in its upside-down archway, closed tight, trying not to exist.

"It's not good to think so much." She reached out a finger toward the moth, its spotted wings. It would have to find a new secret place. Something in the woods was laughing. A distant and hysterical forest sound. A twig snapping. A crow called out. Life might have ended right there, perfectly, before anything else could go wrong.

The Part That Understands

CARRIE AND GUS LOOKED LIKE DESPERATE people trying to convince a more desperate person not to jump off a bridge. But Portia was not standing on a bridge. She was in her living room, on the couch with the lilac cushions, and all she wanted to do was go to bed and talk about it in the morning.

"Do you remember the night that you showed up on my doorstep?" Carrie was asking her. "During a blizzard? You had snow packed inside your shoes."

Portia was still embarrassed about that night at Carrie's, about how impulsive she had been over what she thought was a work of genius. Carrie had recorded it all on her phone and then played it back to her, proving to Portia that her brilliant composition—what had inspired her to wake in the middle of the night and trudge across town with a frozen guitar slung over her shoulder—was just noise. Garbage.

"I got overexcited," Portia said. Carrie looked at the floor. Behind her, Nathan sighed wearily and stood, rolling his head on his neck. He had finished picking up the pills from the floor, having used a flashlight to find the last few, the beam casting little black shadows where the pills would have otherwise blended in with the carpet.

"You scared us, Portia," Carrie said, still looking at the floor. "We were all scared of you that night." Portia could not believe what she was hearing. She had made a fool of herself, yes, but she had not done anything so unforgivable—certainly not frightening. She had also found solace in Carrie's—and even Gus's—tenderness toward her. The wet socks on the radiator. The slow, snowy drive home. Portia had had trouble, all her life, accepting platonic love, but somehow Carrie's remark that night had introduced her to the possibility of that love. Without being fully aware of it, Portia had been carrying that "crazy bitch" close to her heart for the last three years, like a patch sewed onto a fraying sweater. She wondered: Could Carrie have been lying?

Nathan sat beside her on the couch and took one of her hands in between his. Portia pulled away. She saw Carrie raise her eyes to Nathan, as if confirming something with him, silently. Just minutes ago, Portia had felt sorry for her friends. It was a dreadful feeling, watching this overreaction of theirs, like watching a stain swell across a tablecloth. But now Portia was not so sure. It seemed that an awful lot of preparation had gone into this intervention, beginning with Nathan removing Julian from the house. He had taken the dog too. The dog was not there.

Nathan stood.

"It's time to go, Portia," he said. "If you make this difficult, it is going to be upsetting for everyone." He was gathering her things—her bag, her cell phone. He took out her wallet and flipped through it before dropping it back into her bag. He tossed in the pill bottles.

"Are there any medications that you *are* still taking?" he asked her. "Anything that you are going to need overnight?"

"No."

It was Carrie leaning in now, her hands clasped cautiously in her lap: "Have you noticed that your voice is getting louder?" she asked. "You're yelling, Portia."

◆

There was an overturned shopping cart in the river below them, the wheels broken off, maybe salvaged by whoever had dumped it there. Sticks and leaves collected in and around the metal body. A plastic bag, a deflated balloon. What Portia wanted to be was truthful.

"I'm in love with you," she had said to Theo. Then: "I think I'm in love with you." Then: "It feels like I'm in love with you. It feels like being in love with you is changing me." In the past, her straightforwardness had sometimes been confusing to men. As if saying "I like you" or even "I want to fuck you" was too clinical. It may have been what they wanted to hear, but not in the way that they expected to hear it, coming from her. This had happened in college. The boys that knew her there must have had preconceived ideas of what a small, dark-haired woman named Portia would be like. She would be hard to decipher, maybe coy, haughty. They would have to break her down, in a way. And so, when she was blunt, it unnerved them, and they did not know how to respond. Men like Skip, on the other hand, wanted to hear what they wanted to hear and worried little about the shock to their intellect.

Theo took the news gently. Portia could see him weighing it. What she wanted was for him to jump to his feet, take her by the hands, look into her eyes. She wanted the result to be cataclysmic when he said, "I'm in love with you too." But Theo did not say anything, not right away. Portia watched the river. She saw how the banks were falling in. On the opposite side, there was another parking lot to a small shopping center, most of its businesses closed, now rented as offices, with one remaining nail salon at the end, brown paper taped over the door. The shopping center's parking lot was also coming apart and crumbling into the ravine. It might have been that none of the boys in college had truly desired Portia and that their rejection of her was inevitable, whether she was blunt with them or not. They had energy for the chase, the seduction, and perhaps the triumph, but not for her.

"How is your marriage?" Theo asked, finally. The way the sun was shining, it was hard to see his eyes behind the reflection of his glasses. He seemed to sense this and took them off, wiping the bridge of his nose. Portia wanted to say that she did not recognize herself anymore. When Nathan was around, she wanted to turn up the radio in the car, run the water, hum to herself so she would not feel alone, as if she were standing on an empty stage with Nathan as her only audience. She did not like who she was through her husband's eyes, although she could not say if she had always felt this way or if it had happened gradually over the years. She tried to think about how they used to be, when they were first together, how Nathan's heart had seemed so mysterious to her, like a pincushion that she wanted to extract all the needles from, until she realized that that was not what he wanted at all. His heart did not want to be plucked clean.

"There is nothing wrong with my marriage," she said.

A man showed up across the bank and eased himself down the slope to the edge of the water. He looked up at them and nodded, pulling a plastic soda bottle from a bag at his side and pouring its contents into the river. Portia realized that she was nervous, that she did not want anyone—not the quiet, haggard man below—to hear them.

They agreed to continue the conversation on foot. As they left the parking lot, Portia started talking. She talked and talked. She told Theo about how she and Carrie had met in high school, how they had gone to the music store in Albany and told the employee that they wanted to sound like Billy Corgan from Smashing Pumpkins and the employee had led them to a formidable wall of sleek electric guitars.

"One of these oughta do it," he had said to them.

She told him about the giant heart at the science museum, how as a child, she had feared not just its size but its insistence, the burden of mortality that it represented. The embarrassment of being ushered through its red and purple hallways. And she told him that, for the last three years, her day-to-day existence had been shaped around doctors' appointments, mood quizzes, psychiatric assessments, pills—and that she had stopped taking the pills. Just stopped one day without telling anyone. Theo was now the only other person who knew about it.

"You know how, when you listen to music, you can hear the notes and understand the words?" she asked him. "But then there is the other part of you that *understands* the music. The place that gets all stirred up and aching?" Theo nodded. All this time he had been listening, walking beside her, and letting her speak. "Well, when I was taking the pills, that part—the part that understands—just wasn't there anymore. I couldn't stand it," she said. They turned down a side road. It was difficult to tell who was leading or if they had both decided at once to avoid the busier parts of town, where someone might see them together.

"But, without the pills," she went on, "I sometimes believe things—I get too excited. Alby Porter. I started to believe that he was talking to me—about music, about everything. Like he was giving me permission to do something more." They were walking by a tall chain-link fence surrounding a vacant lot. The links were choked with weeds and little white flowers. They were both looking through the fence, into the wild green mess. Theo shrugged.

"That doesn't sound so bad," he said. "Maybe you were right." Portia stopped walking. No one had ever suggested this to her. Her first inclination was to refute him, defend the seriousness of her situation. She saw Dr. Shay every two weeks, so that she could report to him the intensity of her thoughts, whether they were tipping dangerously toward ecstasy or depression. Sometimes she talked to Dr. Shay about how productive she had been—whether her house was clean. Was it *too* clean? How many books had she read, and was it a reasonable amount of books, or had that number become too voracious? Voraciousness, wordplay, confidence—they were all warning signs. Portia did not want Theo to shrug at this. He had to understand that this had been with her for most of her life.

"What I'm saying is that these things have an expiration date," she said with some defiance. "And I am afraid that one day—any day now—I'll wake up and all this will be gone too." She waved her hand in the space between their bodies, almost dismissively, wanting to convey fleetingness. But something was not right. They had stopped walking and were now standing behind the abandoned dye mill, a huge structure in the middle of town that had once been one of the state's top producers of water pollutants. It was now abandoned, despite a slew of out-of-towners who had wanted, over the years, to turn it into a shopping mall, or a culinary school, or a community of artist's lofts. Nothing ever stuck. There was something about Vermont that doused the enthusiasm for these types of projects, as if everyone knew that winter would soon come and dreams would be delayed, all extra money spent on fuel oil.

"What was that?" Portia asked. She waved her hand again in front of Theo and pulled it away. She stepped back and looked at him. He did not move.

"It's okay," he said. "If this doesn't last, I mean." Portia took a small step toward him again and felt the edge of it, like a swarm of electricity between their bodies. She held out her hands, feeling the pull of something, a current all around her, shifting her center of gravity. She looked at Theo, hoping to see in his face a clue to what was happening, but all the confidence was gone from him.

"You have to understand," he said to her. "Nothing like this has ever happened to me."

✦

Portia was going to the hospital. Nathan held the back door open and she was walking through it, to the car. He had her bag slung over his shoulder, his face wiped clean of sympathy. Outside the birds were singing in the dark. There was a fine silvery-blue line beginning over the mountains to the east. When she was a child, Portia's parents did not have air conditioning in their car, so for long road trips, they would leave before sunrise to take advantage of the cool air. Since then, she had associated the very early morning with the excitement that came with stretching a day to its limits, the feeling of being awake—alive even—without breakfast, driving through the empty streets of her town. Leaving it behind in its state of vacancy, the streetlamps still on, as if by accident. Gus opened the door to Nathan's car. Portia was to sit in the back seat, like a child, next to Carrie. Nathan would drive. Gus would follow them in his own car.

The Whore of Babylon

When they arrived at the emergency room, it was unclear at first who would be the one to take charge. Finally, it was Gus who explained to the woman behind the glass that his friend needed emergency psychiatric intervention. Gus had been a social worker, briefly, back in Colorado, and he knew how to deliver these kinds of words with concern but without hysterics. They shared the waiting room with one man, who was wearing dress pants, belted, and a white undershirt, and who did not seem to be in any distress but sat silently and perfectly still, with his right hand cupped to his right ear. After watching him for some time, Portia concluded that he must be holding his ear to his head, to stop part of it from falling off. Perhaps he did not want to make a fuss over it because it was his mistress who had bitten him too hard in a moment of passion. He was taking his time, she decided, composing an alibi to tell his wife as he waited. And then she was wondering how Nathan was going to convince the doctors that she was unwell enough to be committed.

They were soon called in to the emergency room, which was not a room but a sterile hall partitioned by blue curtains. The doctor was a youthful-looking man who looked like he practiced seeming at ease in front of the mirror every morning. He looked like he had all the right intentions.

"My wife has a history," Nathan was saying to the doctor. Portia sat on the edge of the examining table. She was glad that Carrie and Gus had decided to stay in the lobby. Nathan had told them, in a trembling voice, that they could go home, that they had been so helpful and he was indebted to them.

"No," Carrie had said. "We will see this through with you. We will be out here if you need anything." Portia now wondered why Carrie had not said, "We will see this through for *her*." It was so odd to see her friend this way, looking at Nathan as if the three of them, excluding Portia, had all been through something traumatic together. Carrie, who had lived in her car, who claimed to have eaten roasted squirrel at one time because she was too proud to ask her parents for help— that Carrie—was now looking at Portia like she was crazy.

"I know my wife better than anyone," Nathan said to the ER doctor. "She is not herself. I don't know where my Portia has gone." Portia wanted to find amusement in her husband's words. How could Nathan be saying these things that were so obviously untrue? But he went on, describing Portia to the doctor, about what kind of woman she was—and he looked worn-out, opening his hands, holding them as if they were so heavy.

"Years ago, Portia dropped out of college," he said. "So that she could begin a risky affair with a felon who lived in a trailer park."

He must be talking about Skip, Portia thought. But why would he be talking about Skip? She felt as though she were being folded up, stuffed into a little compartment of apathy in her brain. In that compartment was also the part of her that laughed at a gruesome scene in a movie because it was just too unbelievable. She tucked herself next to that free-floating bit of self-preservation, where courage was also cowardice, like how she had once watched Rupert break free from her grasp and run after a kitten, straight through traffic, while she held Julian's hand on the sidewalk. She had not reacted as a loving dog owner should have, but as an exhausted mother, who had only the energy to be thankful that it was not her child in the middle of the road.

Nathan had removed the dog from the house, she reminded herself. He took the dog so that the dog would not bite him.

He was still talking: "When she was hospitalized and separated from her felon lover, she engaged in sexual activity with a schizophrenic man against hospital policy."

Nathan had never tolerated Portia's relationship with Skip. The relationship was not something that Portia had been proud of, but it was also something that she had come to accept. Her acceptance had alarmed Nathan. How could she live with herself? he wondered. How could she not regret how low she had allowed herself to stoop? And Portia had tried to feel regret, but it did not seem worth the effort, to dive in and remember those moments. To muster the energy and the self-loathing needed to reject them. She wanted to move on from it. Also, she did not see Nathan's disgust as jealousy or prejudice but rather as evidence of his innocence; he was not the type who would engage in deviance of that kind. Portia watched her husband's hands as he spoke to the ER doctor, how he cupped them in the air, as if demonstrating all the difficulty he had been made to carry over the years. The little hospital room had become a stage for him, the doctor completely engaged in his story—the story of a man who had lived with a woman for so long and dealt with her problems. Now, he was tired and scared. He had kept it together for Portia, for Julian. She watched his fingers curl. She saw his eyes become bleary, as they did when he was distressed. But no tears ever fell. His sobs were always dry, a hand covering his face, as if to hide his desert weeping. There was a moment where no one spoke. Nathan composed himself.

"And now we find that she has stopped taking her antipsychotics without medical supervision." Nathan took off his glasses and peered through them before putting them back on.

"Ah," said the ER doctor. He looked at Portia. "Is this true?" Portia was not sure if he was just asking about the pills or if he was including all that Nathan had just told him. It occurred to her that she had never talked to Nathan about her encounter with Jerry. Or if she had, she had forgotten the conversation. Jerry had been held, suspended by the men in scrubs, and he had been sweating with fear and adrenaline. His eyes when he looked at her were a ferocious, piercing blue.

"I did not have sex with Jerry," Portia said. Nathan cast his eyes upward and shook his head, helplessly.

✦

Portia thought of all the places that she had searched for herself. The racks of dresses, skirts, and blouses at the Salvation Army. The praise on her teachers' lips and in their written assessments. Sickening words, words like *promising* that required so much hope and commitment. The early, early mornings before breakfast. The windows of other people's houses with their fresh curtains. The fresh space between her bedsheets after a long trip.

✦

Jerry had said, "I know you." He was out of his mind, but in that moment, he had seen something in her that he recognized, and she was drawn to it. He had spat on his captors, but he had spoken to her.

✦

There had been a day in winter, the year Julian was three. The sun was due to set at five o'clock in the afternoon and all day it had been stuck firmly in the sky, like a bleach stain on a gray sweater. It had rained and snowed and then rained again, the wind picking up so that the icicles hung at an angle. Portia had been alone with her son. Julian was sick with a stomachache, and Nathan was discouraged with her for not wanting to drive to the doctor on the icy roads. He had been in court, at a hearing when she called him. She had already left a message with the pediatrician, but she was drained from Julian's screaming. He would scream and then fall silent, turning the pages of a picture book, and then remember that he was sick and scream again. It was impossible to tell what, if anything, was wrong. She wanted to hear her husband's voice. She wanted him to reassure her that she was doing the right thing by waiting for the pediatrician to call back. She did not want to pack Julian into the car, fighting with him about boots and mittens, then backing slowly down the long, ice-covered driveway, unless the pediatrician told her that Julian was, indeed, seriously ill. She was so tired.

Nathan was stressed that day and did not like being called in the middle of a hearing, having to excuse himself from the courtroom to pace the hall with his phone to his ear. There was always that stomach-turning onset of irritation when his phone rang at work, that fear that something had gone horribly wrong. So, when he finally understood what his wife was calling about, her voice quavering with meekness, he made a mistake and he snapped at her. He told her that he would have to hire a nanny to raise Julian, someone with enough competence to know what to do when the boy was sick.

Portia, stunned by her husband's words, made a mistake when she said to him: "Fine. I never wanted to be a mother anyway."

◆

The doctor had left. Nathan remained where he was, standing beside the blue curtain. He pinched the bridge of his nose and took a deep breath.

"I had to do it like this," he said gently. "Sometimes, when someone is having a crisis, it is impossible to reason with that person. I hope that someday soon, you will understand why I had to do it like this."

◆

Portia's biggest crime, perhaps, was that she had not given enough credit to Jerry's illness. She had taken him at his word, or, more specifically, at his actions. He had entered her room and let his pants drop to the floor, and she had interpreted this gesture as if he were a sane man, coming into her room and dropping his pants. From a sane man, this would be an invitation. But it was possible that Jerry was trying to convey something else entirely—something not of a sexual nature at all. Once she had seen what Jerry was doing, Portia had not cried for a nurse or told him to leave. She met him in the middle of the room and wrapped her arms around him.

He was about as tall as she, so she could smell his hair, which smelled sandy and unwashed. It smelled wonderful. She held him tightly, feeling his body against hers. It did not matter what this act looked like from the outside; it was something that could not be defined, not even by the two of them.

When the ER doctor came in through the curtain again, he told Nathan that he had been on the phone with Portia's psychiatrist, Dr. Shay, to discuss their possibilities. Portia remembered how, so many years ago, Dr. Shay had tipped forward, his nose lifted to inhale the stench of her unwashed hair, the sleep crusted like salt around her eyes.

"Boy, you *are* ripe," he had said, smiling, as if he had been expecting her to appreciate his sense of humor in the face of her crisis. He had instructed Portia's parents to leave the room and then explained to her the importance of having a plan, although never once did anyone mention the word *suicide*. The inference had been like a land mine; once the idea was planted, it was beyond anyone's power to ignore it. Action had to be taken, and that action was a broad and clumsy excavation. Portia felt the eyes of her husband and the ER doctor studying her. If either one had asked her a question, she had not heard.

"I don't have a plan," she said to them. But they did not follow her meaning, and Nathan said, "That is why we are offering you one." He stepped forward.

"All we need from you is a *yes*."

The Bridge

◦—◦ POOR ALICE HAD A SHOW THAT WEEKEND, A routine gig that they took every year, playing at a street fair in town. It was casual, with audience members coming and going, drinking lemonades, adorned with henna from the booth next door. Carrie liked for the band to play some improvisational music at these gigs, because no one was really staying for the songs but rather the promise of ongoing sound. They set up under an awning in front of the real estate office. Portia was tired, and when Theo pulled up to unload his car, she saw the same hollowness in his eyes. He walked around the car, glancing at her, and shook his head, as if shaking off the possibility of discussing what had happened. It had been only yesterday that they had stood in the shadow of the abandoned factory and Portia, having confessed her love for him, had warned him that she might fall out of love just as quickly. There had been that strange sensation, like magnetism, in the space between them. Portia had not been able to tell whether she had imagined it.

Theo set up his drums while Carrie arranged her pedals on a piece of wooden board that she had designed to hold them in place. The pedals were attractive and compact, all with a colorful plastic exterior, like old telephones. Amplifiers were switched on. Carrie whistled an A through her teeth and began turning the pegs on her guitar. Soon, they were immersed in a slow, dark tune, Carrie's echo effect turned so far up that her notes seemed to leave spots in the air. Portia closed her eyes and tried to forget about the people watching her. She followed Carrie's lead, the purple blots of her melodies like paint falling onto the surface of water. Portia was so tired that she sat on the ground, resting her guitar in her lap, and, from there, she could feel the bass drum, which sounded as tired as Theo looked. She brought her fingers high up on the fretboard and picked out a little four-note request. She did not know if a crowd was gathering on the street or if no one had stopped. It was difficult being a band in a small town. There was no nightlife, so going out to see live music was, for most people, an extravagance. Portia did not blame them. Being warm and comfortable at home nearly always triumphed over standing in a meagerly populated bar, avoiding the eyes of drunk men. Walking home through the snow with your ears ringing.

Meet me somewhere, she thought, playing another made-up riff that sounded as much like *meet me somewhere* as she could muster. Meet me at the bridge, she added. She repeated these five notes, as if speaking through the guitar. For some reason, she envisioned the wooden footbridge behind the school, not at all close to where they were. But it was that footbridge in her mind, unfailingly.

I will, she imagined Theo's kick drum saying. *I will. I will.*

They took a break after an hour of playing. Carrie went for a beer from the vendor down the street.

"You want anything?" she asked Portia.

"Yeah." Portia handed Carrie a crumpled bill from her pocket. Theo was still sitting behind his drums, talking to Gus, as Portia slipped into the crowd. It was easy to disappear, to take the passage between the tattoo parlor and the drug-rehab center, to cross back over the parking lot behind the lawyer's office. She moved like a person in a dream, being chased by the police for a crime that she could not remember committing. Portia often had these dreams, where she was running from the cops, down the piss trail of alleyways, hopping fences and ducking clotheslines. Soon she would get this tingling on the back of her neck. The tingling meant that she had lost her pursuers, that any ground she now covered would be a bonus, an added security. In her dreams Portia always kept running, through giant warehouses with clouded windows, hearing the bat cry of her shoes turning corners, opening small doors into narrower and more secluded passages until the tingling overtook her, a self-mummifying sense of triumph and solitude.

There was only a thin stream of water running beneath the footbridge. Portia had a memory of releasing a turtle in this area when she was a child, but the water must have been higher at the time. There had been more trees too. She had always assumed that this small piece of land behind the elementary school was a kind of public park—it had of course appeared so much larger when she was a girl. Now, she wondered if she was even supposed to be there at all, if it wasn't a part of someone's backyard. The boards beneath her feet were soft and mossy. There was a dispensary smell of beer. A stash of aluminum pull tabs at the base of a tree. She should have found herself standing there, questioning everything, feeling sorry and embarrassed for believing—for even entertaining the idea—that she could communicate with Theo without words. That they would meet here, by way of powers unknown. But there was no time for that because Theo was already walking toward her.

"You followed me here," Portia said, before he came too close. She wanted to guard herself. She wanted to appear unmoved and stoic. Skip had teased her once, called her an "Ice Queen" and smacked her on the ass, watching her face for a reaction. He pinched her on the arm, then pinched her again, twisting the flesh. Still, she did not change her expression. Her cheeks flushed. Her eyes glossed.

"My Ice Queen," he had said, and she was proud of the title. When he slapped her a second time, not on her ass but on her face, her heart had leapt up in shock, but her eyes did not break. At the time, she had thought that by remaining unaffected, she was winning.

Theo dropped to his knees in front of her, his head bowed. He told her that he had not slept. He had not eaten. These were not exaggerations. They were not the kind of sweet nothings that you say to a woman to express your devotion. His belt had already come in three notches. As if his belt already knew what was going on and was just waiting for Theo to catch up.

"I don't care if this is crazy," he said. He was still speaking to the wooden planks. "I am not sure that I can survive not being near you." Portia did not speak at first. The Ice Queen would have tried to play it cool, to be suspicious of all professions of love. But there was an even older Portia—who had existed before the Ice Queen—who would have crouched on this same footbridge, kissed the shell of her turtle, and told it to be free. She sank onto the bridge beside Theo, exhausted.

"I hear your name beating in my ears at night."

"I feel like I have known you since before I was born."

"The air wakes up when you are near me."

"The world brightens."

"I'm forgetting everything I know."

They fell into these hushed words, like falling into a cool bath. It soothed them to speak such things, as if they had been holding them back their whole lives.

When they came to their senses, they saw that nothing around them had changed, but the color had returned to their faces, and they felt hungry, starving. As they walked back to the stage, they swore that they would not call each other, not ever again. They would never touch—even casually. They would spend as much time together as they could, but only in public, so that they would not be tempted to break the second rule. They kept a distance between them of about two feet, and, the entire way back, that empty space crackled and hummed, as if the air had become electric. They did their best to ignore it.

That night, Portia lay next to Julian in his bed until he was asleep. She put her hand on his chest to make sure that his breathing was relaxed and slow, then got up carefully, filling the empty place beside him with a pillow. She spent a long time looking at her reflection in the bathroom mirror, looking deep into her eyes, as if searching herself for doubt, an air leak in her resolve. How could she be doing this? How could she *not* be doing this? She found Nathan downstairs, sitting on the couch. Portia took the chair across from him and watched her husband, unsuspecting and undisturbed, look up from his book.

"I have something that I need to tell you," she said.

Anniversary Dinner

NATHAN WAS BEGINNING TO SMELL DIFFER-
ent. It was a charcoal smell, a pine tar smell, and it was not
because he was dirty or because he had walked into a forest
or rubbed against something strange but because everything
had changed—and was still changing—and Portia was only
just discovering it. She felt the loss of him, sleeping beside
her, breathing with a soft, almost undetectable whistle. At
the same time, she wanted to protect him from what she was
feeling, her love for him falling away, like the banks of a river
dropping into the water. She could not stop the banks from
falling in, could not hold up one side without letting the opposite shore crumble. So she buried her nose into his hair
and inhaled again, as if trying to hoard something invisible, a
trace of an old feeling. His shoulders tightened and he lay his
hand over the clock beside the bed.

"What time is it?" he asked, getting out of bed, groaning, and he found his pants draped over the armchair by the
window. As he was buttoning himself, he gave Portia a bleary
smile.

"I love you," she said to him, but then turned away, feign-
ing sleep, so he would not say it back to her.

✦

She and Nathan were going on a date to celebrate all the years that they had been married. It was some outrageous number. Seventy years, eighty years. And yet they were not any older than the day they had met. They were young and plain, dark-haired. The restaurant that they had chosen must have been so exclusive that it did not warrant a sign. Patrons were expected to know where to enter without asking. In the foyer, there was an old woman sitting in a chair, looking at you with a slightly startled expression, and you were supposed to give her your coat and hat, even though it felt rude to do so. Even though a part of you suspected that all of it was a hoax. But then, through the back door, in the garden, there was a lovely patio with three tables. White cloths. Long-stemmed glasses already filled with light bubbling drink. They sat at their table and the waiter appeared. While Nathan ordered, Portia admired her surroundings: the miniature picket fence separating them from a grove of flowering trees. The minty grass under their feet. But she was surprised by the tone of Nathan's voice. He was speaking angrily to the waiter, jabbing at the menu with his finger. The waiter smiled politely, bowed, and walked away. Behind them, Portia saw that there were three large crows, perched in one of the flowering trees. When the waiter returned, he was holding a bow with an arrow pulled taut. He fired three times at the birds and hit them each, cleanly, without missing. They fell to the ground, like heavy fruit, and Nathan did not even flinch.

Golden Boy

THERE WAS A STORY THAT PORTIA HAD BEEN told, or one that she had been piecing together for a long time. It was about a boy. A Golden Boy, whose mother adored him. This Golden Boy was bright from the very beginning. He had gone to kindergarten at the age of four and a half, which was much earlier than his peers, whose pediatricians had reassured their mothers that, being boys and developmentally slower than girls, six years old was a perfectly good age to start school. But not the Golden Boy. His pediatrician was astounded by the boy's fluency in abstract ideas, in shapes and numbers. The boy had sat in the doctor's office, his belly straining the tape on his diaper, and recited the alphabet, beautifully. And his smile was so serene and trusting, his hair so curly. His mother was prouder than she had ever been in her life.

When he was four and five months, just a month away from entering school (the teacher had been duly warned about the brilliance of her future student), his mother had a friend over for coffee. The friend had driven all the way up from Florida (not just for the coffee, of course, but for some cheery family reason—a baby shower, maybe, or a reunion) and was wearing a kind of summer pants suit that accentuated her slimness and height. She walked in, like a flowing, upright scarf, laughing already at some thread of conversation that had started before she had even appeared, and placed her sunglasses on the small table in the entryway, as if that table had been meant for her glasses all along. Golden Boy was smitten. He waited outside the kitchen while his mother fussed over the lady from Florida—whose name, Chloe, was as tantalizing as her appearance—noticing how frequently she laughed, just how smart and happy she was. She did not seem to care at all about the peach tart that his mother had spent the morning agonizing over, having ditched her original plans for blueberry cobbler in favor of a more southern fruit. This pleased him. There should be at least one person in the world, he thought, who did not give a hoot about his mother's baking. And then he was hearing his name called— "Nathan?" His mother zipping him around the corner so he could stand in front of Chloe's chair and say his alphabet. He knew the alphabet, of course, and was even able to picture the letters in his mind as they flew out of his mouth, each one with their own secret color and personality. *A* was yellow and brave. *B* was the color of a plum and motherly. But when he got to the letter *C*, he thought he saw a twinkle in Chloe's eyes, as if she also did not give a hoot whether he knew his alphabet or not. As if, unlike his doctor and his family members, she did not understand that small children were not expected to know something so terribly basic. So he decided to do something that he had not tried before: he made his voice sound like a baby's and sang the letters all wrong, waving his hands, sticking out his tongue. For a moment he got what he had wanted, Chloe's sweet laughter, like tropical fruit, like a beautiful green melon sliced open, until his mother spoke.

"That's enough of that," she said, and she began to clear the table in a frigid, furious hurry. Later, when the lovely friend had gone, the Golden Boy's mother sat him on the stairs and scolded him.

"Once a person thinks you're stupid," she said, "they treat you like you're stupid." Before she left him there, she added: "I hope you're happy."

Portia suspected that the Golden Boy was not happy, that sometimes he felt a sense of angry pride that he began to confuse with happiness, when he received a prize or when his teachers acted disgusted at the other children in his class for not being as astute. They sometimes shot him imploring looks across the classroom, like he was the only child who was on their side. This was something that he got used to. Intelligence to him became something more than a way to show off, but rather a sharp knife, a direct line of communication, an absolute that could never fail him.

When the Golden Boy was twelve, a traveling quartet played in an assembly at his school. Afterward, the musicians answered questions. They all had sleek, muscular arms and straight backs. There was something beautiful, the Golden Boy thought, in the discipline of their posture and appearance. How shiny but also antiquated the instruments were, like age-old secrets smelling of resin. He went straight home that day and asked his mother for a violin so that he could practice every day, as the musicians had talked about. He found her on the back patio, smoking (in those days, it was not yet considered harmful or even poor taste). She heard what he had to say and shook her head at him.

"Oh, but it's too late," she said. The smoke poured out of her face and trailed up her arm as she pushed her cigarette into the tray. "You are much too old to master the violin. If you had wanted to play, you should have started a long time ago." There were birds in the yard, flitting around a feeder. Mourning doves and cardinals and chickadees. The Golden Boy watched them while something danced on the edge of his mind, a rule that wanted to break, something that for a very brief instant felt sacred to him and courageous. But he must have put it aside. Blinked it away. There would be a few more moments in his adolescence when he would make this same silent decision, and each time, a little hand came in, like a hand stopping an elevator door from closing. It was full of insistence and rage.

Locked Away

⌒⌒ "All we need from you is a yes."

Nathan's words followed her as she moved through the yellow hallways, across the speckled linoleum floor. Someone who she had not gotten a good look at pushed the elevator button and waited for her to step inside before getting in after her. When the doors opened again, she noticed that the halls were still yellow, greasy with fluorescent waves reflected from the rows of lights above. Everything was the same as the floor below, except the elevator now only had a single button with an arrow for going down. This meant that they had taken her to the top.

"Sometimes, when someone is having a crisis, it is impossible to reason with that person," Nathan had explained to her in the emergency room. "I hope that someday soon, you will understand why I had to do it like this."

A card with a magnetic strip was produced, swishing through a little nick in the wall. There was a green flicker followed by a gratifying clunk as a lock was disengaged, the door opening. Everything was the same as it had been thirteen years ago.

They told her to undress in an empty room directly to the left while they held up a sheet in lieu of a privacy curtain. There were two extra people called into the room for the business of holding the sheet, and Portia wondered whether having two more sets of eyes around her while she stripped down was working against the sheet's initial purpose. She took off her shirt and handed it to the closest person, a young woman with a ponytail who, in reaching for the shirt, nearly dropped her portion of the sheet. But as Portia began to unclasp her bra, they stopped her. They were not concerned with the straps or the underwire in her bra, nor did they need her to give them her sandals. Nothing was confiscated, which bothered her, just a little. The whole morning had seemed to her a perverse injustice—a violation—and she had expected this feeling of violation to fully run its course, beginning when Nathan had brought up her sexual history in the emergency room. As she saw it, Nathan had no right to harbor such judgments over her life, especially her life before him. The way that the ER doctor had nodded when Nathan spoke about her relationship with Skip, as if it were vital information, as if Nathan were so clever to have remembered this telling piece of evidence, lawyer that he was, made her want to scream. Next, two nurses in training had been sent in, wheeling a cart clattering with glass vials. No one had warned Portia that before she could be admitted, she would have to have her blood drawn by girls who did not know how to find a vein, who were appalled when she hissed at them to "stop fucking giggling," as if it had not occurred to them that patients could also be people who were having a bad day. It seemed fitting that she should have her clothing confiscated, as a final injury to her humiliation, to be deemed so extraordinarily insane that she had to be tied naked to a gurney. When this did not happen, the macabre perfectionist inside her thought, How pointless.

Both Nathan and the ER doctor had agreed that it would be best for her to be admitted that night, while everything was in place; Julian was being cared for by her parents; the hospital in Moulton had a bed ready for her. Just an ambulance ride over the mountain, they said. She could rest, they assured her, and Nathan's eyes had softened, pleading, filling the small, curtained-off room with this one request. It was shameful what was happening to her, shameful to have her past dredged up like that, out of context and unsightly, like a squid reeled in on a fishing line. Some things—past things—she thought, made sense only in the dark and the deep. But what was worse—and a notion that had taken shape as they got Dr. Shay on the phone—was the possibility that she had been capable of this all her life. That it was so easy for everyone to accept that she would, one day, succumb to her weaknesses. She remembered how Nathan had threatened to hire a nanny on that dreary day in winter; he wanted someone who knew what to do, who would not bother him at work with silly questions. These words had been spoken to her in anger, which took away some of their potency, but they were still words that must have been in Nathan's head. They had come from a bud of truth, possibly nestled deep inside, she imagined, ready to bloom: a red, rageful flower of blame. Oh, how good it must have felt to say those words to her.

After the search—no one called it a strip search, but that was exactly what it was—Portia was shown to her room. By then, it was late morning, but she got into the bed right away. The sheets smelled like a hotel, which was a non-smell, a hard-water kind of cleanness that she found soothing. She wrapped herself in, as if to stave off the wide-open part of her heart that had complied to this, the part of her heart that must not have been sewed up tight enough when she was born. She could not control it and she could not defend it, and so she had said to Nathan and the ER doctor, "Yes, okay, *yes*. I will go."

As Portia slept, she became aware of a presence in the room with her. She sensed that someone was crossing the room, creating a shadow between her and the window, as if pacing with worry. She was grateful for this presence and its apparent concern for her, but she did not open her eyes. The blinds were closed to keep out the sunlight beating against the western side of the hospital. They shone dangerously, like strips of film in a projector, ready to catch fire, and it made her toss and turn. When she was a child, her afternoon naps had always felt feverish, the toppling into unconsciousness and landing in the soft, red center. She thought about the giant heart at the children's museum, getting lost inside the purple arteries, learning nothing about human anatomy but everything about the runny noses and sticky hands of the other children. Julian's little face showed up behind her eyelids. He would have hated the heart as much as she had, asked her why all the parents were shoveling their children into the entrance, then crossing round to the exit, a slide meant to look like a vein that spat them out the other end, and yelling up through the tunnel, "Hurry up. Get out here. *Now.*"

The figure seemed to be crossing the room more hurriedly, causing the light to blink in and out.

Is that you? she asked him.

Yes, he said. *But don't open your eyes, or they will take me away.*

Have they tied my hands down?

No, he said. *They don't do that anymore.*

There were footsteps in the hall and a brisk knock on the doorframe. Portia opened her eyes and discovered a nurse standing over her, holding a sheet of paper. Sometimes doctors liked her to complete a kind of multiple-choice quiz, to confirm that she was, indeed, afflicted. There were different kinds of bipolar, depending on whether you were more prone to ecstasy or despair or, in some cases, if you existed in a gray area of agitation. But the questions were always the same, more or less:

Are you losing sleep?

Are you experiencing feelings of being very powerful or superhuman?

Are sexual thoughts becoming overwhelming?

Do people tell you that you are speaking too rapidly?

Do you find yourself making extravagant purchases, beyond your means?

Portia never checked the last box. She had learned early on that thrift stores did not count.

But the nurse was not handing her a questionnaire. It was almost dinnertime, the nurse explained, and the kitchen needed to know what to make for her. Portia sat up and took the menu. She glanced to her right, where the pacing shadow had been, but saw through the glowing blinds only a dark shape hurling itself around. She began filling in the boxes on the menu. Thirteen years ago, every Thursday night, the cafeteria had served pistachio pudding for dessert. Some of the other patients had lived for pistachio pudding day, made horrific jokes about postponing hanging themselves in the shower so they could have one more taste of the cold green stuff. They had licked it off the plastic spoons, held a drop of it on the tips of their wagging tongues. Portia was not hungry for dinner, but she was sure that the nurse, who was standing very close and snapping her red fingernails together, did not care what happened to the food as long as she got the order to the kitchen in time. When she left the room, Portia went to the window and pulled the blind. The sun was there, blazing like a pot of hot oil, and in front of it, an American flag whipped around on its mast.

It had been about sixteen hours since she and Theo had parted ways outside the bar. He had wanted to walk her home, but she told him no. It was likely that Nathan knew where she was, even though she had lied to him about where she was going. All he had to do was send a text message and a police officer would circle the area. The police officer would enjoy doing this favor for Nathan because Nathan had helped him in many situations over the years. There might even be a fraternal sense of duty, keeping an eye on the attorney's young wife, making sure that no harm came to her, even though she was with another man. Portia had explained this to Theo like it was commonplace because it had happened before. Before she and Nathan moved in together, Nathan had asked a policeman to patrol the block where Portia lived.

"I asked him if he would do an extra loop on his rounds, for my girlfriend," Nathan told her.

"I'm your girlfriend?" Portia was gleeful. The gesture had not struck her as anything other than romantic.

And later, she had given Nathan permission to track her phone, after a car crash in town had killed the driver, a woman about her age. In Nathan's line of work, he heard about crimes on the police scanner, or by word of mouth, before the public did. He said it would help calm his nerves to know where Portia was, so he could stop fearing that every car wreck, mugging, or body found floating in a lake was his wife. These events rarely happened in their small town, but Portia did not mind.

"You can track mine too," Nathan had said, sweetly. And they had made this small pact between them, as a husband and wife who just wanted to look out for each other.

Portia wondered now, looking out at the hospital grounds, what would happen if she bribed one of the kitchen boys, when they came up with the dinner cart, to take her cell phone and put it on a train. What would Nathan think if he tapped his screen and saw the little red marker running away across the map? Would he feel the loss of her, like watching something dear washed down a river? Was she dear to him?

Portia removed the stockings and the skirt that she had been wearing since the bar, which had become twisted as she slept, leaving waspy lines on her skin. Someone had folded a set of scrubs at the foot of the bed. She put these on, not caring how gawky she appeared with her strappy heels, and she clopped down the hallway, toward the common area where the patients had their meals. But as she walked, she began to feel heavy. The earth—however far down, below the layers of the hospital—was pulling her to it. She got on her hands and knees and felt it still, stronger and more insistent, so she pressed her whole body against the floor. It was cold, vibrating slightly with the hum of the building. She lay her ear down, and the hum became a muffled roar. She wished that Theo would come. He would understand what she was feeling. He would know that she was not bad or crazy. There were voices above her, not nurses or staff but a pair of old ladies.

"Oh, sweetie," they cooed. "Life is worth living. Life is worth living!" They had cool, dry hands, and they touched her arms and forehead, brushing her hair back. Portia struggled to get to her feet. Theo was so far away. He had no way of knowing what was happening. She could call him, she thought. His number would still be in her phone's history log, from when he had called her that day and she had answered from the woods behind her house. She could find his number.

"That a girl!" the old ladies said when she was upright again. They had a soft, halting way of speaking. If Portia had not met them in this way, in the hallway of a psychiatric hospital, where everything was either boring or completely unexpected, then she might have noticed their French accents right away. She might have noticed that they were identical, with their brightly painted lips and their charcoal eyebrows, linking arms on their way down the hall to have their cafeteria dinners. But Portia's mind could not hold any more oddities, and she had no choice but to accept them. She did not turn around to thank the ladies. She would go to the nurses' station and ask for her phone, find Theo's last call. She would tell him that she was locked away.

Signal

◠◠AFTER SAYING GOODNIGHT TO PORTIA AT the bar, Theo returned home to discover that his front door was ajar, his keys dangling in the lock. He would have liked to blame this forgetfulness on the strangeness of the evening, but the truth was that he had done things like this all his life. His ex-wife had sometimes used it as proof against him in situations that were completely unrelated. How, for example, could she trust him to remember to buy the right kind of children's Tylenol, or remember their youngest son's shoe size, if, on some occasions, he could not properly lock the door or figure out where he parked the car when they got out of the movie theater? Theo had wanted to tell her that these instances were of different sorts, kept in different parts of his brain, but he also did not have a map of his brain ready as reference. She liked for information to be easily displayed and backed by facts. He closed the door behind him and hung the keys on a magnetic hook that he had attached to the side of the refrigerator because, whether his ex-wife had been right or wrong, he was still trying to be better.

Theo had not fixed the screen in his bedroom window, so when he entered the room, where the light had been left on, he saw that moths had flown in and landed on the wall above his bed. There was one in the center that had a kind of face between its wings, a pattern of brown and gray feathers that frowned at him as he pulled the covers back. It was hot in his bedroom. He dropped onto the bed with his arms outstretched, dazed at all that was transpiring. It had been only three weeks since he had awoken from that first dream about Portia, where they had been lying together, with the light falling over them. In that dream, his life had come together in a way that made perfect sense, and now it was difficult—nearly impossible—to remember what it had been like to not love her. Up until two weeks ago, he had believed that such a love could not exist, just as he had believed that there was something wrong with him for wishing that it did.

Theo knew that Portia had a young boy. He had seen him a few times, a boy with wide eyes, long lashes—"old-soul eyes," his mother would have said. Theo remembered what his own sons had been like at that age, how his oldest had gone through a phase, suddenly showing up between Theo and his wife in their bed at night, saying garbled sleep-things, eyes glossy and full of worry. But what had broken Theo's heart was how his son, every morning, denied that he had ever been afraid, that during the day, if he fell or stubbed his toe, he sucked in his breath and put his face angrily to the floor beside his mother, knowing that she would bend down to kiss him but never daring to ask her. Theo wondered what it would have been like for his son if the divorce had happened during that vulnerable time, when he needed the world at his fingertips, when he needed both parents to be in the same bed. The false face of the moth continued to stare, so Theo turned on his side, the springs of his cheap mattress nudging him in the shoulder. The water glass on his bookshelf was still overturned from when the cat had walked over it, the picture frame still facedown. He and Portia did not seem to be making the decision to see each other but rather to avoid the discomfort of being apart. There was a difference; he was sure of it. He felt as though their affair—if it could be called such a thing—was a matter of survival. But wasn't that how all love affairs were? Theo assumed that men and women had been creating far-fetched reasons to be together since humans had learned how to lie. This force that was driving him mad, these strange events—were they not more than a cover-up for the truth? An inventive excuse to be in love with a young married woman?

The next morning, Theo woke from a dream where he had come across a beehive, one of those perfect, round beehives depicted in book illustrations. The beehive was hanging from a tree limb, and Theo had walked up to it and placed his hands on either side of it. There was a man there, somewhere next to him, or behind him, who was trying to tell him something, maybe a warning not to do what he was doing, but Theo could not hear him. The beehive was buzzing and causing his hands to buzz, as well as his arms and his chest. He felt the buzzing go straight down through the soles of his feet, and someone cried out, "On the floor!" He opened his eyes. The room was bright. The moths that had populated his wall were gone. Something on the floor seemed to groan twice. He turned over and saw that his phone was vibrating. A white bar appeared across the screen with a message. *NO PRACTICE TODAY.* It was from Carrie. He had been looking forward to seeing Portia again that morning at Carrie's house, where they would love each other silently from across the room, all the while pretending that they were not in love, which was the most wonderful game that he had ever played. He supposed that Carrie's text did not warrant a phone call—in fact, the last phone conversation they had had was three years ago, when she called him to ask him to be in the band—but Theo had already dialed and was listening to a muffled ringtone, waiting for her to answer.

"What's going on?" he asked her.

"I don't know," Carrie said. She sounded distracted, far away. She sounded like she was outside. Theo, probably because he was not fully awake, pictured her taking the call from a ferry, the wind blowing her hair across her face. Gulls in the background.

"Portia said something about not feeling well," she said.

"You talked to her?" His voice was too breathy, too anxious. Carrie must have picked up on it.

"I mean," she paused. "She's fine and all. Hungover, probably."

Theo thanked Carrie and hung up, dropping the phone back onto the floor. His chest was aching. It was an old feeling, something that he had almost forgotten, similar to when he was a boy, riding in the back seat of his mother's car. His mother had had a habit of turning the knob on the radio while she drove, skimming through the stations, through what Theo had always pictured to be a horizon of static. The problem was this: when she came to that little bump of clarity, when a voice or the quick jeer of an electric guitar would come through, Theo's mother would continue turning, back into the static, on and on. Theo never found out if this was a nervous habit of his mother's or if she was just that indecisive, but it had filled him with agony. He would have settled for anything, even a ten-minute commercial for washing machines, just for some peace and continuity. It felt like being jarred from a dream, every time his mother tuned past another clear signal. And now, sprawled crookedly on his bed, the dial was turning in his chest, looking for something but slipping, slipping. When he could not stand it any longer, he got up and put on a shirt. Within five minutes, he was out the door.

The sky was gigantic with stiff cathedral clouds. Theo walked quickly, the radio dial in his chest running along its static highway. He did not know where he was headed, whether what he was doing was an attempt to relieve the discomfort or to find the source of it. He walked past fences with blistered paint, patched screen doors, neglected hedges sprouting green fingers. He walked on roads with sidewalks and some with only a gravely shoulder, until one of the roads came to an end. A surprisingly clean-cut end, he noticed, like the square end of a tape measure. Beyond the pavement there was a deep patch of woods, grown thick with weeds, where someone had dumped lawn clippings and dead brush. Everything was humid and glistening. Theo stopped. He considered charging through it, taking on the thorns and ticks, losing himself in the tangled, suffocating center, but he hesitated, listening. He heard a lawn mower. There was a clicking from the butt of an air conditioner in a nearby window. The quick honk of a car being locked. Children squealing. Something was missing. It was then that he realized that Portia had been with him, in his thoughts—not necessarily in a psychic sense, but more like a steady awareness, locked in, like the awareness of your children or of your faith—and now she was gone. He had lost her. It was possible that she had called off band practice that day not because of a hangover but because she could not face him. Because she was done with him.

On the Floor

NATHAN WAS FRIENDLY WITH THE NURSES. When he visited, he approached the front desk reverently. He had a way of yielding his own authority while exuding it at the same time—Portia had seen him do this with Julian's teachers, with police officers and judges—slipping into modesty at just the right times, tilting his head, opening his hands when he spoke, as if his honesty had reached a level of holiness. The nurse who had given Portia the dinner menu the night before was especially drawn in. Portia could tell that she was responding to Nathan's lean, unshaven face, his apparent perseverance, the love that he had for his troubled wife. The nurse made sure that the chair they brought for Nathan was sturdy and then offered him a cup of water, held gently by the tips of her red fingernails.

"I am sorry you are so upset, Portia," Nathan began, speaking to Portia from the foot of her bed. She lay on her side, watching the shadow of the flag behind the window shade. It thrashed, then softened, then picked up thrashing again.

"I am sorry that you were so upset by the way I responded." He paused, perhaps waiting for her to acknowledge that he had apologized for something. But all Portia heard was, *I am sorry that you reacted poorly.*

"Still, I have been thinking. I know we can fix this, Portia." She sensed that he was leaning forward in his chair, trying to catch her eye. Why had he not moved the chair beside the bed? He had perhaps calculated it this way, that he would sit there and say these things without having to look at her, while making it seem like it was her own doing—that she was the one trying to avoid him. She continued to stare blankly at the window shade.

"In fact," he said brightly, "I am happy that all this has happened. It gives us a chance to be better." His hand on her foot was a strange pressure. A little squeeze. Oh, Nathan, something inside her cried. A small desire kept in a cloudy bottle. *Nathan.*

The night before, Portia had gone to the nurses' station and asked for her phone, which was being kept, along with other small items belonging to the patients, in a deep drawer. As the drawer slid open, Portia spotted the rows of cigarette packs labeled with sticky notes; each patient had their preferred brand, which was handed to them three times a day by a generous gloved hand. Some patients needed only one cigarette on their allotted break, but others would suck down two. They were not allowed more than two. The nurse handed Portia the phone, which was kept in a clear resealable baggy, and told her that she was allowed twenty minutes, that she could not bring the phone back to her room. Portia nodded, already scrolling through the numbers in her history. There were calls to her mother, one to Nathan, and three missed calls from Carrie, from the night before. Theo's number was not there. For a moment, her head reeled with the possibility that she had imagined the conversation. It had been an absurd thing to do in the first place, to answer the phone in the woods, laying it on the dirt. And their conversation had been dreamy and vain, a back-and-forth, like a weightless bug skipping over a pool, as they confessed to each other the same declarations of love again and again.

Portia stared blankly at the phone. She dialed the first three digits of Theo's number but stopped. *Hi, Theo,* she practiced saying in her head. *I'm sorry I disappeared, but I am in a mental hospital.* No. *A psychiatric hospital. I've been hospitalized.* Theo might try to console her. He might begin to tell her how unfair it was that such a thing had happened. He might ask her what he could do to help, and she would have to explain that it was her own doing. She had agreed to the whole thing. Portia imagined the silence on Theo's end as he pieced together the story, wondering if she had, indeed, come to her senses about him or at least admitted to herself that something was wrong. Without him in front of her, without the electricity between them, Portia did not know how to explain to Theo the nature of her doubts, her shame, and the love that she still had for him, how it had all been collected and relabeled, like evidence handwritten on a poster board, thrust in front of a jury. Portia slid the phone across the partition, told the nurse that she had changed her mind. She felt as though a tether had been cut, as if, with his number, Theo too had been lifted from reality. Back in her room, she could not convince herself to get into the bed, which was unmade and spread open, obscenely, like the hide of a dead animal. She stood at the foot of the bed for a long time, trying to visualize where she was in the hospital, which direction the outside wall was facing, and where her hometown was in relation to all of this. It would have to be the west-facing wall, she decided, where the sun had been blazing all afternoon, and likely the closest that she could physically get to where Theo was in the world. She lay down against it. No blankets or pillows. Just her body and the wall.

Portia had closed her eyes and followed her thoughts through the places where she had been—the bar with Theo; the footbridge; the top of the stairs, watching Nathan take off his glasses, ready for her to strike him. She saw Julian's navy-blue bedroom, the numbness of a space that should have a child in it but no longer does. And then, in the way that sleep can sneak up on you, teasing you with indescribable images right before it pulls you in, Portia realized that all the time that she had been thinking, she had also been dreaming, as if her mind were a split screen or one of those illustrations that can be peeled away in layers of transparency. She was dreaming of a man, a beautiful man with a sharp nose and long, bewitching teeth. It was Alby Porter, looking at her in that affectionate way—such a way that could be possible only in her fantasies. His eyes gleamed with ivory eyeshadow. He had come back, after having been gone for almost three years, and Portia wondered why.

"Why me?" she asked Alby. He tilted his head, and his smile made lines in his makeup.

"Why me?" he echoed, pointing to his chest. He was wearing a kind of full-body leotard, striped pink and red. His lips were wet and painted, his cheekbones shadowed blue, mixed with the same ivory as his eyelids. "Why me?" he echoed again. Portia did not understand, but she realized suddenly that he must not have come to her in this vision—he was far too important for that. She must have somehow found him. She felt guilty for appearing in front of him, mortal and ignorant. It was dark where they were, and all this time, she had accepted that the prism of gauzy light coming from behind him was a kind of halo, an indication of his otherworldliness, his magic. But as he turned from her and walked into the light, she saw him take something in his hand, give it a little toss. It was a microphone. He was walking onto a stage, and the roar came up from the crowd.

This was how they found her the next morning, pressed flat against the baseboard as if she were a line of putty, molded to seal a leak. A new doctor had come onto the wing to meet her. Dr. Wilk was a graceful woman, reminding Portia of a retired dancer that she had known when she was at school, a woman who had moved through the world as if at any minute she could step onto a gust of wind, as one would step onto a carriage. Dr. Wilk, with her artistic face and her long legs and her flowing beige trousers, was like a tree coming into the room. What was the trouble? she asked, her expression a little funny, a little tilted. Portia had a feeling that she had come in there wanting Portia to be right in some way.

"It looks like you have had some interesting ideas in the past," she said. Portia had gotten off the floor by then, her neck and hips aching. The doctor had not mentioned anything about finding her on the floor but simply waited for Portia to use the bathroom and return, while she crossed her long legs and studied a folder in her hand. The folder must have been given to her by Dr. Shay, who had recorded in it all Portia's delusions about Alby Porter. Dr. Shay would not be coming to see her. He would not get mixed up in this so close to retirement. Portia wondered though: How many volumes had he kept of her thoughts? She might have just put them down in a diary and not told a soul. It might have saved her a lot of trouble.

"Do you know why you are here?" Dr. Wilk asked her.

"My husband thinks that I am acting dangerously."

"Is that what you believe?"

"No," said Portia. Then she said, "I don't know." She sat on the bed with her arms around her legs, still dressed in the blue scrubs she had been given the day before. The doctor lowered her eyes. "Hmm," she hummed to herself. She seemed to be taking many things into consideration. Her light-brown hair ended neatly at her chin. It swayed a little as she bobbed her head, thinking.

Now Nathan was sitting at the foot of the bed, telling Portia that he wanted to make it right. He had made arrangements with a marriage counselor, and the counselor was just waiting for their call, as soon as Portia was ready.

"As soon as you are on your medication again, we can start over," he said. She looked at him now, sitting confidently in his folding chair, sipping the water that the nurse with the red fingernails had brought him. She wondered what he had thought about on the drive over the mountain, alone in his car. You could not get a radio signal for most of the way, so she imagined that he had traveled in silence. Was it his own voice, deep and pure, that he heard in his head, when there was no other sound?

In the Lobby of the Dream Hotel

᧬───᧭ IT WAS TRUE THAT THE BOTTOM OF HER SINK began to get dirty again, but there was more to it than that. The outdoors opened up; she regained a sense of space and movement. There was an acknowledgment of the outskirts: the tops of the trees, the bottoms of feet, even the fingerprints on the lenses of her glasses. She had not noticed how her sense of smell had been dulled until it came back to her one night, when a dark, firepit odor from somewhere in the neighborhood was blown in by the window fan. She was aware of the odor's varied stages, closing her eyes and breathing in this fire as it aged, became an old fire, and then fouled and died. In the back of her mind, there was a black pelt that shifted from black to blacker, to dark brown, and then to a black so dense that it was purple. This pelt was related to the fire pit, occurring at the same time, proof that she was growing back that felty, private part of her that had been stripped away by the pills—a fine, elusive layer of her spirit that she could not possibly describe to a doctor. You could not complain to a doctor about such a thing. You could not nail up a poster that said:

MISSING: THE LINT OF MY HEART
Last seen under the couch cushions,

inside the O of a sonnet,

hitching a ride on a dandelion seed.

Answers to "my most precious little lamb."

When her sense of sound returned to her she was in her kitchen, her usual place, elbow-deep in the dishwater. She liked singing while the water ran. It felt secluded, a break in the middle of a long day. On this day, she had the public radio station on. The show must have changed, because suddenly she was listening to a lone piano. Someone was steadily striking a note, and, below that note, a lower melody was slowly growing. Every few seconds, the lower phrase would touch the higher part in such a way, like a fish nosing the surface of the water, that Portia felt herself buckling down. She felt those collisions of sound, the melodies overlapping, as if they were braiding their way up her spine. Every part of her body began to wake up again.

◆

When her husband asked her why she had stopped the pills, she said to him: "I couldn't hear music."

◆

"I think I am in love with Theo," she told Nathan, and watched as he had shifted all around on the couch, took his glasses off, pinched the bridge of his nose, crossed and uncrossed his legs, as if what he really wanted to do was pace the halls or fly into a rage or use the bathroom. They talked for so long that, eventually, they discovered that they could not go on until they had both used the bathroom. Portia took the upstairs and Nathan the downstairs, and when they were done, they met up again in the living room, forced to resume the most dreadful discussion that they had ever had. And now, having been to the bathroom, having both admitted, in a way, to being unfailingly human, their voices took on a damp, sour kind of dejection. The blaming started, the reality of what was happening soaked into their voices. Nathan, of course, held fast to the hope that Portia was being foolish and that she would drop back into her senses any day now, like waiting for a balloon to deflate and fall to the earth. He did not believe her when she used the word *love* because her alleged love for Theo was mixed up in a bad crowd of other impossible emotions. He reminded Portia that she had a history of crazy ideas. And he knew for certain that Theo did not love her back.

"Theo is doing what any desperate divorced man would do," Nathan explained to her. "He sees a confused woman, and he is taking advantage of her. Once he gets what he wants, he will have no need for you." It had grown late, and Nathan's voice was deep with hoarseness and fatigue and a timbre of finality that made Portia afraid. He had been slouched over, elbows resting on his knees, when he raised his head, then his eyes to hers. "You will not give him what he wants."

Portia agreed to stay away from Theo. That was how it happened. She agreed because she was married and her feelings for Theo were foolish and wrong. But she had met him at the bar anyway. She had told Nathan that she was going out with Carrie.

"Expect me to be late," she said from the bathroom, combing her eyelashes with a mascara wand. She switched the wand to her left hand and did the left eye, staring into her reflection as she lied, calmly, to her husband, who stood outside the bathroom door. "I need to spend time with Carrie, to think about something different for a change," she said. "You're right. I need to come back to my senses."

When Portia left the house, she almost believed what she had told Nathan. She would drive to Carrie's instead of going to the bar, where she knew Theo would be waiting. Carrie and Gus were night owls, with no children to put to bed and to exhaust them, so they would welcome Portia at their door. They would pour her a drink, choose a record from the stack with great care and thoughtfulness—what kind of night was it? The Moody Blues? Talking Heads? Or maybe the Velvet Underground. Yes, their messiest album—and put the needle on. Besides, Portia thought, she did not have the brashness required to meet Theo now, after her confession to Nathan, which had taken all the brashness that she had ever had.

✦

The world was opening up again, like a peacock, showing off its colors, its *scope*. The world called to Portia, tantalized her with its loveliness—the love affair of two piano notes, the smells steaming up from the grass after a rain, ideas that came to her out of nowhere, like colorful ribbons begging to be handled, braided, interwoven. The world was a child with beautiful locks of hair, and Portia was the lonely old lady who needed to run her fingers through it. In her kitchen, she plunged her hands into the dishwater and longed for so many things.

✦

It did not take courage or brashness to meet Theo at the bar. In fact, Portia knew that she was being a coward because she had done nothing to stop herself. She knew that Theo would be there. Maybe he had told her over the phone that day in the forest, or maybe they had planned this, in the same way they had planned meeting at the footbridge, which was not at all. He was there when she walked in, a beer between his hands on the counter with old froth receding. He had not touched it. She ordered. They tried to speak while the bartender poured, but they could not. The words that they had for each other felt too loud for even that setting, too profoundly personal. There are moments sometimes when you are reading a novel and you find that you must close the book and put it down, even though you are alone and the words on the page are only an invisible stream in your mind. Even then, words can be too much. They demand their own caution.

With drinks and coasters in hand, they moved to a corner table lit dimly by a neon advertisement. Portia slid down the bench, and Theo sat beside her, slowly. She wanted to be nearer to him, but she was kept at bay by the fear that she would be pulled in too rapidly, that they would seize each other and run away, bury themselves into a dream. She would open her eyes the next morning to a spark of sunlight peeking through the fold of a duvet, tucked away in a hidden world of warmth and skin, and she would never come back to earth. Oh God, she thought. She wanted him.

"There has to be some legitimate way," she was saying to him. "I could apply for a job at your company. I need a job. I could be your secretary." While she was saying this, she was also thinking of preposterous, morbid scenarios: Theo would fall ill and he would need a lifesaving procedure. She would donate her blood, her bone marrow. A kidney. That way, they would be connected, *linked*, and she would not have to break any vows.

"I quit my job," Theo said, shaking his head. Portia saw that his glass was almost empty. She saw that she had also been drinking hers, without noticing. They were dizzy from all this grasping, all this impossible wishing.

"We could switch bodies."

"Or die and find each other reincarnated."

"If we could shape-shift, like werewolves, then it would not be wrong."

"We could become lucid dreamers and our dream selves could meet every night, in dream treehouses."

"On dream trains."

"In the lobby of the dream hotel."

By the time the bachelorette party came in, the dingy quarters rolled into the jukebox, and the noise became too great to speak over, Portia and Theo were already absorbed in this kind of talk. In a way, they were serious in their plans. On the other hand, they both knew that they were already letting go. Portia knew about this kind of mourning. Four years ago, right before her grandmother died, Portia had spoken to her on the phone, knowing that it would be the last time.

"It will be Thanksgiving soon," her grandmother had said. "I will see you and Julian then, and all the others."

"What should I bring this year, Gramma?" Portia had asked. "The sweet potatoes?"

"The sweet potatoes," her grandmother said. Because sometimes that is how people say goodbye when there is no other way.

(In Bloom)

⌒⌒ THERE WERE TWO PATIENTS AT THE MOUL-
ton hospital who had been there for a long time. The twin
sisters, Manon and Lou, who must have been in their early
seventies, were not permanent fixtures but came and went,
moving between the hospital and a residential facility. Portia
was never given the full story, but it did not matter because
she knew that no one would believe her if she tried to describe the identical French-speaking septuagenarians. For
anyone who had never spent time in a psychiatric hospital,
the sisters would seem too fantastic, like an amateur screen-
writer's idea of what the inhabitants of a nuthouse should
be like. But most of the patients were truly odd: they wore
eccentric clothing and had outlandish, often misspelled tattoos, and a few kept headphones on at mealtime to drown
out the voices in their heads. They shared stories about hopping trains, being in jail, surviving gunshots. They cared a
great deal for one another.

It was routine for Manon and Lou to sit outside patients'
doorways in the evenings and read to them from a book of
French poetry. They did not announce when they would
begin or whose door they would go to first. Even the most
hopeless, strung-out patients would fall silent and listen,
without comprehension, lulled for a few minutes. The sisters

had a book with them with a frayed binding. They sat in folding chairs, the toes of their slippers aligned perfectly with the threshold of the room that they were facing. They took turns with the passages, reading so softly that if you closed your eyes, it was impossible to tell when one voice stopped and the other began. And every now and then, they read in delicious unison. Portia knew a little French from high school and college—not enough to understand the poems fully, but enough to pick up on the sisters' strange pronunciations. Their French was not quick and dewy, like Parisians, which meant that they were most likely Canadian, possibly Swiss.

They came to Portia's door, straightening their chairs. When they were seated, one sister lifted the ribbon from between the pages, holding the book above her lap and slightly extended, as if there were a possibility that it would take flight. She read—they read—and Portia felt a sense of reassurance because it was lovely and because it was somewhat bizarre. She thought about language, about the power one must feel when slipping back into one's native tongue, like riding a horse without a saddle.

Portia was back in her bed, but just for the poem, she told herself. When it was time to sleep, she would lie on the floor, but, for the moment, the bed seemed to her to be more polite. Its softness was overwhelming. Portia closed her eyes, and the voices of the sisters in her doorway walked all over her, like mouse feet. As if words, said in the right way, at the right speed, could pitter-patter you to sleep.

❖

Carrie and Gus had visited that afternoon. Portia met them in the art room, around a dinged-up table with Scotch Tape scars and lonely, ineffectual messages scratched into its surface: "Nurse Patty likes the D"; "I was here, most of the time"; "Beast River"—whatever that one meant. No one had thought to turn on the lights. The air itself felt unambitious. Carrie looked nice; her short bleached hair was parted and swept to the side. Gus did too, dressed similarly to how he had been in Portia's living room the other night. He remained by the window, however, looking out across the grounds. Carrie told Portia that it had been a dangerous decision to stop her medication like that.

"Without medical supervision," she said. She was wearing a thin cardigan over a Morrissey T-shirt. Dark-wash jeans. She must have taken the morning off to drive over the mountain, to tell Portia this cautionary bit of information that Portia had already been told. She thought about the bottom of her kitchen sink, how well she had tended to it when she was taking her pills every morning and how she had tossed out all the expired sauces and uneaten leftovers from the back of the fridge. Sometimes, during those nights, before she started lying to everyone— before the great Dangerous Decision—Portia would find herself pulling the chain on the bedside lamp and falling asleep, almost imperceptibly. Suddenly, it would be morning and Julian would be asking for her to pour his milk, the dog whining to go outside. It had been wonderful, in a way, to sleep without darkness, without lying awake for hours, trying to pinch close your fears like a resealable bag.

"The music didn't sound very good," Portia told Carrie. She looked at Gus too, as she spoke, not knowing why she thought that he might be more inclined to sympathize with her or understand what she was trying to say. "I like listening to music while I wash the dishes," she added. "And, of course"—she made a gesture across the table between herself and Carrie—"the band."

Carrie was silent. Portia could tell that she was not enjoying this conversation, and she wondered if she was thinking back to the night in winter when Portia had arrived at her doorstep. Perhaps Carrie had dressed cleanly and combed her hair for her sake alone, to fashion herself against the hard truth that she was about to deliver.

"Portia," she said, grimacing in that way to express distaste but also charity. Gus turned his back, and Portia could tell that his hands, although they were thrust deep into his pockets, had closed tightly into fists. "Has it ever occurred to you that maybe it's not worth it? That maybe you just write simple songs, play rhythm guitar, and sing backup?" She shot her hand across the table to interrupt herself. "Of course, that's fine. It's great." But now that she was saying it, she went on, before Portia could answer. "We've been at this since we were kids. If we were meant to be brilliant, wouldn't we be brilliant by now?"

✦

Manon and Lou continued their reading, sometimes trading off midline, alternating every other word. Portia had been confused by Carrie's speech in the art room. There she was, saying that Portia was not a good-enough musician to warrant going off her pills—as if being crazy were worth it only if you could be a genius too. But before, in the emergency room, Nathan had spoken mostly about her degenerate past—Skip and Jerry—as if the moments that she had spent with these men defined her whole, reckless being. He had made it seem like she was out of control. And before that, he had removed his glasses and closed his eyes, ready for her to hit him in the face, like he had been expecting this since their wedding day.

✦

Nathan was already trying his argument from another angle, in the room with the Scotch Tape table. It was so dim, compared to the days before, when the sun had pushed its way in through Portia's blinds, the flag whipping around in the heat.

"You're a mother, whether you like it or not," Nathan said. "Leave your family behind and you lose everything— your money, your security, your home. You might think that you are something special, *important*, but that is just your sickness speaking." Portia suspected that Nathan was not trying to bully her. She could tell because she saw how it pained him to say these things.

"You've not asked about Julian," he added. "He wants to know where his mommy is. Your parents are doing their best, but eventually they have to go back to work." The word *mommy* broke in the back of his throat in a bubble of grief.

It was piling up. It had been piling around Portia for most of her life, this guilt, the awareness of the burden that she was to others. Alby Porter had struggled too, she knew, weighted down by the things that he wanted to change about himself but could not. What he wanted was to be creative all the time, from the moment he opened his eyes in the morning to when the night yielded to the cold pre-dawn sky of the next day. This was not possible, of course, except for during those fevered times when mania overtook him and he strummed his guitar until the tips of his fingers peeled off. But these prolific days always came at a great cost, followed by months of depression and remorse, for when he was on fire, he was also cruel and impatient and narcissistic. Like her, it seemed.

After Nathan had gone, Portia wandered back to her room and was met by a nurse who wanted to give her a pill. A little vacation under her tongue. Why not? Why not?

✦

Manon and Lou had come to a poem by a poet named Ew-go. Portia remembered the poem from her college French class. In it, the sorrowful poet was going to see his dead daughter. Portia had assumed that he was walking, through the meadows and the forests, headlong to his own death, or at least that that was what one's life became once a child died: a journey to the end, no matter how many years it took or what scenery you passed along the way. But there had been a girl who sat beside her in the college lecture hall, who Portia had seen offering free "stick-and-poke" tattoos at a party—little line drawings, about an inch in length, stabbed into the wrist or an upper thigh with an inky needle. The "stick-and-poke" girl said that the poet was literally walking to his daughter's grave. Just leaving his house and walking there, to put flowers on it. Grief did not need metaphor to be valid, she said, her chin held high, aimed at the professor. She scratched at a self-inflicted tattoo on her wrist: a little penguin. Her statement at the time had seemed irreverently wise. Portia had nodded silently, but, inside, she wanted the poem to be grander and more complex—to be *more*.

And that was her problem: she wanted life to be deep and gratifying. She wanted to hear music and be thrilled by it every single time. She wanted a love so big that it came with its own cycles, its own ecosystems. Perhaps not as a child, but certainly as an adult, she knew a part of her longed for the giant heart from the science museum, complete with its sticky tunnels, its lost, howling children. She had thought that Theo might find her there, in that big, impossible love, but maybe she had been wrong. It could be that all she was hoping for was to avoid the maintenance of life. She did not have a job; she could not remember the plots of books that she read, could not find her way in a city—maps themselves looked frightening to her, like a web of fungus on a tree. And when it had come time to bring her only child into the world, she had not been able to do that the right way either. Instead, a man with hairy fingers had cut her open, wrestled her son from her body, and flicked him hard on the bottom so that he would cry.

On the floor.

Portia had been sleeping on the floor to be closer to Theo. There, she imagined, she could feel the vibrations of the hospital, her body could share in the frequency of the building, which was one of the largest buildings in Moulton—possibly the largest of any that were still in use. If her body was humming along with the building, then she herself was bigger. A bigger sound in the night. A bigger fish in the ocean. Theo could find her this way by just looking out his window, by licking his finger and holding it to the wind.

"On floor," the sisters were saying. "On floor," like a question put to no one. They had lovely, leafy voices. Rose-petal voices. Portia opened her eyes, wondering why the sisters had suddenly shifted to English. Her eyelids were heavy—her face felt bloated, like a baseball mitt. She pushed herself up with one hand, shielding her eyes from the harsh overhead lights with the other. The sisters were still there, but they were closing the book, placing the ribbon inside the crease, moving on.

"Wait," Portia wanted to say. Her tongue was fat and dry inside her mouth. She rolled it around. But they had picked up their chairs and were shuffling their slippers to the next room. In the poem, the narrator reached his destination and placed holly on the grave, along with heather, in bloom: *"en fleur."*

White Rabbit

❧ It was becoming harder for Theo to picture Portia in his mind. Sometimes he looked for her and all he saw was the outline of a girl in a yellow dress scratching her heel on the sidewalk. That was fifteen years ago. Her hair had been shorter then, cut close to her head with some small pieces in the front, which he did not know how to describe. Had he thought that she was beautiful then? Or just strange and therefore worthy of note? He should not have been thinking of that Portia because that Portia was much too young, barely eighteen. A splash of yellow, a swirl of a skirt. A freckle from his past. But Theo had not heard anything from Portia. There had been the text from Carrie, her cold excuses over the phone—"a hangover," she had said. Finally, he had tried to call Portia's phone and it had not rung but gone straight to voicemail, which should have been enough of a sign that she was done with him. She had warned him that this might happen, that she might suddenly change her mind, and he had been stupid enough to believe that he could bear it. That somehow, Portia could stop loving him and he would take it as a lesson, or a beautiful, fleeting dream, and move on with his life.

The cat had showed up again, slinking through the door when he opened it. It dashed around him, under the kitchen table, where it stayed, hips low to the floor. Its eyes were large amber drops. They flashed at him, like opinions that he did not want or need.

"I know," he said to the cat, as if it had scolded him for something. He hung his keys back on the hook, not sure where he thought he was going anyway, and kicked off his shoes. He had been wanting to call Carrie again, hoping that she would say something—anything—about Portia, but he could not come up with a good reason to be calling. Neither he nor Portia had told Carrie about what was going on, and he certainly did not want her finding out now. It would be humiliating, how easily he had allowed himself to believe that something of great importance was happening. Carrie would see right through it. She would see him for the lonely, desperate man that he really was. But here was something, he thought, growling at him from under the table. Carrie and Gus had lost one of their cats last winter, when a car struck it during a blizzard. They had found the poor thing in a snowbank, pushed there by the plows. He picked up the phone.

"Hi, Carrie," he said. "Do you need another cat?"

◆

It was summer break, so Theo's sons had been in and out, spending most of their time with friends whose parents owned large houses with basketball hoops and in-ground swimming pools. His sons were kind boys, and Theo knew that they held no resentment toward him, but he also knew that it was not any fun for a fourteen-year-old and a fifteen-year-old to be sharing a room in their father's shitty apartment, their father who sometimes baked them a chocolate cake for no reason or made them a three-course dinner with a can of cranberry sauce on the side. Who also made them Pop-Tarts at midnight and was open with them about drugs and sex and personal failures. It was not that this father was trying too hard, or missing the mark, but that most of what he had to give was mixed with sadness. Theo could see in his sons' eyes, as they stuffed forkfuls of cake into their mouths, the effort it took for them to smile at him. What a drain it was to have a sad father. He did not want to be a burden for them, so he did not pester them about being home more often.

＋

The cat rubbed itself on the leg of the table, ignoring Theo's hand when he reached toward it. It purred and growled and mashed its forehead into the wood. Carrie wanted to know if Theo had called the animal shelter or the veterinarian's office. She sounded annoyed, not her usual self.

"No, I hadn't thought of that," Theo said.

"Have you asked your neighbors?"

Theo sighed. According to the clock on his microwave, it was a little after noon. He was probably catching Carrie on her lunch break. She was a physical therapist. His mother had been one of her clients years ago, after a knee surgery.

"No," he said. "You're right. I'll try the neighbor first." There was a pause. Static on the line again, maybe an air conditioner in the room or a bad signal. He was about to say goodbye, apologize for wasting her time, but Carrie cleared her throat.

"I know why you are calling," she said. "And I think you should drop it."

The cat redirected its headbutting from the table leg to the sliding glass door. Theo never used that door because the weedy patio on the other side of it did not get any shade in the summer and was concealed from the neighbor only by a flimsy piece of lattice. The neighbor behind the lattice had an ashtray the size of a birdbath that she never cleaned. It probably had been a birdbath at one point, but it was now filled with tarry rainwater and swarming with gnats. It was not so much the smoke or the foul odor of the waterlogged cigarettes that kept Theo away but that he feared being caught in conversation with his neighbor, the awkwardness of staring at the filth that was her side of the patio and the scorched desolation that was his. He slid open the door, and the cat slipped out like an eel. He was only just putting Carrie's words together in his mind.

"Drop it?" The cat dashed round to the neighbor's half of the patio, flopping down beneath the wooden folding chair there. Maybe if Theo had talked to the neighbor, even just once, he would have known that the cat belonged to her.

"You and Portia," Carrie said. "Whatever you think is going on between you two. Isn't."

"Did Portia talk to you?" he asked. He should not have been astounded. He should not have expected any of the things that he had allowed himself to expect over the last few weeks. But it did not sit right with him that Portia would not tell him herself. Even if she was angry or ashamed or remorseful. Carrie's voice softened.

"Theo," she said, gently now. "I've known Portia for a long time. Whatever she told you—" Theo heard the pity in her voice, a shade of condescension, as if she could see through his desires, see that they all came from the same stunted root: the last little bit of him that believed that he deserved something good. He did not know what to say. He wanted to shout at Carrie, tell her that she was wrong. What had happened between him and Portia had taken them both by surprise and in the same way. They had not been beside themselves with infatuation. They had not been giddy. They had been trying, with great care and sobriety, to understand what was happening to them. But Theo did not say any of this to Carrie. Instead he heard his voice, squeaky and adolescent, saying the stupidest thing that he could say in that moment: "I love her."

At the same time that Carrie started laughing, Theo's hands began to tingle. The phone became warm against his ear and in his grip, then hot, burning. He let it drop, throwing up his hands as if he had touched an electric wire. The phone landed flat on the kitchen floor, Carrie's name facing upward.

"Theo?" He could hear the phone talking in its parrot voice. "Hello?" Theo backed away, his hands still in the air. They felt charged, not like hands anymore but like radio antennae. He did not know what to do with them.

◆

When he had first separated from his wife, Theo's friends told him that he should make it easier on himself by "playing the field." Some of the friends were envious that he had suddenly been given this gift of sex with other women. They shook their heads as if they knew already that it would be wasted on him. Still, they were generous, and they did their best to set him up, writing phone numbers across the damp napkins under their beer bottles—divorced cousins, friends of their wives. There was a cute receptionist at the dentist's office. She was the younger sister of a friend of a friend, who, according to a highly reliable source, had had a crush on Theo throughout high school.

"It's a sure thing," they said. "Maybe not long-term, but you'll have fun."

Theo, at the time, had wanted none of it. The last ten years of his marriage had felt like he was living with a stranger. Why would he want another stranger stealing her way into his life, with her new smells, her unfamiliar laugh, a whole life behind her? He imagined that these aspects—larger than life in their novelty—would be trying always to barge into their small talk, their flirtation, like a grizzly bear breaking into a parked car. His friends did not believe him. They were frustrated by his resistance to something so painfully necessary. Even Gus had been critical, and Gus had the happiest marriage of any of them.

✦

By now, Theo's hands felt as though they were on fire. His phone lay on the kitchen floor, the screen blank, because Carrie had dropped the call. It was one of those terrible moments, when the question of what to do is so intimidatingly vast, that the solution feels as though it needs to be just as dramatic. He might climb up to the roof and hope for a lightning storm to roll in and strike him down. He might start digging his own grave—not so that he would die, but just to do something with his hands that felt heroically purposeful. Instead, he plucked his keys off the hook, put his shoes back on, and, leaving the phone where it lay, went to his car. He would not turn around for the phone, he told himself, even though its absence in his pocket felt like the cold reeling of rock climbing without a harness, the foggy terror of driving without his glasses. It felt like making a commitment that he was not ready for, but that was exactly what he was doing. He opened the car door. I will not call her, he thought. He sat behind the wheel. I will not humiliate myself by calling her. He twisted the keys in the ignition. I promise not to call her. As he backed into the street, Theo decided that, if the universe really wanted him to be with Portia, it would lead him to her, just as it had in Moulton. He would drive and drive until something made him stop—maybe a roadside sign would alert him to where she was or tell him what to do.

He began with Portia's street. He almost expected to find Portia's house surrounded by flashing police cruisers, the pillars on the front porch tangled in caution tape, the windows barricaded; she could not just disappear so easily, he thought. If she were going to disappear, even of her own will, there would have to be some evidence of struggle or strife. People who were obliterated by atomic bombs left shadows on the sidewalk, he thought. And then: Oh, how awful. His mind wanted to wander into the darkest, most sadistic corners, as if Portia had been torn from him, when all that had transpired was a band practice cancellation, a phone call in which he had been scolded by Carrie in the mildest way.

Portia's house stood quietly, removed from the road by a grassy slope. It had the stillness of a house that has just been rained on and is waiting for its occupants to open the windows again. Theo caught sight of the green plastic slump of a sandbox in the shape of a turtle, the turtle shell closed tightly. No one was home.

He continued to drive, toying with the radio, wondering if he had what it took to discern a sign from the universe from the cries of his own fraught and needy heart. It felt good to drive, at least. Theo rolled the windows down, which still felt

like a luxury after almost two decades of his wife insisting
that they stay closed. His wife had not liked the dampness
and roadside rot thrumming in her skull as they drove, or
hearing the crunch of the tires, smelling the headache of rag-
weed and goldenrod. She was a mother. The boys had stinky
socks and peed all over the toilet seat. She had just wanted
peace and air conditioning, which Theo could not argue
against. He let his arm dangle out the window as he drove,
inhaling the outdoors. He liked how you could drive along
some woods and suddenly smell the cool mineral smell of a
river and know it was there, even if you could not see it. He
was a father. He had worked in the Antarctica of all office
buildings for most of his adult life, where the women's arms
looked like plucked chickens and the elevator was plastered
in Suicide Hotline posters. He just wanted to feel alive.

For a while, there was nothing, meaning that there were
mountains on either side, blue flowers coming up around
the guardrails, and a feeling of deep quiet behind the trees.
Sometimes another car passed him on the left and he would
hear the motor straining with a kind of righteousness, calling him out for driving the exact speed limit. One of these
passing vehicles was a white pickup truck that ducked back
into the lane in front of him and seemed to slow down, which
Theo thought was especially cruel.

He remembered how Portia had been with him at the
bar, wavy with purple and red in her hair from the neon
lights, so smooth with her speech and her movements. She

had been like someone in a dream. She *had* been exactly that, for he had dreamed of her in the bed, in that cabin with the skylight. Dreams, he had noted, were full of realistic light and shadows. But they could also access a certain core of perfect understanding, like incubators for feelings that you have not had since childhood. Perfect love. Perfect acceptance. Things that he had not thought were possible but that he had wanted so badly. His attention shifted back to the truck in front of him, which was braking unnecessarily when there was nothing in its path but open road. It was a New York license plate with the word *RABBIT* written across it. Theo wondered, drearily, if this could be the sign that he had asked for. If so, it was a confounding one and he did not like it. He would probably give up, he told himself, go home, buy himself a television before his money ran out. But then the white truck swerved onto the shoulder and arched wide into the oncoming lane, turning completely around. It continued to drive in the opposite direction, as if nothing had happened, like a fish that had reached the end of its tank. Theo had almost come to a complete stop during this and was beginning to speed up again when it occurred to him that he was about to do something stupid, because the truck was white and the license plate said *RABBIT* and everyone knows that white rabbits are meant to be followed.

Never Give Up

When Portia was first hospitalized, Dr. Shay had not understood that he was only furthering Portia's humiliation by deeming her "heartbroken," when it was clear to her that the nature of her crisis was uniquely and sophisticatedly tragic. In Portia's experience, only Victorian women and very small mammals were susceptible to the dangers of heartbreak. Dr. Shay sometimes visited her in her room, patting her back lightly when she was crying and twisted in her bedsheets, once touching her hair but then removing his hand swiftly, catching himself in this act of unwarranted affection. One day, he entered her room with the gleam of someone who had brought a new solution to her problems. He sat beside her bed and produced a piece of paper.

"Someone left this in the photocopier at my office," he told Portia, handing her the paper. "I thought of you."

Now, thirteen years later, Dr. Wilk was sitting in her room, with her sleek arms, her legs that crossed and recrossed at the ankle. She was wearing a chestnut-colored blouse with gold trim around the collar. She looked like an autumnal fairy queen. Dr. Wilk was nothing like Dr. Shay, and it occurred to Portia that all doctors had their own agendas, that there would never be any continuity to her treatment. If Portia were a book and her doctors were not doctors but English professors, they would teach her differently, their highlighters finding vastly different passages to examine.

"You are highly imaginative, Portia," said Dr. Wilk. Portia did not know if she should say "thank you," so she said nothing.

"I think that people who are highly imaginative sometimes take it for granted," the doctor continued. Portia was drowsy from her medication. Her eyelids felt like blisters. Like opening your eyes in chlorinated water. She remembered how it had been, lying in the deep end of Alby's pool, watching the bubbles of his remaining breath riot to the surface. She remembered how it was to feel that your own breath was a traitor, to watch it swim away while you sank to your death. Had this memory attached itself to her when Alby died, when he transferred some of his energy onto her?

"It's not always my imagination," Portia heard herself speaking. She felt that her voice was uninhibited; whatever gate was usually positioned carefully between her thoughts and her tongue had been removed by the medication. Dr. Wilk looked pleased. She recrossed her legs and leaned forward.

"What's not?"

Portia did not want to talk, but she found that if she opened her mouth slightly, the words were there, heavy and ready to roll out.

"I mean that most of the time, I feel like I am watching TV in my head: I just sit there and the ideas and images come to me. That's not imagination. I don't know what that is."

"Alby Porter," said Dr. Wilk. "He was a real person. You didn't make him up."

"No."

"What if I asked you to close your eyes and envision a nice slice of cherry pie? Could you do that, Portia?"

Portia huffed. She was not stupid. Even sedated, she could see miles ahead of Dr. Wilk's line of reasoning. Like a game of chess, she recognized her opponent's move and where it was leading, and she wished that they could scrap the whole thing, fast-forward to the part where her doctor delivered her point, scribbled a prescription, and nothing changed. Portia was tired of being evaluated, diagnosed, then disappointed. Thirteen years ago, Dr. Shay had strode into her hospital room and given Portia a piece of paper that he had found in the photocopier. His smile had been all hope, his voice all warmth, as he described how the image on the paper must have been meant for Portia to see. But when she had it in her hand, it was nothing more than a grainy black-and-white cartoon: a mouse holding open the jaws of a cat who was trying to eat it. A caption that said, "Never Give Up."

"I was meant to have this?" she had asked him, doubtfully. The cat and mouse reminded her of Tom and Jerry, which reminded her of Jerry sitting at the breakfast table with his juice box, who claimed that he did not know which was the mouse and which was the cat. Jerry had also said that he knew her, then called her the Whore of Babylon. She needed to stop finding connections where there were no connections to find.

"Yes," said Dr. Shay, "because I don't want you to give up."

"You went to medical school for this?" She folded the paper in half, creasing it with her fingernail, unable to look at her psychiatrist's face. She did not mean to insult him.

"I know how to daydream," Portia told Dr. Wilk. "I know the difference between daydreams and fantasies. Fantasies and delusions."

Dr. Wilk flexed her fingers, tilted her head.

"I can think of cherry pie and see it in my head."

"Okay," Dr. Wilk said. "But please . . ." Her eyes focused softly on Portia, who was sitting on the bed, holding her pillow against her chest. "Humor me. Take me on a tour of one of your daydreams. It would interest me greatly."

Portia would have rolled her eyes if her eyes did not feel like overripe tomatoes. She knew that Dr. Wilk was flattering her so that she would talk. She tried to press her ego down, to flatten it against the bottom of her soul, but the drugs had made her weak, and there was something lovely about Dr. Wilk's bronze-tinted gaze. Her probing kindness. Her desire to understand. Despite everything that was wrong, Portia wanted to help her understand. "Sometimes, I daydream about what it would be like to leave my husband and live by myself. Just me and Julian."

Dr. Wilk raised her eyebrows. "Julian?"

"My son," Portia added. "I haven't forgotten about him."

"No one suggested that you had," the doctor said. "Talk to me about this daydream. Narrate it, as if you are watching it unfold."

Portia found that it was easy to do. The apartment where she lived in her imagination was set up in her mind, just as she had left it, three stories above the street. The street resembled downtown Moulton because there had been a time when she thought she might live there, start over. A fan rattling in the window. A mattress on the floor, where she played guitar in her underwear. Somehow, the daydream always began with Portia returning home from waitressing, after Julian had gone to bed. Paying the babysitter, with gentle, single-mother exhaustion, like she had seen beautiful actresses do in movies.

"I am still wearing my apron when I get home," Portia said to Dr. Wilk. "The apron is wet and foul-smelling. I will have to wash it in the bathroom sink and hang it on the wooden rack in the kitchen if I want it to be dry for tomorrow evening."

"Where do you work?" Dr. Wilk asked. "And why don't you have a washing machine?"

"At a big restaurant on the outskirts of town, where tourists like to eat. And because my apartment didn't come with one." Just because it was a daydream did not mean that it could not be realistic. In fact, Portia had discovered that there was a specific pleasure to be had in daydreaming within the parameters of reality. There were hallmarks of poverty to be endured, if she were to divorce her attorney husband, and these hallmarks made Portia's desire for freedom all the more palpable. Dr. Wilk nodded.

Portia continued: "It was a busy night at the restaurant. The kitchen was backed up with orders and the cooks were taking out their frustration on the dish-pit boys, who had then targeted some of the waitresses by splashing them with putrid water from their troughs of food runoff—ketchup, steak juice, clumps of gravy and potato skins—until the cooks intervened, meaner than ever. So the dish-pit boys went after the bussers instead."

"Okay," said Dr. Wilk. "That's good. But what about you? Go back to you."

Portia closed her eyes and brought the gray hospital blanket around her, smelling its institutional soapy nothingness. She saw herself tossing her apron on the floor of her imaginary apartment, then stooping down to retrieve the wad of tip money from inside the pocket.

It's not safe to walk to your car with all that cash in your apron. One of the kitchen boys might follow you out the back door, Corrina, the waitress, had said to Portia years ago, after Portia had made extra tips from taking over Corrina's abandoned tables. Corrina had tried to explain away the red mark on her neck by saying that one of the other girls had slammed into her while she was carrying a tray of food, that the edge of the tray had bruised her neck. No one had seen this happen.

You know a lot about kitchen boys, Portia had said.

This conversation had occurred in Portia's past, and not in her daydream, but she found, as she slipped into her narration for Dr. Wilk, that something had pushed its way into her vision. Something that she had not intended.

"I am giving the wrinkled bills to the babysitter," Portia told Dr. Wilk. "They are damp from the dish-pit water. But the babysitter is looking at me funny, and it's not about the wet forty dollars. After I lock the door behind her, I go to the bathroom and look at myself in the mirror. There, on my neck, is a big red mark, like a hickey."

Lemonade

⟲⟍OUTSIDE THE HOSPITAL, PORTIA COULD hear the flag flapping loudly in the wind. It snapped, like a whip, and there was a metal chain that clanged against the post. Portia, along with some other patients, had been allowed to take a walk along the path that followed the edge of the parking lot and looped through the woods. Staff members accompanied them, but quietly, and the talk among the patients was minimal; none of them knew each other, and it was risky to form any sort of long-lasting friendship, even though the temptation was always there. Portia had been in the hospital now for four days, but it was enough time for the outdoors to regain its sense of wonderment. She liked the warmth rising from the blacktop and the dandelions growing in the seam of the walkway. It was still June, so the sky had not fully dropped with the humidity of July. The heaviness of midsummer in Vermont could feel like a looming pregnant belly, the storms hormonal, the heat prickly and nauseating. This kind of weather surprised visitors not from the area, who had expected any season that was not winter to be forgiving and picturesque. Portia followed the line of patients into the woods, which were not deep but gave the illusion, once you were surrounded by trees, of cover.

Dr. Wilk had arrived shortly after breakfast. She wanted to hear more about Portia's daydream, about the hickey that Portia had found on her neck.

"What caused you to think of that?" she had asked of the hickey. Portia struggled to find an answer. It was true what she had said, about how her daydreams often got away from her, taking on a life of their own. In the French picture book that Julian liked at bedtime, there had been an illustration of a dark-haired woman in a blue dress, gazing out her window. Imagining herself as that woman had been a kind of longing, a chance to flex that version of herself that wanted to cook mushrooms and read books and live plainly, honestly. But then the woman in the blue dress had appeared in her dreams at night, as if she would not resign herself to being forgotten. And even as the picture book lost its tier in the bedside pile, Portia felt the presence of this character that she had created, living in the cracks of her awareness: the woman in the blue dress would exist with a certain rebellious chasteness, watering the pansies in her windowsill, writing lists in spilled flour. She would live, whether Portia cared or not.

"The red mark. I didn't put it there," Portia had told Dr. Wilk. "I don't know why it keeps coming back. I never got a hickey like that in real life."

"So the hickey is intrusive. Something that you cannot control."

Portia had not wanted to admit to this, not until she

knew how Dr. Wilk would use the information, but once again the words were rolling out, freely. Her head was a barrel of apples that had been tipped, her thoughts scattered for all to see. She hated feeling this way.

"Yes. That's right," she said. She remembered how she had dreamed of Alby Porter while lying on the floor of her room, pressed against the wall. How he mimicked her question: *Why me?* Like a piece of AI technology that had reached the limit of its programing. As if *he* were asking *her* to come up with the answer. It was not reassuring. But she had not been in control of this either. Portia's thoughts began to take on a shimmering mirage of paranoia. It was possible that everything that had happened to her was not a carefully choreographed miracle. It was possible too—now that her mind was tipping over with hard truths—that her love for Theo was just as random and intrusive.

Were the moments they had shared somehow a trick of their own minds? She could not deny that the two of them were alike, but maybe the alignment of their particular strain of foolishness had made them all the more gullible.

"And what if this has nothing to do with delusion?" Dr. Wilk was saying. "What if this is more about control? If you took back control of your daydreams, what might happen to your life?" The doctor's demeanor had changed. Her feet were planted firmly on the floor. Some cloud had evaporated from over her eyes, and her face was naked with epiphany. Portia's neck and back hurt. Her brain hurt. She stretched her arms over her head and tried to get a peek of the doctor's silver wristwatch, hoping that she would not miss the walk into the woods that she had been promised. She agreed with Dr. Wilk: the question of delusion was not important. What was important was that Portia was a mother who was away from her child. A wife who had wandered into temptation. What was important was that she had brought suffering onto her family and friends. Nathan's message was becoming clearer to her. He had told her that she should not expect to see her parents anytime soon.

"They have been given just about as much as they can handle," he had said. "It would not be wise for them to see you like this, again." But of course, Portia had thought. Her parents could not be there for her because they needed to stay strong for Julian. Motherhood, it seemed, was not a walk on the moon, was not an enchanted forest, but another rock to load into your pocket as you waded into the ocean; once you were under the water, you might as well sink to the bottom. Once you had a child, you should no longer expect to be allowed to catch your breath. If Portia was remembering correctly, it was Virginia Woolf who had walked into the river with stones in her pockets, whose suicide was enveloped now in a tragic, scholarly covetousness. If only everyone could die in such a way, with such immensity of brain. Dr. Shay had liked to talk about Virginia Woolf because Virginia Woolf shared something in common with Portia, having been afflicted in the same way. She had seen Dr. Shay's face brighten with fascination, just as Dr. Wilk's was brightening. What did they want from her?

The woods did not last long. Portia was already stepping out of the trees, back into the opposite side of the parking lot. She shielded her eyes from a hundred flashing suns, reflected off the windows of parked cars. It was hotter now that the wind had died, and she was feeling weak from sleeping poorly, from whatever little yellow "vacation" she had been slipping under her tongue every day. The drug collected the edges of the world around her, like tightening the mouth of a net, something knitted and soft. If she could take those pills for the rest of her life, she thought, then she might just stumble through unscathed.

"Portia." Someone was calling her name. There was a figure coming toward her through the glare of the parking lot. For a brief moment, she did not recognize him—maybe due to the sun spotting her vision or because not only was she not expecting him but she was under the false impression that somehow she was untraceable out there, on that smutty path on the outskirts of the hospital. But there he was, with his arms out, smiling. He stepped into the fringe of shadow at the end of the parking lot and she could see him more clearly.

"Nathan."

He was addressing one of the nurses who had led the walk, asking for permission to join his wife on their way back to the side entrance. As he spoke, something caught Portia in her belly, like a fishhook tugging, small but painful. Nathan walked beside her, with his hands in his pockets, looking down at her, warmly. The fishhook tugged again. *How easy it would be to go home with him,* it said. *To pretend that none of this had happened. Back to the way things were.*

"Will you try something else for me?" Dr. Wilk had asked her that morning, her eyes shining.

"Do better than your waitress daydream. Dream bigger. After your walk, come back here and write everything down." She handed Portia a yellow legal pad. "I'll have the nurse deliver you a pencil."

They had reached the side entrance, where the walk had started, just a gray doorway with a pointed wooden overhang. Portia hung back as the other patients filed through so she could say goodbye to Nathan. He was not allowed into the building this way, and it was not worth the trouble for him to go around to the front, to sign in, take the elevator, when he could give her the photograph right there. He handed it to her: a picture of Julian on what appeared to be a rocky beach, the lake behind him streaked with glittering sun. He was wearing a brown sweater stitched with red flecks— flea-bitten, she might call that pattern if it were the coloring of an animal. Portia could not place the sweater. She could not remember having seen Julian in such a sweater. Perhaps she had been looking at the photograph for too long, trying to figure out this mysterious beach, trying to remember if the sweater had been a Christmas gift or a hand-me-down from the neighbor, because Nathan touched her chin with his thumb so that she would lift her eyes to him.

"Are they giving you something strong?" he asked. By then, the other patients had gone inside, and the one nurse who had stayed behind waited, looking at her cell phone, with her shoe propping open the door. Portia felt the unsteadiness in her legs. Her body was heavy. It reminded her of being covered by a lead blanket at the dentist, which always made her feel sleepy, and the world feel mercilessly lightweight and cold, once the blanket was removed. She nodded, and Nathan let his hand fall back to his side.

"Just be careful," he said. "Remember what those kinds of pills do to you."

"What do you mean?" she asked him.

"The lemonade?" He gave this word such strange emphasis that the nurse at the door raised her eyebrows without looking up from her phone. "You don't remember throwing a half-gallon cup of lemonade at the nurse after Julian was born?"

Portia thought back to the day after her C-section. The nurse who came in to dress Portia's incision had scolded her in some way. Something about how Portia should just be happy that she was alive and forget that she was in pain, that the birth of her child had felt all wrong, like the surgeon was digging around inside her, looking for change to put into the vending machine. Portia had been angry at the nurse, but she had not thrown anything. She had pushed her drink onto the floor because that was all she had the strength and mobility to accomplish, with the IV in her arm, the catheter tube, and the stiff bandages keeping her belly from splitting open.

"I didn't throw anything," she said to Nathan. He narrowed his eyes in concern, studying her for a minute.

"You really don't remember, do you?" He took a step toward her and she pulled back, dropping the photograph onto the grass at her feet. Dr. Wilk had wanted Portia to take control of her daydreams, but she barely had control of her own memories. Had she thrown the cup at the nurse? It was hard to dispute a man like Nathan, whose job it was to dispute people all day long, who kept facts in his head, dated and preserved.

Nathan stooped to pick up the fallen photograph, wiping it gently against his sleeve.

"You don't have to take it if you don't want to," he said to her. "I only thought—" but Portia had snatched it back. Nathan put up his hands and stepped away, as if Portia had taken a swing at him. He glanced at the nurse, who had not seen the exchange or was pretending not to see. Portia looked again at the photo of her son. He was smiling. His hair was long, covering his left eye. He did not usually smile for pictures, unless the picture was taken quickly—not candidly, but swiftly enough so that the boy did not have time to consider that he should be appearing to enjoy himself, before he could remember that his life was also someone else's memory.

Portia still did not recognize the flea-bitten sweater, but she did not dare ask Nathan about it, in case he was ready to catch her in her forgetfulness. The nurse slipped her phone into her pocket and took the door handle, holding it wide. She smiled, as if to say, *I am not insisting, but it is time to go.*

Lois

⌒〜⌒ THEO THOUGHT THAT HE WAS GOING TO FOL-
low that white truck right back into town. He would not have
been surprised if the truck had led him back to his street, pulled
up in front of his own apartment. If he had watched himself—
as if out of body—get out of the white truck and walk through
the front door that he had neglected to lock. As if the universe
were telling him to go home, to surrender quietly, without
kicking and screaming. But the truck pulled off the highway
before making it into town, at a restaurant, a steak-house-type
restaurant with a long deck lined with yellow umbrellas. Theo
watched the truck stutter over the gravel driveway and come
to a dusty halt. He parked his own car farther down the lot,
where he hoped that he would not be noticed, and waited to
see if the driver would get out. For a moment nothing moved
at all. Theo thought that maybe the driver was intentionally
stalling, as if he or she was aware of Theo and calling his bluff.
Finally, he decided that it did not matter; he would go into the
restaurant because he had made it this far.

It was not a place that he frequented, unless his office had
reserved one of the dining rooms for a party. It was the kind
of restaurant where you brought your in-laws so they could
fawn over the view of the mountains, or maybe you brought
a colleague because the place was big and American, without

being too tacky, and there would be no surprises. The bar itself was oversize, a great polished wooden slab lit too brightly, so that the people seated around it looked small and inadvertently guilty. No one at a bar wanted to be well-lit. Theo did not mind, having no business being there in the first place. He made eye contact with the bartender and found a stool. Besides the afternoon drinkers at the bar, there was a long table set up along the window, on the other side of an empty karaoke stage. There seemed to be a party going on at the table. A girl was pulling crumpled tissue paper out of a gift bag and letting it fall to the floor. A graduation party, Theo guessed. Even though the group was at the opposite end of the dining room, Theo still felt like an imposter, sitting awkwardly on his stool, like a man sitting above a target at a dunking booth. He might have left, but the bartender had already slid a beer toward him in a tulip pint glass. He had not ordered the beer. The girl at the far table was pulling the last rosette of tissue paper from her gift, tossing it at her feet as she ducked her nose into the bag to see what was inside. Theo had been toying all day with the notion that he was going mad, as if it were a small achievement to let go of reality, to be so unconcerned with it. But now the possibility flashed at him, dangerously close; maybe he had ordered the beer without knowing. Maybe he knew the bartender but could not, for whatever reason, recognize his face. It was called face blindness. His mother had read an article about it once. She was intent on learning about new psychiatric conditions—the different strands of narcissism, limbs that moved with their own agenda, people who could not dream—in the same way that her best friend, Margaret, kept abreast of what hat the duchess had worn to a christening. Theo was about to thank the bartender all the same for the beer when he saw that the bartender's forehead had turned red. He was a younger man, with gelled black hair and a silver post in his bottom lip. Theo's mother had said that sufferers of face blindness often had to rely on piercings, tattoos, and hairstyles to recognize the people around them, even close family members.

"I'm so sorry," the bartender said. He reached for the glass and dumped its contents into the sink at his station. "I thought you were someone else."

The graduation party was beginning to disperse. A small group lingered, taking pictures in front of the window, women of different ages with their arms linked. Theo was aware of them only peripherally, as the camera flashed. He had decided to order from the flustered bartender, if only to show the poor man that he was not offended, but he did not plan on staying long. The allure of the white truck had faded (the driver turned out to be a woman around Theo's age who was taking a call on her cell phone) along with any hope of discovering what he was supposed to be doing. When he felt the tap on his shoulder, he expected it to be another person who had misidentified him, now that it had occurred to him that he might have stumbled onto the turf of his doppelgänger. Sure enough, it was a woman he did not know, smiling tentatively at him, a dimple appearing like a comma in the side of her chin. Theo did not know that dimples could appear in such places, but he found that his keenness for it was immediate and involuntary.

"Theo?" she was saying to him. She had a cardigan draped over her arm. Theo could tell that she wanted to place it on the back of the barstool beside him. She reached out a small pointed hand for him to shake. Her name was Lois, which did not ring a bell but seemed to suit her—her stature and her mildness. Of course, he said to her, she could sit beside him. He was not waiting for anyone, although as he said this, he realized that some belligerent part of his mind had reserved the spot for Portia, for when she decided to swan her way into the restaurant and rescue him from his loneliness. As Lois climbed onto the stool, Theo felt the same private sense of pain that a child would feel if some real person were to sit upon a chair occupied by an imaginary friend. Lois waved goodbye to the young woman from the graduation party and asked the bartender for a glass of water. She had already had two margaritas, she said. Her cheeks, now visible in the light, were rosy. She was rosy right down to the triangle of skin above the neckline of her dress.

"You don't remember me," she said once the water was brought over. "But you used to hang out with my older brother, Gary Strout." Theo had seen that name recently. He wondered if maybe it had been in the newspaper—hopefully not in the obituary, or the court proceedings, which was where Theo was beginning to see more and more of his high school acquaintances. Lois sipped her water, looking as if she were both calculating her next sentence and completely unsure of why she was sitting there. Theo knew that sometimes women pretended to have conversations with strangers, or quickly joined groups of people, to avoid someone who might be pestering them, oftentimes a man who would not take no for an answer. He glanced over his shoulder and down the bar, but there did not seem to be any suspicious person. Everyone from the graduation party had gone.

"You were the only one who didn't ditch Gary that day he got hurt on his skateboard," Lois said. "Everyone else ran like hell. I still think about that sometimes."

Lois Strout. Theo remembered, with some shame now, that the name Lois Strout had not sounded like someone that he wanted to get to know. The name had reminded him of a tea kettle. *I may be divorced,* he remembered thinking, *but that does not mean that I want to date a tea kettle.*

"You work at the dentist's office," he said.

"Oh." Lois looked startled. "No," she said, "But yes. I do." She shook her head quickly, as if shaking off a stupor. "I quit six months ago."

"Why?" Theo asked. About a month ago, Theo had left his coworkers a note on his desk, telling them to keep his African violet and to get rid of the rest. He was sorry, but he could not come back to the building for any reason. It would kill him. If they should, by chance, find his body at the bottom of the stairwell, then it just meant that he had not made it out in time; the building had killed him in the same way the tundra kills: by disorientation, hypothermia, and a complete failure to sustain life.

"I don't know why it is always so hard for me to explain," Lois said. She poked at her ice with her straw. "One day I just couldn't stand it there anymore—I mean, the people were nice."

Theo told her that he understood, probably better than she could imagine. He was starting to get the feeling that he was meant to be having this conversation, with this woman, whose name had been written on a bar napkin and shoved into his shirt pocket just months before. *Not a long-term thing. But you'll have fun.*

Lois seemed to be encouraged because she began to explain to Theo how, for the last six months, she had been trying to lead a different life. Eating healthier, canceling her cable subscription. One day, she had driven almost four hundred miles to visit a medicine woman, who had performed many different acts of cleansing. Thrashing Lois's arms and legs with a bundle of weeds, spitting a mysterious milky liquid under her hairline.

"Then the medicine woman took a chicken egg and rubbed it all over my body," Lois said. "Like it was a bar of soap." She leaned in, excited, or perhaps relieved to be telling someone about the experience.

"After she had rubbed the egg everywhere—and I mean

everywhere—the medicine woman broke the egg into a glass jar and showed me the yolk. To me, it looked normal, but the woman said that the yolk was telling her that I had digestive issues. That I should start by never going for a walk on an empty stomach." She leaned in even closer. "Do you want to know why?" she asked Theo. Theo could smell the margaritas on her breath and then another powdery smell, like makeup or maybe deodorant. Like a sly, female shimmer drifting into the space around him. A thought crossed his mind, something that he would not allow to fully form but could not dismiss entirely, and so it stayed, just on the edge of his heart, like a silhouette lingering outside an open doorway.

"Why?" he asked.

Lois looked firmly at him, as if about to divulge something somber but essential. The dimple on her chin had the pinched look of a scar when she set her mouth straight. She was looking Theo in the eye, which he did not try to avoid.

"Because if I go outside without eating, then I will get too much bad wind in my stomach." She could not control her smile any longer. "Bad wind!" She laughed and leaned back again on her stool. Theo thought he saw her eyes dance over the tiers of bottles behind the bar. He knew that if he ordered another beer for himself then he would be making a commitment to stay. He would continue talking to Lois, and she would settle into another margarita, and then there would have to be some acknowledgment of what to do when their glasses were empty once again. He excused himself, smiling at Lois, to make sure she knew that she had not frightened him with her story, told her that he would be back in a moment. If he had still been a smoker, he would have found someone to give him a cigarette, maybe asked the hostess if he could borrow her long candle lighter, and gone to the parking lot to walk back and forth and smoke. He would relish the feeling of standing outside time, of peering down his nose at the world. But he was not a smoker, so he decided that he would make a call. The parking lot was more desolate now. The white truck was no longer there. Theo listened to the slick rush of cars on the highway and felt the cool air on his skin; it must have rained while he was inside. He had decided that he would break his promise to himself and call Portia one last time. He trusted that he would know what to do if she did not answer. There would be a finality to her failure to pick up, like dropping a penny into a well and hearing nothing, having to choose between the madness of dropping a second penny and then a third or abandoning it for good. And if she did answer, well, then he was ready to be tossed back into the raging sea, to do whatever she commanded, even if it meant leaving her alone. Halfway across the parking lot, however, he remembered that the phone was not in his car. He had left it on the kitchen floor after letting it fall from his hands. Carrie had been laughing at him, her voice clammy and full of pity, and it had made Theo disgusted with himself. He had run out the door, to his car. There were cars surrounding him in the restaurant lot, with vacant faces.

Their license plates had no messages for him. Their colors were muted under the cloudy sky. Theo thought about the egg from Lois's story and turned back to the restaurant.

◆

Before the divorce, when the separation was still in its experimental stage—when Theo was staying temporarily in his mother's guest room—Theo had visited a woman who lived at the end of a deeply rutted dirt road called (quite intimidatingly) Beast River Hollow, to have his fortune read. The sixty-five-year-old, whose name was Tina, looked less like a fortune teller and more like someone about to go hunting for the day, in her puffy vest and her shin-high muck boots, but Theo found her dress and her demeanor promising; she was gruff, with all the signs of someone devoted to honest work. She had been splitting firewood on the porch when he arrived, and she did not wash her hands before making him a cup of tea. He had focused on the dirt caked into her knuckles as she lay tarot cards across the kitchen table, tapping them and telling him what each one meant, like a tracker pointing expertly to a pile of animal scat.

"You have made a decision already," she said, fingering a card. On it sat a sorceress in a blue robe with a black crescent moon marking her forehead. "You may have made this decision long ago, even if you think that you are only making it now." Theo had thought that Tina was talking about the separation from his wife. He had nodded, accepting that there was probably some truth to this; he knew that couples sometimes practiced falling out of love long before they were brave enough to do so officially. But Tina had gone on, looking closely at the lines in Theo's palms, closing her eyes and letting her lips tremble, as if speaking in a dream. Theo remembered how she had raised her eyes to him again, seeing something anew, it seemed, in his face. Her irises were light brown, like leaf-stained water.

"There is something that you don't yet know about yourself," she said. Her attitude had softened by then, and Theo wondered if she had seen something catastrophic and was feeling a bit sorry for him. "You have the potential to do great things, but I wouldn't be doing you any favors by telling you what they are." She wiped her hand over the cards, sliding them back into a pile, and disappeared into another part of the house. When she returned, she was carrying what appeared to be a dark slab of bark in a plastic bag.

"It's venison jerky, made by my brother," she explained, handing Theo the bag. "I'm sorry. It's all I could find, but they are telling me that you need to eat this. You should eat it on the drive home."

"Who's 'they'?" Theo wanted to know, but Tina just shrugged, wide-eyed. It occurred to him then that maybe her mysticism was not something that she had chosen, that she might be just as bewildered and helpless as he was.

◆

"What happened next?" Theo was back in the bar, ready to order Lois another drink and listen to the rest of her story. "What happened after the egg?" Lois's purse was open on the bar. She was putting her wallet and a round, salmon-colored compact mirror back into it. Had she been touching up her makeup while he was outside? Theo knew—the knowledge was like an anvil in his gut, blunt and without magic—that if he tried, he could find Lois beautiful, that there was nothing at all wrong with her. He imagined that she could be warm and honest and would probably always see him in a generous light, as the boy who did right by her older brother all those years ago. The bartender brought over a second beer and a margarita in a stemmed glass. Lois smiled a little self-consciously.

"I was being optimistic," she said about the drinks. Theo liked that. He also liked how she jumped back into the story, without pleasantries or false modesty; she wanted to talk, and she was not going to apologize for it.

"Believe it or not, I took the medicine woman's advice and made sure to always eat before I went outside. I said to myself, 'So many people are looking for big remedies. What if the answer is simple, after all?'" She paused to clink the rim of her glass against his beer, as if to remind him that it was there. "But the only thing that shifted was my waistline. I gained ten pounds from all the snacking. I realized that I didn't even know what I was trying to fix. How would I know if I was better?"

"So what did you do?"

"I did what people do: I sought a different opinion."

"Another medicine woman?" Beyond Lois, through the tall dining room windows, Theo could see that it had started to rain again, this time under a dark and muscular-looking sky. Some of the other patrons had noticed too, with glassy acceptance, before turning back to their drinks or their plates of chicken bones. There was something about how Lois spoke that made it impossible for Theo to guess whether her story would take a bad turn or whether she was about to reveal to him a life-changing secret.

"A medium this time," Lois said. "He was going to get in touch with my spirit guides, and they were going to tell him what was wrong with me." At the word *spirit*, she had waggled her hands, as if to convey that she was certainly not expecting Theo to take any of it seriously. As if, although her story was true, he was welcomed to enjoy it for entertainment purposes only. The sky had darkened even further. On a regular day, Theo would have been at work at this time, staring at a computer screen, separated from the storm by three panes of glass: his office window, the frosted glass divider outside his office, and then the tall, runny windows overlooking the parking lot. On the same such day, only a few years before, he would have been protected by three panes of glass and comforted by the knowledge that his wife was in her classroom, teaching second graders, wearing her brown clogs and her red sweater; that his boys were at their desks in school, watching the storm, watching the clock, the youngest chewing a hole in the sleeve of his new shirt.

"What did the spirits say?" Theo asked, as humbly as he could ask such a question.

"Well, there were only two of them," Lois said. "A man and a little girl. And they told the medium that I was lost—'lost like a woman caught in a blizzard, who cannot see that she is only inches away from her front door.' The man spirit, I was told, had been alive once, a long time ago, and that exact scenario happened to him. Except he actually froze to death, minutes from his house, where his wife was cooking him a goose." Lois groaned. Her shoulders hunched. *A goose*, she must have thought, helplessly. Theo could not tell if it was all laughable or if she was groaning because none of it—neither the medicine woman nor the medium—had helped and here she was, three margaritas into her weekday afternoon. There was a slap of rain and wind against the side of the restaurant. The walls creaked. The restaurant had gone quiet, and Theo could hear the clinking of wineglasses as the bartender polished them and slid them carefully into the rack above his head. Why any of this was making his hands ache, he did not know. He rubbed them against the sweat of his pint glass, but it only caused them to feel hotter, more agitated. He placed them flat on the bar.

"Are you okay?" Lois laid her hand on his shoulder. It felt small, like a leaf. She was a woman in a blizzard, standing outside her door, Theo thought. He remembered then how her brother Gary had been trying to climb a gravestone so that he could reach the mouth of the angel and stick his tongue in it. There was no skateboarding accident. They had given up the skating to smoke pot outside the Perkins Mansion, which was private property but vacant for most of the year. The stone angel had come as a surprise, hidden by rows of solemn hedges, pointed and tall, and Gary, perhaps embarrassed by having been taken off guard by a statue, had wasted no time in climbing the base of it, throwing his arms around it, and gurgling obscenely. He was the kind of boy who seemed to fight off his day with over-the-top acts of defiance, like someone wrestling out of an itchy coat. Theo had followed him and the two other boys that were with them into the strange grove. He liked the spot. It had felt insulated, sacred, and depressing. The gravestone was old, but not more than eighty years; the base, where the angel stood, which had been carved to resemble a natural piece of rock, was still sharp at the edges. Everything was wet, too, even though it had not been raining. It seemed that the sun did not penetrate the spot enough to dry the dew. Gary's foot slipped on the stone. The first part of his body to break his fall was his chin. His teeth went through his tongue. The two other boys, one of whom had the marijuana in his jacket, left while Theo was making a kind of ball gag out of Gary's sleeve to soak up the blood.

Waitress

⟋◠⟍ PORTIA HAD BEEN GIVEN ANOTHER PILL TO dissolve under her tongue, and the sweet, chalky taste was filling her mouth with saliva. She swallowed and felt the medication chip at her thoughts, sending them afloat, like ice floes. Even in this state, Dr. Wilk expected Portia to talk, to slap together something coherent. "After the babysitter leaves, I find Julian in his room, sleeping in his closet on a twin-size mattress," she said. "It only fits halfway inside, but he likes it this way. I let him sleep in the closet. It's a kind of silent deal: Julian will put up with the divorce, the new apartment, and I let him roam around half-wild; sit in corners with a banket over his head; eat his lunch under the table; collect coins, pebbles, and especially the tufts of lint from the laundry room downstairs."

"Yes," said Dr. Wilk. "I want to hear more details like that." She had brought with her a thin cushion, which she placed between her bottom and the hard chair. It was after breakfast, and the nurse in charge of the floor that morning had said that Portia could go on a walk around the grounds. Portia had been in the hospital for four days without incident, which meant that her name had been swept away from the red dry-erase board and written anew in black marker, on a different board. Also on this black board were the names of Manon and Lou, and everyone else who had proven to no longer be a threat to themselves, those who were permitted to sleep through the night without a flashlight scanning the room every few hours. It was a silent graduation, going from red to black—from dangerous to not so dangerous—and one that was made without announcement or ceremony. Portia could hear the voices of the old sisters as they made their way down the hall to their shared room. The rhythm of their soft-spoken French had taken Portia out of her narration, breaking her concentration like snapping a bar of chocolate. She looked toward the door.

"And then what happens?" Dr. Wilk leaned in to catch Portia's eye. "What do you do after you check on your boy?"

Portia watched the old sisters walk, arm in arm, by her doorway. Their faces turned in, almost touching. As close as lovers sharing the same pillow. She waited until they were out of sight to continue. It was not a difficult scenario to imagine, she found, because she had been running through this same daydream for years. The only part that ever changed was the age of her son.

"I get a beer from the fridge, drop the bottle cap in the sink. I should wash my apron, but I go to the couch instead. It's where I sleep. I gave the bedroom to Julian."

"You don't think you could manage a more comfortable life?" Dr. Wilk interrupted. "Give yourself your own bed, at least? Your own space?"

Portia could not seem to explain that to be by herself in

these modest conditions was a luxury. To drink beer on a tattered couch, your feet throbbing from a night of work, and to have no one there to tell you that you were doing it wrong, was a gift.

"I am watching television. A rerun that I am barely following. I am too busy thinking about how my band broke up after the divorce, after my husband—my ex-husband—had me committed to a mental hospital."

"Why would the divorce affect your band?" Dr. Wilk shook her head. It seemed that something about this conversation was not working out the way she had anticipated. "Reruns?" she asked. "Portia, this is *your* daydream. This is *your life.*"

But Portia could see so clearly how it would play out. Carrie would come by with some of Portia's equipment—a dusty practice amp that she had left behind, her little mason jar of guitar picks—and she would be wearing that expression of concern, her forehead so creased with reluctance and worry that it was turning blue.

"It's not that we don't love you," Carrie would say, still standing in the doorway. "It's just that Gus and I need to be careful about getting caught up"—here, she would stop herself, bite at a hangnail and inspect it; maybe she would be torn up about it, deep down—"getting caught up in toxic situations." And she would be implying that Portia was the toxic situation, with her mania and her dysfunctional relationship. Wasn't there a common bit of advice that warned happily married couples about spending too much time with divorcées?

Portia could see how she would lose her little terrier. Maybe Nathan would insist on keeping Rupert after the divorce. Portia's new apartment might not allow dogs. Maybe Rupert would nip Portia's mother-in-law while Portia was in the hospital, and Nathan would say that the dog was untrustworthy, biting his poor mother like that—right on the ankle—when she was only trying to help. Portia's own parents, who had been too overburdened to come visit her, might have the same trepidations about her, wondering if she could be trusted with their grandchild. They might return him to her, watch the boy run up the driveway to his mother, and they would stand stiffly, holding their breath, as if waiting to see how she would embrace him. Would their daughter shed tears of happiness over her little boy? Would her arms be gentle and safe? Portia imagined that everyone would be watching her upon her release, wondering how she would behave.

It was here that Portia began to suspect that the doctor's exercise might be a trap. Perhaps Portia was being asked to daydream these scenarios so that she would realize how much she had to lose if she continued along these foolish paths: falling in love with her bandmate, stowing her pills away, believing herself to be half as worthy as a legend like Alby Porter. It was possible that it was all a ruse to get her to start taking her medication again. To make it seem like it was her own idea.

"I'm not playing this game anymore," Portia said to Dr. Wilk. "I quit."

She tossed her pillow down and, with her legs trembling from sitting too long, walked down the hallway toward the common area. At the nurses' station Portia asked if she could have a cigarette. The nurse seated at the desk slid her glasses onto her nose and began to push the contents—cigarettes, pens, cell phones, and prepaid phone cards—around in the big drawer.

"I don't see a pack with your name on it," the nurse said. She looked up, frowning slightly. Portia knew that she had not brought any cigarettes with her. She had not touched a cigarette since before Julian was born. But she wanted a smoke more than anything, if only to seize the swaying, liquid feeling in her head. To put a stop to the daydreaming that Dr. Wilk had encouraged. She could still see herself half lying on the couch, a beer gripped in her hand, the changing colors of the television dyeing the wall behind her, dyeing the whites of her eyes. The truth was that Portia could not dream herself a better life. She had dreamed so many outrageous things—believed so many outrageous beliefs—but she was too much of a coward to change.

"Jerry said I could have one of his Camels," she told the nurse, who dipped her hands back into the drawer before pausing once more to look at Portia over her glasses.

"Is Jerry a patient here?" she asked.

Jerry had been a patient there thirteen years ago. Portia

understood this, but time was beginning not to matter. Dr. Wilk had said that all that mattered was control. Portia wanted to reach over the partition, into the nurse's big drawer of goodies, and snatch one of the packs for herself, but she knew that they would grab her arms, that if she continued to fight, they would lift her off the floor, her legs pedaling uselessly in the air. She must have lunged, scrambling over the partition for the drawer without realizing, because they were already grabbing her by the arm, pulling her back. Portia cried out. It felt as if it had been years since someone had touched her. Not even Theo, who she had wanted more than any living soul, had wanted to touch her, afraid as he was of what might happen. And now, Portia thought, he never would. They would strap her down, roll her into the "quiet room" with the white walls, like they had done with Jerry. She had seen him that night, thirteen years ago. She had crept down the hallway in the early hours of the morning and, through the sliver of double-paned glass on the last door, saw Jerry tied to a kind of padded table. He was tied in three places: across his chest, his hips, and his ankles. By then, he had stopped struggling and spitting, and his eyes were open, but glassy, looking somewhere beyond the ceiling tiles. There was a large, urgent bulge right above the middle strap. The only part of him that was still awake.

"I only wanted a cigarette," Portia was saying. "I'm not trying to hurt anyone."

"Of course you're not." It was Dr. Wilk speaking. She had

followed Portia to the common area and was not trying to re-
strain her but had reached out only to get Portia's attention—
Portia, who had not scrambled madly over the nurse's desk,
after all. Dr. Wilk backed away, startled by Portia's sudden
show of emotion. She looked especially huddled and small.
Her shoulders barely came out past the outline of her hair.
Her hands, peeking out from the sleeves of her gold-trimmed
blouse, were small and impractical, like the hands of a Barbie
doll. If Dr. Wilk had worked there thirteen years ago, would
she have talked to Jerry in the same way that she was talking
to Portia? Would she listen to his daydreams, encourage him
to spin fantasies that, in his case, might very well end up being violent or lurid? Jerry could have overpowered the doctor
if he had wanted to, crushed her. Portia remembered how
badly she had wanted the hospital staff to take her seriously
back then, how insulted she had been at Dr. Shay's theory
that she was merely heartbroken, his grainy cat and mouse
cartoon. His foolish hope. You would not dare to give someone like Jerry a cartoon and tell him that he was heartbroken.

Still Drowning

⟲⎯⎯⟳ THE RAIN WAS CRASHING AGAINST THE SIDE
of the restaurant in sheets, creating a sound like marbles
hitting a hard floor. Theo guessed that he had probably left
his car windows cracked, but it was too late to do anything
about it. It was also true that the part of him that cared about
whether the inside of his car got soaked was shutting down,
slowing to a halt. Lois had left to use the bathroom but had
not brought her purse with her. It hung on the back of her
stool by a thin leather strap attached by shiny clasps. Theo
looked at it. He imagined Lois coming back from the bathroom and slipping the purse over her shoulder. Asking him
if he would drive her home, maybe laughing at herself for
inadvertently setting him up in this way. Lois seemed to be
a woman who was self-contained without being rigid. There
was a delicate balance to her humor and gentleness that Theo
found steadying but also alluring. He knew that he wanted
something from her, only it was difficult to decide exactly
what it was, as if he could not tell whether he was drawn to
her or drawn to the situation: how he had stumbled into this
place by chance, been handed a drink, as if he belonged there.
And then Lois's little tap on his shoulder and her eagerness
to tell him about her life. Perhaps fate was like sitting in a
train, he thought, feeling yourself moving backward, only to

discover that it was a second train outside your window that had been moving, creating an illusion, a whole-body sensation of going somewhere that was not real.

Lois appeared beside him. She looked briefly at the rain breaking against the window and then dipped her hand into her purse, feeling for something. She paused.

"I had expectations about this day," she said. "I was going to get up early, go to the gym, get some things done. You know, do something useful with my day off." She frowned and then caught herself. "I'm so sorry. That must have sounded awful."

"It's fine. I know what you mean," Theo said. There was a song playing on the radio. It was familiar to him, but the melody was not loud enough to untangle from the rest of the noises in the bar. He wished that he could hear it, in case there was a message there for him, maybe in the lyrics or in an association that he had with the song. Theo found that he was still desperate for something strikingly meaningful to occur, more so than the thrashing wind and rain or the relentless, baffling sensation in his hands. It was serendipitous, this chance meeting with Lois Strout, a woman whose number had been sitting idly in his wallet for months, but it was not enough to put his mind at ease. He wanted something or someone to appear before him and tell him outright that he was exactly where he was supposed to be.

"What do you do now?" he asked Lois.

She looked puzzled. "What am I doing now?"

"I mean, what did you decide to do, after everything?

What did you do with your life?" Lois leaned against the barstool: a woman in a blizzard, according to the spirits, who needed only to take a blind step forward to find her true calling. Theo realized just how eager he had been the whole time to hear the end of Lois's story. Where had her decisions led her? What epiphanies had she reached?

"Oh, but I went back," she said. "I was lucky to even have the chance."

"To the dentist's office?" The disappointment must have been in his voice because Lois's demeanor changed, the comma on the side of her chin pinching tightly in self-defense. She pulled three dollars from her purse and placed them on the bar under her empty glass.

"Like I said, I was lucky to get my job back." She zipped her purse, sighed. "Dreaming leaves you in debt."

They had waited by the coatracks for the rain to let up so they could make a dash for the parking lot. Right away it was clear to them that Theo had, as he had feared, left the windows down; the inside of his car was drenched. Lois had gasped, horrified at Theo's bad luck, then stifled a laugh. Her mood had lifted, possibly from the thrill of leaping over the puddles with her cardigan held taut over her head.

"Ride with me," she insisted. She did not want Theo to have to get into his cold, soggy front seat. "I'll drive you back tomorrow morning with some towels." Theo considered her, standing with her keys held confidently, the silent language of the keys thrust forward like that an invitation in itself. There was no reason for him to refuse her offer or to doubt the implications of what it meant to find themselves together in the morning, with towels. The rain was still falling on them, the drops widely spaced, but fat and powerful, rolling down the back of Theo's neck, hitting him in the eye. He wished that he had a thousand years to make his decision whether to accept her offer. His friends would want this for him. He might even want it for himself. But all he could think about was Lois walking back into that dentist's office after having been away for six months. How her coworkers might have hounded her, lightheartedly, for thinking that she could escape the mundane. They would have patted her on the back, ordered a cake from the grocery store, and Lois would have been grateful that her reception back into normal life had not been worse.

+

Theo had suspected at first that the strange feeling in his hands was caused by all the time they spent hovering claw-like above a keyboard or clutching a computer mouse. At the urging of his wife, he had seen a doctor, and the doctor had agreed that it could very well be carpal tunnel syndrome. They made special splints for that, worn around the wrist. But the longer the sensation lasted, the more Theo could not help wondering whether his hands were aching for a more mysterious reason, if they had minds of their own, which was not something that one could explain to a doctor. He could not go to his doctor and say, "My hands feel like they are receiving a signal from space, like they are trying to tell me something." His hands often flared up when something significant was about to happen, but there was no exact science to it, nothing to pin a real theory on. Sometimes, for example, he would be upstairs when his wife came home, and his hands would feel hot and uncomfortable and he would know, before he even laid eyes on his wife, that she was angry about something. Other times, he would pick up a kind of excitement through them, as if whatever he was thinking or hearing at the moment had a current of truth to it, his hands the conductors for that truth. Playing drums for Carrie and Portia had given his hands something to do, and, for a time, Theo expected that that was all he had needed: a hobby.

Your Lover, Your Alien

March 2, 1983

Dear Emile,

I have sent this letter to your mother's address because I know that she is the kind of upstanding woman who will deliver it to its rightful recipient, no matter the circumstance. She will likely deliver it by hand, and you might even read it this time, for her sake, if not for mine. You see now how desperate I have become.

I am self-aware, as much as I am not self-aware. A mirror of myself and a reflection that wants to shed its source. I am not a cruel man, but sometimes I use people. Sometimes I surround myself with friends for the sense of audience they award my ego. This, and more, I have learned from the hundred sessions I have had with our goat, my psychoanalyst. It has taken me a hundred sessions to realize that he has no sympathy, that the world has no sympathy. And why should they? I have become a monster. Which you already knew. Have you ever considered this: that my quest for fame is nothing grander than a desire for love? But fame requires creation, creation requires madness, and madness alienates. The act of creation pushes love away, makes it shimmering and abstract, like the dull roar of the stadium when the lights come down and you realize that it's only you onstage.

Because of your silence—no, let me rephrase—in the aftermath of your silence, I have fallen upon a new rule, like falling on a sword of sad and inevitable truth: to be great, you must give up part of your humanity..

On my next go-round, I will try again. I promise to be greater, by which I mean better: the monster and the hero. Your lover. Your alien.

Please write back.

A.

Poor Alice

◦——◦ SOMETIMES PORTIA AND NATHAN WATCHED courtroom dramas together and Nathan would complain.

"That's not how it works," he said, his hand sailing through the air in frustration. "The judge would never allow that."

Sometimes they watched hospital dramas where mental patients shouted about conspiracies while being dragged down hallways against their will by muscular men in scrubs. Portia wanted to say that it did not happen that way, that patients were never wrangled by medical staff and jabbed with needles, like you see on TV. But sometimes it did happen that way. Exactly that way. And sometimes, if you were a young woman like Portia, tormented by silly ideas, people did not know what to do with you, so they strung you along, asking you to daydream out loud. They kept you talking, hoping that you would begin to hear yourself, hear the pettiness of your problems.

And it might have been that Portia simply did not know what to do with Nathan, and that, as his wife, she had failed to deal with him properly. She should have been firmer with Nathan in the beginning of their marriage. If she had stood up to him, told him to bandage his own finger, for example, when he cut it carelessly with a paring knife, then maybe he would have grown to respect her. If, when he scolded her for wanting a kiss or accused her of being spoiled when she expected a hug from him, she had only rolled her eyes, then maybe he would have found her resilience attractive. Maybe he would have found himself suddenly wanting to kiss her, after all, because there was no longer the distasteful obligation to do so. They might have developed into the kind of couple that could have disagreements without being devastated. They might have found a new and surprising kind of love for each other, like a pair of hardened police officers on a television series who had been through so much of each other's shit that they merged into a loyal partnership.

But, as her days in the hospital grew numbered, Portia's guilt began to pile around her. She felt sorry for lying to Dr. Shay about taking her pills, for walking into his office, week after week, and lying without remorse.

She felt sorry for, years ago, having smashed an empty wineglass in front of Nathan. It had disturbed him. In his line of work, victims of domestic abuse often reported similar acts of violence—toasters, blenders, cake dishes hurled at their heads. Angry words shouted. These were actions to be taken seriously.

Portia had also thrown a cup of lemonade at a nurse, although in her version of the story, she merely knocked it off the table. Portia's version, however, should be considered with a grain of salt, because she had been heavily drugged at the time. The effects of the drugs may have altered her perception.

She felt sorry for having been involved with the type of man who threw blenders at his girlfriend. Skip may not have done this to Portia, but he had done other things. Called her derogatory names, slapped her across the face to see if she would shed tears. This may have been excusable if she had been trapped in the relationship, but she had walked into it voluntarily, perhaps even enjoyed it. Later, when she could no longer see this man, she had been receptive to the sexual advances of a man named Jerry, who suffered from severe mental illness. Portia should have known better.

Perhaps the most serious of Portia's crimes was that she had been unfaithful to her husband—if not physically then emotionally—and it would have certainly gotten worse if Nathan had not put a stop to it. He had put a stop to it in the only way that he knew how. You could not blame him for doing everything in his power to save their marriage.

And you could not blame him for deleting Theo's call from Portia's phone when he was packing her bag for the hospital. A swipe of the finger. Such a small thing. It need not be mentioned.

Beacon

ᕲ─ᕲ It had almost stopped raining, but the sky was still dark. Theo watched the red brake lights of Lois's car flash twice before she turned onto the highway. He heard the sound of the wet road, like a piece of tape being stripped.

When Theo had told Lois that he would find his own way home, she looked as if she did not understand him but also as if she had never expected to understand him—him or any man, for that matter. Theo had watched her face change as she shook out her damp cardigan and got into her car. Her eyes had stopped their dancing. Her lips were sealed and untrusting. She checked her mirrors, gave him a wave.

His hands had been aching dully the entire time that he and Lois had been standing in the parking lot, but now that he was alone, they became quite painful. He was afraid that he would not be able to hold on to the steering wheel for long enough to get home, so he decided to wait outside until he felt better. There was a bench to the side of the restaurant by the deck, which was empty, the deck's yellow umbrellas cinched against the storm. Theo sat and let his hands catch the light drops of rain, hoping that the raindrops would cool them. He remembered how he had dropped his phone on the kitchen floor earlier that day and stood helplessly, his hands burning, as if commanding that something be done, only he had not known what that was. He still did not know. There were actions that could be taken. Theo tried to calm himself by listing them in his mind: he could go back inside the restaurant and order a meal, now that it was nearing dinnertime; he could sit on this bench, getting gradually wetter, until the restaurant closed and the last members of the waitstaff left for the night; he could get into his car, sink into the soggy upholstery, and hold on to the steering wheel for dear life. But these thoughts did not comfort him, for he realized that there were too many options—going home, not going home, existing in one way or another—and they all led to that same dreadful sense of uncertainty and loneliness; there was no one in the world who could tell him what to do or why his hands hurt, why he wanted to cry. When he was a boy, in elementary school, a teacher sent him on an errand to return a bag of plastic ring-toss pieces to the gym teacher. The gymnasium was at the opposite end of the school, and Theo had liked the trek through the hallways, the mesh bag slung over his shoulder, as if he were setting out on an adventure. When he arrived with his bag, he found the gym teacher in a climbing harness, ropes attached to an older boy who was scaling a rock wall. The gym teacher told Theo to bring the bag to the storage closet down the hall but to watch out because the door to the closet was propped open with a wooden wedge. He said to keep it propped, or else Theo would get locked inside. Theo nodded and swung the bag over his other shoulder, spinning on his heels, full of importance.

He remembered how empty the hallway had been, and the odors of rubber, sweat, and dust from the storage closet, as he poked his head inside. They were the odors of total isolation, away from his classroom and the noise of shouting and squealing sneakers from the gymnasium. Of course, what he would tell his mother, later that day—what he would tell the principal and the school nurse and everyone else—was that the door had closed on him, all by itself, and locked. *Clunk.* And the truth was such a slight deviation from the story that he had told—so slight that its only difference seemed negligible enough to keep to himself—that for years afterward Theo forgot what had really happened: that he had stood inside the closet and watched the door inch slowly shut and done nothing. That the door closing had felt to him like an answered prayer because he knew that from the moment the lock clicked into place until the moment that it was opened again, nothing in the world could be his fault. At nine years old, he had never considered just how much responsibility he assumed for the actions of others, the weight that he carried, the phantom feelings of guilt and shame that had nothing to do with him. For the hour that he was missing, he did not bang against the door or shout or cry in despair. Instead he did absolutely nothing. He let the black ink of his mind drain into a larger pool of black ink. Afterward, the school nurse would tell Theo's mother that Theo likely blacked out from shock, as if it were a bad thing.

When Theo looked up, a light had appeared on the

mountain. It was a slowly flashing red beacon atop a tower, above the trees, for alerting airplanes—of the presence of the mountain peak or the tower itself, Theo did not know. The restaurant's deck was positioned facing east so that the patrons could enjoy the view of the mountain while they ate, especially in the autumn, when the colors of the trees turned orange and red. These patrons were called *leaf peepers*, and they came in huge buses with tinted windows. Sometimes they stood in the road to take pictures, cameras pointed at the highest branches, and you had to drive around them, as if they were loose cattle.

Theo was already halfway up the mountain, his hands burning against the steering wheel, his pants and the back of his shirt soaked through from the car's wet interior, when he understood where he was going. He felt like he was waking up from a trance, and he laughed at himself. He imagined that if his ex-wife knew what he was doing, she would call him crazy. If his friends knew, they would say the same. The headlights of his car formed a kind of binocular shape of light across the road, skimming the tree branches, causing the darkness to jump and tremble. Theo laughed at this notion. He wanted to say to his ex-wife and his friends, *You're right! I'll prove it! Look how crazy I can be.*

The Big Heart

⟲—⟳ WHAT WAS DR. WILK ATTEMPTING BUT THE same thing that Portia's parents had done when they brought her to the science museum and pushed her into the hallways of the artificial heart? Those tight, grubby pathways were no substitute for a real education, but the novelty of it must have been useful. Where an anatomy textbook would have failed the children, this blown-up exaggeration would reach them at the core of their understanding: their own sense of terror.

I am the woman in the blue dress from the French picture book. I live with my son in an apartment above the marketplace, where merchants sell baskets of foraged mushrooms and little songbirds in wooden cages. Today I have decided that it is time to take my son to the museum.

Dr. Wilk had instructed a nurse to bring Portia a pencil so Portia could continue with the strange assignment that she had been given. An assignment that seemed to have no end to it. It might have been that Dr. Wilk's methods were not the trap that Portia had feared but that her doctor was just naive. How, she wondered, could the doctor expect all her patients to have the time and luxury to daydream themselves out of a crisis? She had not even begun to talk of medication—that Portia had stopped taking hers—or diagnoses. There had been none of the usual mood charts and questioning, the tests to see if Portia's thinking was grounded in reality or teetering on the edge of it or if she had already taken off with strapping confidence, in mania, like a hot air balloon. Dr. Wilk reminded Portia of the kind of friend who might stop you in the grocery store and want to gossip, even though you have a screaming child in your shopping cart, because she somehow cannot understand that your day-to-day is not as lenient as hers.

The nurse who had delivered the pencil to Portia was the same nurse with the red-painted fingernails who had brought her the dinner menu on her first day. The same nurse who had been sympathetic to Nathan, making sure that he had water and a sturdy chair when he came to visit. She handed the pencil to Portia but then lingered, watching her, as if suddenly curious about what Portia might do with it.

"It must be hard," the nurse said finally. Portia looked up. She noticed the nurse's pleasant but inscrutable expression, how young she was, probably in her early thirties. The closeness in age made Portia feel shabby in comparison, conscious of how she must appear, sitting cross-legged on the tile floor with her unbrushed hair, the bags beneath her eyes, her ashen face. The nurse continued: "To be away from your little boy?"

Portia held the pencil tightly in her hand. She tested it on the corner of the yellow paper, noting the dullness of the tip. She hoped that she could write all that she wanted to write before the lead ran out or broke. She did not want the interruption and indignity of asking this woman for permission to use a sharpener.

"Yes," she said to the nurse. "I miss him very much."

I tell my son that we will ride on a fast-moving train to Paris.

"It will be the smoothest train that you have ever taken." We pack our breakfast into paper bags and walk to the station, my son stopping now and then to pinch off pieces of bread from his bag and toss them to the pigeons. He has never left his home this early and with his stomach empty. I wonder if he will, for the rest of his life, associate this time of day, just before dawn, with the clean feeling of hunger, the warm lights from inside the bakery, the birds dropping down and taking off in a surge of flapping wings that sound like the pages of a book. He might remember, as I will, the train pulling in, warm and silent, the lights in the cars still on, and the few people sitting inside. It is comforting to know that the world is calm and gray at this hour, like a grandmother.

I am taking my son to the same science museum that I used to visit as a girl, which had always seemed deep and velvety but also startling, like the startled glass eyes of the taxidermy bobcats and mountain goats. In the center of the museum, there is an exhibit made especially for children, where a giant heart, constructed from fiberglass and papier-mâché, is installed. It is large enough for children to crawl through its narrow arteries and find themselves inside a red padded room, where speakers play a low, muffled thumping. The heart had always been a source of great anxiety for me, for its constancy; it had seemed that once such a thing was built, the beating switched on, then there was a responsibility for it to endure, even though I knew that it would someday, in some capacity, have to be destroyed, as all things would have to be destroyed.

"Do the museum guards turn off the thumping every night, before they lock the doors?" I used to ask my mother, and my mother said, "I suppose they must."

It is not my intent to introduce my son to this same worry, but there is an inevitability about it, a rite of passage. We sit across from each other on the train, eating from our paper bags, feeling the subtle and expert tilting of the train car. The guards are just unclasping the chains at the museum's entrance when we arrive, which is just how I had envisioned it. I had not envisioned, however, that there would be a small black sign just outside the heart exhibit, informing the public that the heart was undergoing a routine "surgery," a kind of housekeeping to keep it safe from the hundreds of little feet that pattered through it every day. We stand, reading the sign, and for a moment, I do not know what to do.

The nurse had gone. Portia sat on the floor with the pad of paper in her lap, feeling the slight vibrations of the hospital. Below her were the other floors, where other patients slept and ate and took pills. It reminded her of a boarding school, in a way, how you could go to the cafeteria, or to the recreational room, and see someone from another section of the hospital in passing, like seeing a student from a different grade. Looks of reluctant curiosity were exchanged, as well as looks of envy—which was not real envy, but the kind that children exhibit, a directionless wishing.

Portia was only doing what Dr. Wilk had asked of her because she had already made up her mind. There would be no more frantic visits from Carrie and Gus, no more gauzy visions of Alby Porter in the night. Portia's future had been scrubbed clean, bleached like a bloodstain in a bathtub, and soon it would not matter what she said to the doctor or what she wrote on the notepad. She wrote quickly, this new daydream, but then it was not so new, because she had always known it. She wrote it all down. "Dream bigger," Dr. Wilk had said, and so Portia did, in the only way that she knew how. When she was done, she tore out the pages, folded them into a small, tight square, and stashed them behind a loose baseboard, like the niche where she had discovered the lone razor blade, years ago. There was a finality to it: like making one last list before you lose your memory. Before you lose yourself.

◆

Nathan had stopped Portia outside the hospital, after her morning walk around the grounds, to give her a picture of Julian. He told her that he was troubled by what seemed to him to be gaps in her memory, events that she was forgetting.

"Do you remember the birth of your own son?" he had

asked her, and waved apologetically at the nurse who had been holding the door for them. This wave was also authoritative, such as when a civilian takes it into his own hands to direct traffic. The nurse gave them a short nod. Portia had a sense that most of the nurses felt sympathy for Nathan; he carried his handsomeness with such weariness, bearing his love for Portia like a cross. She could see that it was impossible for the nurse at the door to refuse him this conversation with his wife—to refuse him anything at all.

"Of course I remember," she said.

"Then you remember what I said to you while you were on the operating table?" The sun was still behind him, simmering the blacktop, spraying off the rows of windshields. She knew that just beyond the parking lot, across the lawn, there was a fountain, a large granite sphere that trickled water from a hole. She thought back to the night that Julian was born and blinked, as if seeing the bright lights of the operating room again, pointed at her face, her insides exposed and spread all over.

"You told me that my hands would come back to me." She looked up at her husband and found that his face had softened. She could not tell if it was out of pity or love.

"Is that what you remember?" he asked.

"Is that what you said?"

"Is that what you remember?"

She had grown hot, suddenly, even though they were standing in the shade of a tree. Her face was flushed and her eyelids felt swollen, as though she had been crying—which she had been, on and off, for days—but this was different, the heat and pressure like a fever. She put her hand over her forehead.

"Stop this," Nathan said. "It's time for you to stop this." He took the photo of Julian from her hand and held it while he spoke, directing it at her, as he made his points.

"Once things get difficult, you start to lose your grip. Every time life gets hard." He was jabbing at the air with the photo, Portia's own son an actor in the delivery of this terrible message. "You go off—*poof!*—somewhere else."

Portia tried to stay focused, but she knew that beyond the parking lot there was a fountain, and beyond the fountain there was a street, lined with shops. If she could only see that far, she might see that Theo was there, crossing the road again. For all she knew, some version of herself was over there with him, waiting for him on the opposite sidewalk in her yellow dress from the Salvation Army. What Nathan was saying was probably true; it was much easier to look at the little figures in her mind, going off together around the corner, than to face the problem at hand. She wondered if what she had thought was a burning desire for Theo had been, all along, a very sophisticated system of denial. She thought of the way that Rupert sometimes stuck his nose into Julian's paper lunch bag and then could not get the bag off his head, how he walked backward, blindly, and how the bag remained. Portia knew that if she did not intervene and remove the bag herself, then her dog might keep walking backward until he dropped dead, rather than pause for a moment to solve the problem rationally. She laughed at this notion, it being so close to her own patterns of self-sabotage.

"And this is funny to you?" Nathan asked. He had put the photo of Julian back into his shirt pocket, perhaps without thinking.

"No," Portia told him. "It's only that I understand now." She reached for him and felt his cold hands in hers. How long had it been since they had held hands, facing each other, like this? Since their wedding day? She remembered what Alby Porter had said to her, gazing affectionately at her over his surgical mask. Perhaps this was what he had meant about her hands. Could this have been what he meant? She gave Nathan a squeeze. "You're right," she said, struggling to keep her eyes open, even though they were heavy—every part of her was heavy with the desire to look away, to fall asleep and start dreaming again. "I want to get better."

I am about to steer my son away from the giant heart exhibit when a man in a white mask appears from behind the heart, waving urgently.

"Un moment," he calls to us. He meets us at the sign and introduces himself as le chirugien, the surgeon. Only, he explains, he cannot continue his job until his assistant returns with his cup of coffee. He invites us to enter the room—here is our chance to have a private tour of the heart, he is saying, without the noise

and distraction of the regular crowd. The heart is the reason that we have come all this way, so I urge my son toward the circular tunnel that leads inside to the red, puffy interior. And as we get closer, I notice that the sound has been there in the background, all along: the same deep, muffled thumping that haunted me when I was a little girl. But of course, they would not stop the recording for a little maintenance. My son is on his hands and knees now, peering into the tunnel. He looks up at me.

"I don't want to go alone," he says. I glance over at the surgeon, who is holding a rag and an unmarked spray bottle. I realize then that he is not any kind of specialist brought in to operate but one of the museum's own custodians, probably tasked with prying up old pieces of gum and wiping up mysterious stains. Somehow, this seems disappointing but fitting. I crawl inside with my boy.

Nathan was smiling. He pulled her in and held her, and she felt that wonderful relief—something much quieter than happiness, entrenched in shame but lovely too; all her faults had a chance to be put right again. Portia could see how taking her pills again might be a gesture, a demonstration of the strength of love that she had for her family. Every day there were women lauded for their great sacrifices; it was noble to give up your freedom, or your potential for greatness, to care for your family. Of course, the higher the potential, the bigger the sacrifice, which made Portia's sacrifice, in the end, a small one. She would likely have to give up music and the pleasure that it brought. The band would fall apart (which it would, she knew, regardless of her decision), and she would not be allowed to see Theo anymore. These were direct and simple rules to follow. There was something attractive about having a straight path before you, even if it was a desolate one.

They said goodbye at the door, and Portia had a moment to watch her husband walk away, through the parking lot, until it became difficult to see him against the shadows and waves of heat. She knew that the next time she saw Nathan, they would be together again. He might even grant her the kindness of forgetting her transgressions, or at least stomaching them as he had never done, with the knowledge that, morally, she had no chance of catching up to him. He would always be far ahead of her in that regard, having never lied nor been led astray, but for once they would both understand why it was better, and easier, this way. And it was fleeting but she felt it, stepping back into the cool darkness of the hospital stairwell: her conscience for a moment clean, like black water beneath ice.

In the Center

⟲──⟳ THE CENTER OF THE HEART IS SMALLER THAN *I remember from childhood, and a bit too similar to a padded cell for my liking. In here, the beating sound is louder but still somehow dampened, like having a pillow wrapped around your head. It smells in here also—not bad—like someone's bedroom. It is a familiar smell of bodies sleeping and, for an instant, before I see him there, I remember what it is like to wake up wrapped in someone else's scent, my face buried in someone else's hair. The man lying on the floor hears us come in and turns, his eyes blinking as he takes in his surroundings. At first, I think that this must be the custodian's helper, that somehow he has not gone out for coffee but has come in here to take a nap instead, but the man is speaking now, in English. He is dressed nicely, although his clothes are wrinkled, it seems, from his position on the floor. I grab my son and hold him close, and I must look afraid because the man puts out his hand. He says: "It's okay. You don't have to be afraid. I'm only lost, that's all." His voice is thick, and he breaks into a yawn. My son wrestles free from my arms and goes to the wall to examine a diagram that is there: it depicts the chambers of a real heart but also acts as a map for the artificial heart that we are all now crowded inside.*

"We're here," my son says, pointing to the middle. He does not seem interested at all in the strange man in the corner, who

is now rising to his feet. The man pulls a pair of black-rimmed glasses from his shirt pocket and puts them on. He is too tall to stand upright in this red room built for children, so he sits back down, with his legs crossed. There is something forlorn about him but also resigned, and I wonder if maybe I have walked in on a ghost.

"What are you doing here?" I ask him, noticing that my son does not look away from the sign, as if he has not heard me speak. The man looks at his hands as he explains to me that he had come to this museum once as a child and lost his mother in the crowd.

"I was holding her hand and then I was holding on to her skirt," he says. "And suddenly everyone around me was different, speaking to me in a language that I did not know. We had just been to the heart—" here, the man opens his hands and looks up at the red padded ceiling, indicating that he is talking about the place that we are now occupying. "So I went back to it and waited there—not inside, but right by the entrance—for my mother to find me. It seemed like the safest place." All I can do is nod. It feels as though we have been having this conversation for hours, while the deep thudding continues all around us, as if the heart is everywhere: in our ears, on the other side of the wall, outside the museum windows, pressed to the glass, larger than life. My son has moved on to another diagram. There are buttons on the wall that he can press that light up small red lights, alerting him to new bits of information.

"Can I go to the other chamber?" he asks me. I nod again

and watch him crawl through a second tunnel, apparently more at ease now.

"My mother found me," the man continues. "And she put her hands on my shoulders and said, 'Theo, that was the smartest thing you could have done.'" He pauses, a faint smile on his lips, as he relives the pride of that moment. "So now, almost forty years later, I've come back, because I don't know what else to do."

"Have you been here all night?" I ask him. I am beginning to feel a strong affection for the man, although I am certain that we have never met. I step toward him, half expecting him to vanish—a ghost, after all. He remains.

"Yes. I must have fallen asleep. It's very warm in here." He laughs at himself, then looks at me. "And now you're here," he says, almost as if it is a question. Just then my son appears in the tunnel and waves. I do not get the impression that the giant heart will have the same agonizing effect on him as it had on me. I predict that he will sleep soundly tonight, peaceful and unchanged. I look back at the man, at his wrinkled pants and the shadow of stubble on his face. If he has spent the night, then perhaps he can tell me whether the museum turns off the heartbeat when it locks the doors. I kneel in front of him, so that we are eye level, my face warm, drumming with the sound, my mind now burning with the question—does the heart beat through the night?—and it occurs to me that I have always wondered this. I will never stop wondering.

Acknowledgments

I want to thank Anne Mishkind, who has been my friend since I was two (and a half). She was the first to see that this book was a book, even before I had the confidence to see it myself. I want her to know that her courage and intelligence have helped shape me.

My agent, Reiko Davis, has been a most needed and steadfast advocate. A centering force. At times, a mind reader.

My editor, Leigh Newman, helped this story to thrive on all levels. Every good thing that I write after this will carry a spark of her guidance.

Thanks to Rebekah Tracy, for the walks, the phone calls, and the bunker. For starting a band with me and trading guitars. Sometimes, I am convinced that this all started with the Telecaster.

Thanks to all my friends and coworkers who believed in me. There are too many to name. I am so grateful. Also, to the booksellers, especially Linda Foulsham and Phil Lewis, for their warmth and enthusiasm.

Enormous thanks to Anna Hogeland, Caitlin Horrocks, Clare Beams, Christie Tate, and Rachel Yoder, for their brilliant writing and for their early support. To Kendall Storey, Summer Farah, and the team at Catapult for their hard work

gmENTS

and their many talents, and for making my work feel understood and cared for.

Thanks so much to Ava for her love and her faith in me. Thank you to my parents, for raising me around music and strange things, and for always valuing my creative endeavors.

To Jamie, for dreaming and dreaming and dreaming with me.

To Wilson and Frances: My whole heart and every word.

354 ·

© Jamie Granger

GENEVIEVE PLUNKETT is the author of *Prepare Her: Stories*. Her fiction has appeared in *The O. Henry Prize Stories* and *The Best Small Fictions*, as well as such journals as *New England Review*, *The Southern Review*, *Crazyhorse*, *Colorado Review*, and *Electric Literature*. She lives in Vermont with her two children.